BONDED HEART

A nineteenth-century Cornish romance

Circumstances have forced once-respectable Roz Trevaskis to turn to smuggling. When she is called on to nurse local Justice Branoc Casvellan's brother, Roz sees a chance to improve her lot, not anticipating the effects of such close contact with her handsome employer. But how will Branoc – and his family – react when the truth about Roz's past, and her involvement with the local smuggling trade, comes out?

BONDED HEART

Jane Jackson

Severn House Large Print
London & New York

This first large print edition published 2010
in Great Britain and the USA by
SEVERN HOUSE PUBLISHERS LTD of
9-15 High Street, Sutton, Surrey, SM1 1DF.
First world regular print edition published 2009 by
Severn House Publishers Ltd., London and New York.

British Library Cataloguing in Publication Data

Jackson, Jane, 1944-
  Bonded heart.
  1. Smuggling--England--Cornwall (County)--Fiction.
  2. Cornwall (England : County)--Social conditions--19th
  century--Fiction. 3. Love stories. 4. Large type books.
  I. Title
  823.9'14-dc22

  ISBN-13: 978-0-7278-7882-3

Severn House Publishers support The Forest Stewardship Council
[FSC], the leading international forest certification organisation. All
our titles that are printed on Greenpeace-approved FSC-certified paper
carry the FSC logo.

Mixed Sources

Product group from well-managed
forests and other controlled sources
www.fsc.org Cert no. SA-COC-1565
© 1996 Forest Stewardship Council

FSC

Printed and bound in Great Britain by the
MPG Books Group, Bodmin, Cornwall.

One

Though the inn door stood open and the small-paned windows were flung wide, there wasn't a breath of wind to stir the summer heat. The aromas of ale, cooked food, illicit cognac, and the pungency of boiling tar drifting up from the slipway, were layered with tobacco smoke. The thick fug dried Roz's throat and made her eyes sting.

Beneath a faded calico gown and coarse linen apron, her shift clung to damp skin as she set plates of steaming beef stew in front of two fishermen whose checked shirts and forearms bore smears of the black pitch they were using to seal the hull of their fishing boat.

'Can I get you anything else?'

'No, my bird. Look 'andsome it do.' Winnen rubbed scarred hands together.

As Roz nodded, smiled and turned to gather up empty tankards from the table behind, his mate spoke. ''Ere, maid, bring us another mug of ale, will 'ee?'

'Certainly, Mr Bosanko.' She waited.

He glanced up. 'Go on then. Dry as a boot jack, I am.'

Roz smothered a sigh. It was almost two and she had been at work since six that morning. Her back ached and her feet were throbbing. How could she have imagined she would ever get used to it? 'The money, Mr Bosanko?'

'Tell Jack I'll pay'n later.'

'With respect, Mr Bosanko, I don't think he'd believe me.'

'She got 'ee there, boy.' Winnen grinned as he caught Roz's eye. 'Mean, he is. Tight as a gin. 'Tis some terrible affliction.'

'I aren't,' Bosanko bridled. 'No such thing.'

Digging into his pocket, Winnen slapped a handful of coins onto the scarred tabletop. 'Go on, my bird. Take for two pints. Us'll be here all day else.'

Roz delivered their ale. Then, resting her tray on a vacated table, she began scraping and stacking used plates. The inn was always crowded at meal times. The past three months had been particularly busy as masons from Helston and surrounding villages had arrived to assist local men with rebuilding the harbour wall and quay destroyed by the terrible storm in March.

More fishermen were coming in now that the mackerel season was almost over, though a few of the old men still went out with hand lines and sold their catch on the quay. Boats were being repainted and the nets and sails steeped in vats of boiling oak bark to preserve them before the fleet headed west to the Irish sea to fish for herring. This preparation was demanding work that created both a thirst and an appetite for Nell's savoury pies and rich stews.

As Roz loaded her tray she had a sudden vivid memory of gleaming mahogany covered in crisp white damask, delicate bone china and beautifully presented food. But the faces around the table had been tight-lipped and unforgiving. There was so much she missed. But not that: not the lack of *charity*.

'All right, my beauty?' An arm snaked around her waist.

Roz batted the arm away before it could pull her closer. 'That's enough, Jim Kellow.' Keeping her tone light, Roz moved swiftly to put the table between them. Jim was an appealing rogue. But Roz had no interest in him or his games. Instead she treated him in the same no-nonsense manner she used on her young half-brother when he was naughty. 'It's your Susan you should be hugging.'

'I would, but she's mad at me.' The young man pulled a face. 'Awful teasy she is.'

'Then you'd best go home and apologize.'

'But I haven't—' he broke off as Roz raised her brows at him. 'Well, maybe I did. But it never meant nothing.'

'All the more reason to tell her you're sorry,' Roz advised.

He winked. 'I'd sooner stay here.'

'You must do as you wish.' Shaking her head, Roz picked up her tray and shot him a look that warned him to keep his distance. 'If you want ale, ask Jack.'

'Some hard-hearted woman you are.'

Roz said nothing. If she were as tough as he imagined, she wouldn't be here. She would have turned her back and walked away.

As she carried the heavy tray out of the

7

taproom into the short stone-flagged passage leading to the kitchen she asked herself once again what madness had brought her to this? She had given up a secure, comfortable life for the sake of the mother who had abandoned her, a woman difficult to help. Yet, demanding though it was, didn't her life have more meaning here than in the stifling propriety of her grandparents' home?

The kitchen was an inferno. Curls that had escaped from her frilled white mobcap stuck to her temples and the nape of her neck. Perspiration prickled her skin as she rested the tray on the edge of a table alongside a vast wooden tub half-full of scummy water and began to unload the tankards.

Keren, the scullery maid, her skinny arms red to the elbows, wiped a pewter plate with a grey rag, plunged it into a smaller tub of cleaner water then slotted it into a wooden rack to dry.

Nell Hicks, the landlord's wife, a short square woman with work-worn hands and a kind heart hidden behind a commanding manner, clattered the lid onto a cauldron hanging over glowing embers in the huge hearth. She turned to Roz, her face crimson from the heat. 'Still busy is it?'

Roz shook her head. 'Just a few left now. The rest have gone back to work.'

Nell released a gusty sigh. 'Right, Keren, leave they plates and get this floor swept and washed.' She glanced round as another woman bustled in from the private dining room carrying a tray. The dishes stacked on it were not pewter, but patterned china, and the cutlery was silver.

'Everything all right in there, Annie?'

Plump and beaming, Annie nodded. Instead of the coarse linen Roz wore, Annie's apron was crisp white cotton. Her gown was pale blue, and frizzy fair hair peeped out from beneath her neat cap. 'Both gentlemen said it was the best stew they'd tasted. Had two helpings of strawberry tart, they did. Soon as they've drunk their coffee they'll be gone.'

'Paid have they?' Nell demanded.

Annie nodded. 'Jack's with 'em now.'

'Who's looking after the tap, then?'

'Toby. And there's only a few in there. Stop your fretting, Nell. Looking fagged to death you are. Why don't you go and have a sit-down?'

'I wouldn't mind,' Nell admitted. 'Me feet is giving me gyp.'

'Go on, then. We'll finish up here. You got a couple hours before you need to start cooking for tonight.' Annie set down the tray of china.

As she waddled wearily towards the door, the landlord's wife looked back at Roz. 'Mind they dishes, won't you?'

'As if they were my own,' Roz promised. Satisfied, Nell nodded and went out.

While Keren fetched the soft broom and a dustpan from a cupboard, Annie helped Roz carry the tub outside. After the fug in the tap-room and the kitchen's heat, the air tasted sweet and fresh. Roz breathed deeply, filling her lungs.

'I seen Jim Kellow in the tap,' Annie said, as they tipped the dirty water into the gutter. 'Susan mad with him again, is she?'

'He says she's teasy.' Roz's tone was dry.

9

'She always was.' Annie sniffed as they returned to the kitchen and set the tub down. 'I reck'n she thought she'd tame un. But a man don't change, not less he want to.' She clicked her tongue. 'If that girl had a lick of sense she'd offer'n kisses instead of scolds.' She glanced at Roz. 'He idn' giving you no trouble, is he?'

'Jim's easy enough to manage. I only wish—' she broke off, shaking her head. Crossing to the hearth she picked up a hessian pad and wrapped it around the handle of a large black kettle suspended from the chimney crane. She needed both hands to lift it down.

Annie hefted a pail of cold water and emptied half into the tub. 'Only wish what?'

As Roz tipped the kettle, turning her head to avoid the steam, her gaze met Annie's. 'Will Prowse,' she mouthed.

Annie set the pail down and straightened. 'What have he done?' she whispered.

'Asked me to marry him.' Roz shuddered.

Annie's eyes widened. 'He never did.'

Roz glanced at Keren on the far side of the kitchen, but she was humming to herself as she swept, happier now Nell was not there to chivvy and scold her.

'I wish he hadn't. I can't imagine why he thought—' Roz shrugged helplessly. 'He must have known I'd refuse.'

'What did you say?' Annie hissed, agog.

'I was polite, of course. A proposal of marriage – even from a man like Will Prowse – deserves courtesy, especially when it's declined.'

'See, there you are. You got this lovely way

with words. But are you sure he knew you was turning him down?'

Roz tightened her grip on the kettle's handle. 'He pretended he didn't. But I know he did. He *must* have done. Anyway, the point is I said no and I meant it.' She shuddered again. 'Annie, I couldn't marry him. I just couldn't.'

'Course not, my bird. Hey, don't take on so.'

But Roz knew there would be no escaping Will Prowse. For she owed him. And one way or another he would make her pay.

As Annie went out to the pump to draw more water, Roz pushed her sleeves up past her elbows, wet her hands, and worked the block of hard yellow soap between her palms to create suds. After soaking a coarse cloth in the steaming soapy water, she gathered up the silver cutlery from Annie's tray and carefully wiped each piece clean.

This job had fallen to her as soon as Nell realized she knew how to take care of the china and silverware kept for visitors of quality.

'Jack never said where you was working before,' Nell had stated, her gaze suspicious. 'Somewhere decent, was it? Only I don't want no trouble.'

Recognizing the warning, and understanding Nell's reservations – for in her heart of hearts, didn't she share them? – Roz had told as much of the truth as she dared. 'It was the house of a reverend gentleman, Mrs Hicks. The family was very particular. I was not dismissed. I left because my mother needed me.'

It was Mary-Blanche who had insisted they

come to Porthinnis, who urged Roz to try for work at the Three Mackerel, who said she knew Jack Hicks and to mention her name, but not in his wife's hearing. Weary, disheartened, and anxious to secure any kind of work for her meagre savings were almost gone, Roz had chosen not to ask questions whose answers she feared would reveal more about her mother's life than she was ready to hear.

After an instant's pause, Nell had nodded. 'Right, well, do what you're told, work hard, and we'll get on.'

Roz had earned Nell's trust and found a friend in Annie. But her mother's behaviour meant that no matter how hard she worked, she simply couldn't earn *enough*.

Toby stuck his head round the door. 'Any beef stew left? Two of they masons working on the quay just come in.'

Annie frowned at him. 'How didn't they come up with the rest?'

'Waiting for stone they were. Couldn't leave till it was checked.'

Annie clicked her tongue. 'I got four pound of strawberries waiting to be—'

'It's all right, Annie,' Roz broke in. 'I'll do it. You see to the fruit.'

Wiping her hands dry, she took two clean plates from the rack and ladled stew onto them. Swiftly cutting hunks of bread from the loaf, she piled them onto another plate, placed the three plates and two spoons on a tray and carried it down the passage to the taproom.

The two men were sitting by the open window.

As Roz approached, a man passed by outside.

'Bit of all right that is,' one of the men beamed up at her.

The other nodded. 'Starving I am.'

Roz smiled as she put down the tray and set the steaming plates in front of them. A male figure filled the open doorway, briefly cutting off the light.

Looking up, Roz's smile froze as she recognized Constable Colenso. Her stomach clenched with the all-too-familiar sense of dread. *No, please no. Not again.* She straightened, picking up the empty tray.

In his fustian breeches and brown coat, his hair drawn back into a queue above a wilting collar, the parish constable looked hot and uncomfortable as he crossed to the bar where Jack was drawing a pint of ale.

'Any butter is there?' one of the men asked. 'Miss?'

Roz dragged her attention back to her customers. 'I'm sorry, what—?'

'Butter? For the bread?'

'Yes, of course. I'll fetch it.' Maybe the constable was here for something else entirely, nothing to do with her at all.

But as she started towards the kitchen passage she saw him turn from the bar and start towards her. She gripped the tray like a shield. Then realizing the futility of her gesture, she let it drop to her side.

'Sorry, Miss.' In the dim smoky light she thought she saw pity behind the constable's frown. 'You're to come with me.'

13

Even as fear leapt, so too did a spark of hope that this time the reason for the constable's visit had nothing to do with her mother. 'Is Tom—?'

'Boy's fine. He's downalong with blacksmith. Sorry, Miss. 'Tis your mother.'

Again. He didn't say it, but Roz heard it in his voice just the same. She swallowed the dryness in her throat. *Yet another fine to pay. How was she supposed to* ... The room swayed.

His hand caught her arm. 'Steady now. All right are you?'

She sucked in air. It tasted thick and stale. 'Yes.' The lie slipped easily from her tongue. As all her hopes had come to nothing and every effort had been flung back in her face, her ability to pretend that it didn't hurt had become second nature. *Where had her mother got the brandy from this time? And how had she paid for it?*

'Thank you, Mr Colenso. I'll come as soon as I've finished here—'

'No, miss.' He shook his head. 'Now. The Justice said he wants to see you right away.'

Roz pressed one hand to her stomach as dread spiked. Dread, and something else. Something *foolish, hopeless.* Mr Casvellan had been kind – so far. But he would hold her responsible. She had given him her word. And she really had tried. Yet what was she supposed to do? She couldn't lock her mother in. 'I—' she gestured towards the kitchen. 'I'm still— I have to—'

'Want me to tell Jack, do you?'

'No!' Struggling for control she repeated more quietly, 'No, thank you. I'll do it. Will you wait outside? Please? I'll be with you directly.'

14

'Quick as you can, miss.' With a nod he turned and left.

Edging between the tables Roz hurried to the bar.

Jack continued wiping up spills on the polished wood as he jerked his chin forward. 'Trouble?'

Roz nodded.

'Bl— your mother?'

Roz nodded again. 'Mr Casvellan wants to see me.'

'Right now?' Jack paused, his hand still. 'John come to take you up there, has he?'

Roz guessed his thoughts were echoing hers. Never before had the Justice demanded she leave her job during working hours. So why had he this time? What was so urgent? *What had her mother done?* Fighting panic, Roz dipped her head, her face burning. 'I'm really sorry.'

''T'idn' your fault, girl. Go on then.'

'Thank you. I'll make up the time. I'll—'

'Never mind about that. Quick now, don't keep'n waiting.'

Roz hurried down the passage, untying her apron and pulling off her cap. 'Annie, the two men who just came in want some butter for their bread. I have to go.' She hung cap and apron on a hook behind the kitchen door.

Annie's forehead puckered. 'What's on, my bird?'

'The constable – I have to—' Roz shook her head, unable to continue, her throat stiff with tears of rage, frustration and grief.

'Dear life!' Annie snorted. 'Not again. I know

she's your mother and all. But she's a bleddy nuisance. Need a good thrashing, she do. Knock some sense into her.'

Keren had stopped washing the flag-stoned floor and was gaping at them.

'Catching flies, girl?' Annie snapped. 'Get that floor wiped. If 'tis still wet when Nell come down she'll give you what-for.'

As Keren bent again to her task, Annie patted Roz's shoulder and went to fetch the butter from the slate-shelved larder.

Her heart thudding, Roz dipped her hands in the pail of cold water and pressed them to her cheeks, her throat and the back of her neck. If only she had time to change and tidy her hair. *What difference would that make?* Shaking out her faded calico gown, she put on her hat. Her hands trembled as she tied the ribbons beneath her chin.

How many times had she been summoned to Trescowe? Each time her mother had promised it was the last, that from now on everything would be different. Roz had wanted so much to believe her. But despite all her support and encouragement, here they were again. No matter what she did, it was never enough.

'You don't understand,' her mother would sob or snarl. 'You have no idea what I've been through.'

Roz couldn't argue. She didn't know. So she bit her tongue, put her mother to bed, cleaned up the mess, and tried to find new hiding places so there would be enough money to buy food and pay their rent. But Tom was growing so fast. He

16

needed new trousers, and his boots were falling apart.

Up till now she had managed to pay the fines. But doing so had put her in debt to Will Prowse. She knew the Justice was losing patience. How much longer could she hope to keep her mother out of gaol?

Swinging a muslin kerchief about her shoulders she crossed it in front of her gown, tied the ends behind her back, and tipping her hat forward so her face was in shadow, she walked outside into hot sunshine where the constable waited.

Two

Seated at the large table he used as a desk, Branoc Casvellan signed the document placed in front of him by his clerk.

'What else, George?' The sun had moved round and no longer filled the room with bright light. But the afternoon heat still lay sufficiently heavy to have forced Casvellan out of his dark green frock coat now on a wooden hanger on the back of the door. Had he been alone he would also have shed his striped waistcoat. But he wasn't, and he had no wish to offend his clerk who cared deeply about the dignity and the respect due to a Justice.

Crow-like in black, his greying hair neatly tied back in a black ribbon, Ellacott retrieved the document.

'About Quarter Sessions, sir—'

'I shan't attend. It's a day's ride each way, then at least half a day wasted on pomp and ceremony that does little but remind certain dignitaries of their own importance. I've too much work here.'

'You'll be attending the Midsummer Coinage in Helston?'

Casvellan nodded. 'There's also a dinner at the Angel Hotel to discuss billeting French

18

prisoners of war.' He leaned back, flexing his shoulders. 'Tell Varcoe to prepare for fifteen. He can use the old stable block. The tack room should allow enough space for three officers. Remind him to check the stovepipe. It may have rusted through. If they are here for the winter they'll need warmth and somewhere to dry their clothes. What's next?'

The clerk glanced down at the open ledger he was holding.

'The matter of repairs to the moor road, sir, the uphill stretch above Porthinnis? We've received four complaints in the last two weeks. Two refer to broken axles and two to broken wheels caused by the depth of the ruts.'

'Who has the contract?'

'William Jory bid for it, sir.'

'Well, the work obviously hasn't been done. Has Jory given a reason for the delay?'

The clerk shook his head. 'I wrote to him two weeks ago requesting that information, but he has not replied.'

'Has he been ill?' Casvellan knew his clerk would have made enquiries.

'No, sir. However, I understand he bid for several additional contracts, among them were two for Sir Edward Pengarrick.'

'Did he indeed.' Casvellan tried to ignore the mingled enmity and irritation that inevitably followed mention of the baronet's name. 'No doubt those have taken precedence. But the road must be mended at once. This dry weather won't last indefinitely. If it's in such a poor state now, little rain will be needed to make it impassable.

Who else bid?'

'Henwood Berryman. Anticipating your wishes, sir, I took the liberty of drafting a letter.' He set it in front of the Justice. 'And another to Mr Jory informing him that his contract is voided and the work transferred elsewhere.'

Reaching for his pen, Casvellan scrawled his signature on each of the documents then glanced up as Ellacott cleared his throat, uncharacteristically hesitant.

'What is it?'

'As you were busy on the estate all day yesterday, sir, you probably won't have heard.'

Leaning back in his chair, Casvellan stretched long legs clad in buff-coloured breeches and black topboots in front of him. He planned to ride later. Raad needed exercise and so did he. A good gallop would loosen his muscles and perhaps relieve some of his frustration.

'Heard what?' he enquired. As he saw his clerk swallow he knew the news must be bad.

'Four Mousehole men sentenced to transportation.'

Fury catapulted Casvellan from his chair, the movement so swift and sudden that his clerk flinched. 'Damn Pengarrick to hell and back!' He raked a hand through black hair that fell over his shirt collar in thick waves. 'Were they regular offenders?'

'As to that, sir,' the clerk replied carefully, 'I couldn't say. But if you are referring to previous appearances before a court, I understand only one of them had been arrested prior to this, and that was for disturbing the peace.'

Casvellan paced the room, anger churning inside him. 'God's blood! What's wrong with him? Pengarrick *must* know those men would never take such desperate risks were it not for the high prices caused by this war.'

'Of course he does, sir.' Anger clouded Ellacott's normally placid features. 'Just as he knows you would have treated them far more leniently.'

Casvellan turned. 'And that's why he's done it.' Inhaling deeply, he fought his rage and returned to his seat, his gaze rising to that of his clerk. 'You're right, of course. Those men and their families mean nothing to him. They must bear the punishment, but it's me he is aiming at. Any questions I raise concerning *his* sentencing would give him carte blanche to interfere with mine. I cannot – will not – permit that.'

He made a conscious effort to set the matter aside. He could not waste time and energy on a situation outside his control. Looking up once more he smiled, and saw his clerk relax. 'What would I do without you, George?'

'It is my sincere hope that such a circumstance will never arise, sir.'

'So, what else?

'Ah. The – er – matter of Mary-Blanche Trevaskis.'

Rising once more from his chair, Casvellan crossed to the window. Folding his arms, he looked out, but did not see the lofty trees, their leaves unstirred by the slightest breath of wind. 'What am I to do with her?'

'Well, sir—'

'It was a rhetorical question, Ellacott,' he said gently. 'If she were a vagrant I could send her back where she came from.'

'Penzance was her last place of residence, I believe, sir.'

'Quite so. But she is not a vagrant. So, much as I might wish it, that avenue isn't open to me. Nor, as she lives with her daughter, could I send her to the workhouse even if there were room.' He gazed down onto the gravelled circle and felt a muscle jump in his jaw. 'Pengarrick's policy of gaoling or transporting men for comparatively minor crimes has thrown scores of women and children onto the mercy of the parish. If he cannot see how short-sighted and counter-productive his actions are, then he's even more of a fool than I thought.'

The clerk remained silent.

Casvellan blew a sigh. 'She's a damn nuisance, Ellacott.'

'And must be a sore trial to the young lady, sir.'

'Young *lady*, George?' he questioned, intrigued by the slight softening in his clerk's tone.

'Indeed, sir.' Ellacott regarded his employer steadily. 'However, should you consider I have made a misjudgement then I will apologize and beg your pardon.'

Casvellan shook his head. 'That will not be necessary. We both know you are rarely wrong.'

The clerk bowed. 'That is most gracious of you, sir.'

Casvellan turned from the window. It had been immediately clear to him that despite her

22

obvious poverty and her job at the inn, Roz Trevaskis came from a far higher station in life. *What had happened? What had brought her to this?*

The first time she appeared before him to plead on her mother's behalf, making promises he knew she would find impossible to keep, he had sensed a mystery. In addition and to his astonishment he had experienced a powerful tug of attraction. He had instantly dismissed it. A heavy workload meant he was simply too busy to inquire into matters that did not directly concern him. Instead he had confined himself to deciding how best to deal with the older woman's public drunkenness and disturbing the peace.

But Mary-Blanche Trevaskis had proved to be a recurring problem. In drink the woman was a menace: noisy, coarse and aggressive. Yet on the few occasions he had seen her sober, she radiated a sadness that had led him to hope she might respond to warnings. Unfortunately she hadn't. Perhaps the public ridicule of a period in the stocks might bring her to her senses.

Noting the girl's flushed cheeks and lowered eyes as she supported her mother, he had recognized both her shame and her anger, and found himself moved. She didn't belong here. Then his gaze had flicked to Mary-Blanche whose slow blink and vacant expression proclaimed her still intoxicated. Even as he spoke stern words of warning he had known he was wasting his breath. Mary-Blanche Trevaskis would be back, regardless of her daughter's promises.

23

Aware of tension across his forehead, Casvellan realized he was frowning and made a deliberate effort to relax. He and Ellacott understood one another well, and he relied on his clerk where points of law were concerned. But there were certain matters he would not discuss. How could he, when his thoughts were confused and his emotions – so long untouched – were oddly unsettled?

'Colenso is fetching Miss Trevaskis?'

'Yes, sir. They should return within the hour.'

Casvellan knew that had he not issued the order to have the girl brought here, Ellacott would have made the suggestion. It was a logical move given that Mary-Blanche Trevaskis currently lay sprawled and snoring on a pallet in one of the cells downstairs.

'The prisoner had no money in her possession?'

'No, sir.'

'She has no work that you're aware of?'

Ellacott coughed delicately. 'Not of the usual nature, sir.'

They both knew what the clerk meant. But recalling Mary-Blanche Trevaskis's appearance the last time she had appeared before him, Branoc doubted that even the most desperate seaman would be willing to risk his health for a few minutes in an alley with her.

'One cannot help but wonder how she comes by the brandy, sir.'

'Right now I'm more concerned with the fact that if she has no work, her fines are being paid by her daughter.'

The clerk cleared his throat. 'With respect, sir, the law provides for this eventuality with punishments of a more physical nature.'

'Yes, Ellacott. I am aware of that and have it under consideration.'

'I beg your pardon, sir.'

Casvellan pushed a fallen curl back from his forehead and rubbed the nape of his neck where tension had knotted the muscles. Knuckles tapped on the door. He froze, but only for an instant. *It wouldn't be. Not yet. It was too soon.* Ellacott was nearest the door and Casvellan waited while he opened it.

The clerk turned to his employer with a smile. 'Miss Casvellan, sir.'

'I'm not interrupting, am I?' Cool in white muslin trimmed with blue ribbon, her fair hair cropped into a helmet of curls, Deborah held up a crystal jug of cloudy liquid. 'I thought you might like some lemonade.'

'Deb, you're an angel. Did you bring glasses as well?'

Smiling, she offered two crystal tumblers. 'Mr Ellacott, I'm sure you would welcome a cold drink.'

'That's most thoughtful, Miss. With your permission, sir, I'll take it to my room. There are several matters requiring my attention.'

When the clerk had gone, Casvellan regarded his sister thoughtfully as he pressed the cold glass to his forehead and cheek. 'Is something wrong, Deb?'

'Yes. No. Well, it's just ... Mama will keep talking about Richard. I *know* it's a year since he was killed. Does she imagine I have forgotten? How could I when every newspaper we see carries news of the war?'

Draining his glass, Casvellan set it down. Over the past few months Deborah had regained the weight stripped from her by grief. Bones and angles were softened now by firm flesh, and she looked all the better for it.

'Talking to you about Richard allows her to relive losing father.' Reaching for his coat he put it on.

'Well, I don't wish to seem unfeeling, but there is no comparison. Papa had been out of the army for three years. He was living here at home and died while he was out hunting. Richard was killed aboard his ship during a battle.'

'Captain Whitby's letter spoke of him as an excellent officer loved and respected by his men,' Casvellan reminded gently. 'I know it's small comfort—'

'Yes, it is.' His sister's eyes glistened with unshed tears as she turned to him. 'I *know* he was brave and loyal. Just as I know that though the French had a fleet of thirty ships and the British only six, we still beat them. It was wonderful that we had only twelve men killed or wounded. But Richard was one of them. How *can* Mama claim the events are alike?' She shook her head. Then taking a deep breath she tried to smile. 'I'm sorry. I shouldn't get upset. It's just ... I do still think of Richard. But all the grieving in the world won't bring him back. Sometimes I go a whole day without—'

'Until our mother stirs up unhappy memories,'

Casvellan's tone was grim.

Deborah nodded. 'If there was anything I could do for her, I would. But—'

'There isn't and you can't. Perhaps she genuinely does miss father. Though why that should be so, considering he spent most of their marriage abroad with his regiment, and after he came home—' he broke off. His father's lechery had been an embarrassment his mother dealt with by refusing to acknowledge it. Responsibility for paying off the housemaids his father had seduced, impregnated, then discarded had fallen to him.

Handsome Harry Casvellan had been an excellent soldier, a selfish husband and an absent father. Deborah missed him, for their father had doted on her. Her elder brother did not. Forcing his anger aside, Casvellan smiled, knowing it softened the natural austerity of his features. 'But then, I find women a mystery.'

'Of course you do.' Deborah patted his arm. But her expression told him she didn't believe his claim for an instant.

'Seriously, Deb. Our mother revels in playing the grieving widow. Let her get on with it. But don't permit her to drag you down as well.'

She looked up at him, her gaze thoughtful. 'You sound so harsh. Yet I know you're not.'

One corner of his mouth quivered. 'Don't let the miscreants I have to deal with hear you say that. I'd lose all credibility.' He opened the door for her. 'If Mama has taken to her bed, why don't you enjoy your freedom? You might perhaps call on Mrs Varcoe and see how she's settling in.'

'I already have. She's a delightful young woman, and so looking forward to the birth of her child. Though her mother— No. I promised myself I would make an effort to be charitable.'

'Don't bother on my account, Deb. The woman's a nightmare. She will *gush*.' Glancing out of the window he saw two figures approaching in the dappled shade beneath the oaks and limes that lined one side of the drive. His gaze slid past the stocky constable. Beside him, slim as a willow, walked Roz Trevaskis. Even from here he could sense her anxiety. It showed in the set of her shoulders and her rigid spine. He felt an odd leap beneath his ribs. Deliberately ignoring it he turned to his sister. 'Will you excuse me? I have a case to deal with.'

'Of course. I'll see you later.'

As she closed the door behind her he moved away from the window, not waiting to see Deborah emerge onto the gravelled drive.

Preferring to keep all matters relating to his work as a justice away from the house, he had adapted this building to that purpose. Here in this large room on the upper floor he dealt with the many and varied demands that kept him busy for three or four days a week. His clerk's office was on the other side of the landing with a storeroom next to it. The ground floor contained one small and two larger rooms with stone floors and barred windows in which prisoners were held.

A building on the far side of the gravelled circle housed the brewhouse and laundry. Behind it, the old stables and coach house surrounded a paved yard on three sides. It led onto the back drive used by tradesmen and estate staff.

Loosening his neckcloth a fraction Casvellan tugged the bottom edge of his striped waistcoat down. As he realized what he was doing, and recognized the uncertainty and agitation behind his actions, he didn't know whether to laugh or curse, and mocked himself for a fool.

He was almost thirty years old, a man of the world and a justice. The unmarried owner of a considerable estate, he could spot a designing mother with hopeful daughters at twenty yards.

Fortunately his natural reserve – which he had heard described as aloofness, taciturnity, and by one disgruntled mama as snobbish disdain – proved a challenge too great for younger girls newly out in society. That suited him. He was no baby-sitter. But nor was he a brute. Indeed, those maidens would have been astonished had they known just how much he sympathized with their predicament. Thrust into society, the expectations of anxious parents resting on their shoulders, it was little wonder that those who didn't lapse into nervous giggles pretended sophistication with a forwardness guaranteed to attract the wrong kind of attention.

But there were limits to the amount of blushing and simpering a man could stand. As a gentleman he knew how to flirt and flatter without raising false hopes or straying even close to the limit of what was proper. He had enjoyed occasional affairs with married women who understood the rules of such encounters. But

29

only once had he been in love, tumbling headlong at the age of twenty for a vivacious widow
nearly twice his age. Recognizing his passion for
the calf-love it was, the lady had treated him
kindly, taught him to give pleasure as well as
take it, and ended the affair with a smile. She
had re-married and they were still friends.

In fact she had introduced him to Ellen. Had
Ellen lived would they have married? Been
happy? Such musings were pointless. As his
mother reminded him with increasing frequency,
it was time he married and produced an heir. She
had a point. But providing the estate with an heir
was not sufficient incentive. Having seen at first
hand the damaging effects of a marriage
between people totally unsuited, he had vowed
he would not make the same mistake.

From Easter onward, despite the fact that the
household was barely out of mourning, invitations had poured in. Though some had been for
Deborah, the majority had been addressed to
him, much to the disgust of his younger brother,
Davy.

Casvellan had only accepted those to which he
could escort his sister. Her fiancé's death,
coming so soon after the loss of their father, had
hit her hard. But Deb had never wanted for
courage. She apologized for using him as both a
prop and a shield. But watching her respond to
both the tactful and the crass with grace and
dignity had inspired in him both admiration and
bemusement.

'How do you stand it?' he murmured after
watching one dowager, resplendent in a plumed

turban and numerous sashes of multi-hued gauze, pat Deborah's arm briskly while announcing that though four-and-twenty, given her handsome dowry she need not fear being left on the shelf.

'She meant well. And in all honesty, Bran, it's no more than the truth.'

Nor, if he were seeking a potential bride, did he lack choice. At every social event there were girls of every shape, size and colouring, all from good families. They wore pretty gowns and bright hopeful smiles. They had been drilled in deportment, dancing and social etiquette. They could play the piano, sing or paint watercolours. They all hoped to marry well, and if treated reasonably would not cause their husbands a moment's unease.

So, despite knowing all that, and despite his disgust at his father's behaviour, why in the name of all that was holy did he find himself drawn to a girl so completely and utterly unsuitable?

The sound of the constable's slow tread on the stairs brought him up with a start. A few strides took him behind his desk. Should he sit or stand? Ellacott had referred to her as a young lady. But reminding himself that Roz Trevaskis was the illegitimate daughter of a drunken whore, Casvellan resumed his seat.

Three

Standing in the passage behind John Colenso, Roz could feel her heart thudding uncomfortably against her ribs. She adjusted her kerchief, making sure it covered her to the hollow of her throat. She did not want the Justice to think — noticing the tremor in her fingers she instantly dropped her hands, clasping them tightly in front of her. What did it matter what he thought? He would believe what he chose. He would assume, as so many others did, *like mother like daughter*. But she wasn't. And that alone was sufficient reason not to marry Will Prowse.

As the constable knocked on the closed door, Roz swallowed. Her throat was painfully dry. She moistened her lips with the tip of her tongue. What would she do if the Justice demanded a fine? She couldn't afford to pay it. She had just enough for bread and eggs between now and the end of the week when she got her wages. Asking Will for another loan was out of the question. She had yet to settle her current debt. She hadn't told her mother about his proposal, but someone had. Mary-Blanche had been furious.

'Are you mad?' she had shrieked, her face mottled, spittle gathering at the corners of her

32

mouth. 'Christ almighty, girl!'

Roz had flinched at the profanity.

'We could have got out of this pigsty,' Mary-Blanche had shouted. 'We'd have had decent clothes and proper food. How could you be so selfish?'

'I'm sorry,' Roz had whispered. Her mother was right. It was selfish. But just the thought of Will Prowse touching her had made her stomach churn and her skin crawl.

Nor could she contemplate the alternative her mother had flung at her. That she could even suggest it ... Shaken and appalled Roz had managed to hide both reactions. She had no right to judge. Her mother's situation had been desperate. She had been on the verge of starvation. During their early weeks together, listening as her mother described the terror and loneliness, the things she had been forced to do to earn enough for something to eat and a place to sleep, Roz had often found herself in tears. She had vowed to take care of her mother and Tom so that never again would they feel hungry or afraid.

Two years had passed since their dramatic reunion on the street in Penzance. Two years that had cost Roz her illusions, her idealism and every penny she had. But despite the painful realization that life without the cushion of money was far more brutal, and that her mother's memory could not be trusted, Roz clung to the hope that one day they would be a proper family.

Meanwhile, other than sell herself or marry

Will Prowse – which in Roz's mind amounted to the same thing – there was only one way she could earn enough to repay Will.

In a few days, at the dark of the moon, another cargo of contraband was due. It was her task to lead the string of pack animals. But if she were caught she would not be fined. She would go to gaol. Then who would look after her mother and Tom?

Anxiety clutched her heart like a fist and her breath caught in her throat. She coughed to disguise it as John Colenso looked round. Then she heard Justice Casvellan's voice – how deep and stern it sounded – bidding them enter.

Constable Colenso opened the door and stood back, gesturing for Roz to go in first. Entering the room she had come to know all too well, Roz did not lift her gaze from the floor.

'Thank you, Constable. You may wait downstairs.'

Was the Justice angry? He had every right to be. So did she. But she had learned not to show it, for either her mother shouted and raged at her, or wept quiet, heart-rending tears. Roz wasn't sure which was worse. Both left her helpless and emotionally wrung out.

'Sir.' The constable withdrew, closing the door quietly. Roz felt a moment's relief that no one else would hear whatever the Justice had to say. For surely he would criticize. She could not blame him. Less than a month ago her mother had agreed to be bound over. But as the constable had explained on the walk from Porthinnis, far from being of good behaviour, Mary-

Blanche had been found down at the harbour, drunk and raging at one of the masons.

'I would have took her home, Miss,' the constable said. 'But the foreman wasn't having it. He complained she'd been distracting the men. Said if I didn't arrest her, he'd go hisself and fetch the Justice.'

Shame for her mother had made Roz's face burn as she nodded. 'I understand, Mr Colenso. You had no choice.'

'Sit down, Miss Trevaskis.' Casvellan's voice broke into her thoughts.

Doing as she was told, Roz sat straight-backed on the wooden chair placed at an angle to his desk. Tucking her feet to one side, she stared at her hands folded tightly in her lap.

'You are aware your mother is downstairs in one of the cells?'

'Yes.' Roz's throat was so dry that the word emerged in a hoarse whisper. She cleared her throat. 'Yes, sir.'

'Kindly look at me when I am addressing you.'

She knew she had been guilty of discourtesy, but it was so hard to meet his gaze. She had made promises on her mother's behalf, and they had not been kept. By helping Will Prowse with the contraband she had broken the law, and must do so again. Like the constable, she too had no choice. How else could she pay her mother's fines and still put food on the table?

She raised her head. His eyes were the dark blue of storm clouds, heavy-lidded and fringed with black lashes. He had a way of narrowing them that made him appear sleepy. But it was misleading for his glittering gaze was as sharp as an unsheathed blade. He linked his fingers on the desk in front of him, his expression bleak.

'Miss Trevaskis, this cannot continue.'

Roz screwed up her courage. 'Sir, please, I beg you, not gaol. Bodmin is almost a day's ride away. How am I to keep my job and still find the time to visit?' Driven by fear, the words tumbled out. 'Sir, if she is confined in a small dank cell with hardly any light and no proper food, her mind will break as surely as her health. I've heard the place is rife with fever.' She stopped and chewed her lip, gripping her hands so tightly the knuckles ached.

Leaning back, he tapped his fingers lightly on the polished wood table where several neat piles of documents rested alongside a number of thick volumes. 'I am running out of patience and alternatives, Miss Trevaskis. I understand your mother has now been barred from the Three Mackerel, the Bell, *and* the Red Lion.'

Roz's breath hitched and her head snapped up. She tried to hide her shock, but she had forgotten how observant he was, how shrewd.

'You didn't know.'

'No.' No one had told her. Like him, they probably assumed she knew. But if the three main inns in the village were refusing to serve her mother, then where was she getting the brandy? There were a number of small ale-houses in the back streets by the harbour where no doubt a keg or two of cognac was kept under the counter. One day, unable to find her mother, she had asked Annie if Mary-Blanche might be in one of them. Annie had shaken her head.

'No, my bird. She wouldn't be let over the step. 'Tis men only.'

'Miss Trevaskis,' Casvellan's cool tone pierced the clamour in her head. 'You are clearly not suited to your current circumstances.'

Before she realized it, Roz was on her feet. 'No, I'm not. But I'm doing my best,' she cried. 'If anyone had complained about me I would have been told. Nell – Mrs Hicks – is very—'

'Sit down.' Though he didn't raise his voice it was an order nonetheless.

She sat, her heart pounding. Heat scalded her cheeks as a lump formed in her throat. If she lost her job what would she do? How would they manage?

'You misunderstand. I was not referring to your work. Indeed, Mr Hicks speaks very highly of you.'

The Justice had spoken to Jack about her? When? More importantly, *why*? She dare not ask.

'However, it is clear to me that the job you are doing, indeed your present way of life, are not— Have you no relatives? No one to whom you could apply for assistance?'

Roz recalled the day she had pleaded with her grandfather to help. Though it was two years ago the scene was still vividly clear. It haunted her dreams.

'No one can help your mother.'

'Please, grandpapa, don't say that. Mama's state is truly desperate. She needs all the support we can give her.'

Suddenly haggard, her grandfather had slowly shaken his head. Lines of suffering etched deep in his face had shocked her. 'My dear, your intentions are good and do you great credit. But what you do not possess is experience of life. Your mother's situation is of her own choosing.'

Incredulous and indignant, for the first time in her life Roz had defied him. 'How can you say that? And how can you, a clergyman, turn your back on your own daughter?'

Bracing herself for anger she was startled when he laid a gentle hand on her shoulder.

'Hush, child. Perhaps you have forgotten that despite the shame and sorrow Mary-Blanche caused us by eloping then returning home unmarried and – though we did not know it then – expecting you, I accepted her back into the family. You were born here in the vicarage. We did not put you out for adoption. You were raised as one of our own because, regardless of your mother's behaviour, you were an innocent child. But despite our best efforts, before you were a year old, Mary-Blanche abandoned you and left our protection. Until she returns, truly contrite, and accepts responsibility for her actions, no one can help her.'

'But—'

'No.' He had been firm. 'You have said your piece, now you must listen. Roz, I am three times your age, and thus know a great deal more of the world. You have a kind and generous heart. It would grieve me to see it broken, especially by your mother. And that is what will happen if you pursue this.'

But the image of her mother as they had seen her in Penzance, filthy, clothed in stinking rags, and begging on the street, was one she could not put out of her mind. If her grandfather would not help, then she must.

How right he had been. Every day for the past two years she had lived with anxiety, fear and broken promises. Coping with her mother would have been hard enough. But there was Tom as well. Seven years old and half-wild when she met him, it had taken months to win his trust. She could not abandon him. So she worked long hours at a job she loathed but was grateful to have. Without it they would surely have starved. Yet no matter what she did it wasn't enough. For here she was again, pleading with the Justice.

Sometimes the weight of responsibility was almost more than she could bear. Mr Casvellan had shown remarkable forbearance, certainly more than her mother deserved. But even while she pleaded with him not to send her mother to gaol, she was committed to helping Will Prowse move the next cargo of contraband. Was it possible, she wondered, to die of shame?

Digging the nails of one hand into the palm of the other, Roz shook her head. 'No, sir. There is no one.' Since leaving the parish of Lanisley she had not been back. Her grandparents' lives and those of her two aunts and their families would be easier now she was no longer there as a tangible reminder of her mother's sin and shame. She had ignored her grandfather's advice and left the protection of his home. Like her mother she had made a choice. Now she was living with the consequences.

Anger darkened his face. She held her breath.

'Your mother will remain here in the cell over-night. When she recovers consciousness, she will spend two days in the stocks. At least this time she, and not you, will bear the punishment.'

After a brief knock the door opened and the clerk entered. 'The papers you requested, sir.' Placing them in the Justice's outstretched hand he acknowledged Roz with a brief smile and left the room.

Roz rose to her feet and prepared to leave. 'Thank you, sir.' The words did not begin to convey her gratitude. But she dare not say more, fearful of betraying emotions that had nothing to do with her reason for being here.

Glancing up he motioned her back to her seat. 'Not yet, Miss Trevaskis. We are not finished.' He returned his gaze to the document.

Roz sank down onto the chair. Nervousness tightened her stomach and dried her mouth. What now? Had her mother done something else? Something she didn't know about? But surely he would have mentioned it before. So if it wasn't her mother, what—?

He lay the document down in front of him. 'Your brother, Miss Trevaskis, how old is he?'

'I believe he is almost ten, sir.'

'It has been brought to my attention that he is too often seen in the company of some older boys bent on mischief.' Again she would have spoken, but once more he raised a hand, fore-stalling her. 'I don't doubt you are doing your best. But with an absent father and a mother who

40

cares little for his welfare—'

'Not the workhouse!' The words were out before Roz could stop them. 'Sir, I'll do anything—'

He sighed. 'Then be good enough to let me finish.'

'I'm sorry,' Roz whispered as heat rose like a tide from her throat to her cheeks.

'I understand the boy spends much of his time with the blacksmith. Is that correct?'

Roz nodded. 'Yes, sir. Tom is very fond of horses and loves to watch them being shod. Sometimes Mr Tudgey gives him small tasks and pays him a halfpenny if he does well. Mr Casvellan, I admit he can be a handful. He—he—' Roz was torn. If she told him the truth, that as soon as he could walk Tom was left to fend for himself, this would surely make matters even worse for her mother. 'He has not had the best start in life. But I would not have you think he is always in trouble.'

'I don't. But he will be unless something is done now to stop the rot. Are you acquainted with Daniel Eathorne, my head groom?'

Roz nodded. 'I know him by sight, sir.' A wiry man with a weathered face and bandy legs.

'Both he and Mr Tudgey are of the opinion that Tom has potential. He is intelligent and has shown that he's not afraid of hard work. An apprenticeship will give him the discipline and skills he needs to build a secure future for himself.'

'Apprenticeship?' Roz whispered, staring at him. 'Where?'

'Here, at Trescowe. One of the stable boys has recently completed his term, so Mr Eathorne is looking for a replacement lad.'

'Sir, I—' As her eyes prickled and her vision blurred, Roz looked down. The guilt was almost unbearable.

'Every week I have to decide how best to deal with boys brought before me, Miss Trevaskis. Boys who, for want of guidance and training, slip from mischief into crime. You will not wish your brother to be one of them.'

'No, indeed, sir.' She swallowed hard. 'W– What happens now?'

His features hardened imperceptibly. 'When your mother recovers her senses, my clerk will give her the papers to sign. I do not anticipate any reluctance on her part, do you?'

Roz heard his disdain and felt heat burn her cheeks. No, her mother wouldn't object. Half the time she had no idea where he was or with whom. But Roz would miss him. It had taken months to win his confidence. But her patience had paid off. When she was home it was her he confided in and came to when he hurt himself. She had taught him to say please and thank you, to count to ten, and using a stone and a slate from the beach, how to write his name. So how could she begrudge him this opportunity?

Pride forced her to meet his cool gaze. 'You are most generous, sir. We are greatly in your debt.'

His brows snapped together. 'That is not—' He stopped abruptly, his eyes darkening, his expression unreadable. 'Mr Eathorne will expect the boy at four o'clock next Sunday.' He rose from his chair and stood, tall and forbidding, behind his desk. 'That is all. You may go.'

'Thank you.' It was totally inadequate. He had no idea how much worry he had lifted from her shoulders, or how much shame he had added. Dropping a brief curtsey, Roz turned to the door just as it opened once again to reveal the clerk.

'Good day, Miss Trevaskis.' Carrying a sheaf of documents, the clerk smiled.

'M–Mr Ellacott,' Roz bobbed another curtsey and crossed to the stairs. She heard the clerk's voice.

'Sir, about Master David—'

'What's he done now?' Casvellan interrupted.

Roz paused between one step and the next. How weary he sounded. Then the door snapped shut and she walked quickly down the stairs.

Four

'How many miners?' Branoc Casvellan demanded of the breathless sweating man who had just run into the Angel Hotel where local justices had gathered with the mayor and aldermen.

'Hundreds!' the man gasped, his eyes wide and full of anxiety. 'Dressed in their mine clothes they are. All carrying staves or axe-handles.'

Several of the men seated at the big table pushed back their chairs. 'We must—' began one of the dignitaries.

'A moment, if you please.' Cutting him short, Casvellan rose from his seat and turned to the panting messenger. 'Where are they now?'

'When I seen 'em they was down by the cattle market. But—' He broke off glancing towards the open window as fear paled his face. 'Hark. Coming up the street they are.'

Moving more quickly than the others, Casvellan strode from the room and along the passage to the hotel's open front door. Standing under the pillared portico he looked down the street. The Midsummer Coinage was underway and Helston was crowded with people and strings of pack animals loaded with tin to be assayed, stamped and assessed for tax.

The milling throng prevented him from seeing

44

the miners. But he heard them clearly: the rhyth-mic thud of heavy boots and chanting voices harsh with anger.

'This is ridiculous,' Sir Edward Pengarrick snapped, reaching Branoc's side and craning his neck to see over the heads of the crowd. 'I'm going to send for the dragoons.'

As the rest of the assembled party nervously muttered agreement, Casvellan turned to his old enemy.

'For what purpose?'

Pengarrick's narrowed eyes glittered beneath bushy grey brows. 'I'd have thought that was obvious.' His tone held contempt. 'To remove the ringleaders and send the rest back where they came from.'

Casvellan detested Pengarrick. Despite being a justice, supposedly an upholder as well as administrator of law, the baronet was shameless in his corrupt use of power, dealing harshly with the lower classes yet lenient towards his own. But a public argument in front of the mayor and aldermen would achieve nothing. Casvellan lowered his voice. 'Many of the dragoons are local men. It's very probable that some will be related to the miners. If we order them to open fire and they refuse—'

'I'll have them shot.'

Hanging onto his temper, Casvellan spoke through gritted teeth. 'Which would make a bad situation even worse.' He turned to the clustered dignitaries, scanning their wary faces. 'Those miners and their families are starving. Surely instead of adding to their grievances, it would be wiser to sell them the grain they need at a fair price? One they can afford?'

As heads began to nod, Pengarrick snarled. 'You're bowing to mob rule, Casvellan.'

'I haven't suggested *giving* it away.'

'That's not the point,' Pengarrick snapped. 'If their tactics succeed this time, they'll be back for more.'

'Why?' Casvellan demanded. 'They want bread, not a battle.'

'What can we lose?' the mayor rubbed his hands together, visibly anxious.

'It must be worth a try,' an alderman added.

'Go on, Casvellan,' the mayor urged. 'Speak to them.'

Casvellan glanced at him. 'Wouldn't you prefer to—?'

'No, no,' the mayor said hastily. 'It was your idea.'

So if it failed he would be held responsible. 'As you wish.'

'You'll regret it,' Pengarrick warned.

Ignoring him, Casvellan walked out.

'Where are you going?' the mayor shouted.

'To the market-house. That's where they will be heading because that's where the grain is.' As he angled across the road, the crowd parted to let him through and he saw his agent, Devlin Varcoe, coming to join him. His twin in height and build, Devlin wore fawn breeches and dusty boots. His brown frock coat was fractionally tight across muscular shoulders.

'Market-house?' Devlin mouthed.

Casvellan nodded, then pointed. 'Help me up.

I'll stand on the wall.'

'You're taking a chance,' Devlin warned.

'They'll never hear me if I stay down here.'

Devlin linked his fingers like a stirrup for Casvellan's booted foot and boosted him up. Immediately Casvellan bent to haul Devlin up beside him. Gazing down the street over the heads of the crowd, he could see people straining to see what was happening and sensed unease turning to alarm.

'There's going to be trouble,' Devlin muttered.

'Not if I can stop it,' Casvellan retorted grimly. The miners were forcing their way up the packed street. People shouted as street stalls toppled. Separated from their parents, children were screaming. Unsettled by the noise, mules and horses whinnied, plunging and kicking as they pulled against their handlers.

Panic began to spread. Casvellan nodded at Devlin who cupped his hands round his mouth and bellowed for silence. Instinctively people turned, nudging each other and shushing those next to them. The miners kept coming.

Casvellan raised his hands, palms out. 'Everyone stand still. There is no need for alarm or—' he gasped as a stone hurled from amid the crowd caught the side of his head. Hard and painful, the blow rocked him.

'I'll have the bastard,' Devlin crouched, preparing to jump down.

'No.' As he gripped Devlin's shoulder to hold him back, Casvellan felt a trickle of warmth down the side of his face and knew he was bleeding. Those who had seen what happened told those near them who hadn't. As everyone waited, anxious and expectant, he took a deep breath hoping it might banish the dizziness.

'As I was saying—' he paused as a murmur rippled through the crowd. At least he had their attention. 'There will be no trouble.' The words were an order invested with all his authority. 'The grain in this warehouse is not for export.'

''Spect us to believe that, do 'ee?' a miner yelled.

'Yes, I do,' he roared back. 'The grain brought here for storage is for the local market.'

'So why can't we buy it then?' another miner shouted.

'You can,' Casvellan replied. 'In a few minutes the stores will be opened. You may buy at twenty-four shillings a bushel. On one condition,' he bellowed. 'You are to remain orderly. There is enough for everyone. Once you have received your grain you are to leave and return to your homes.'

'You'd trust the word of this rabble?' Pengarrick sneered up at him, protected by his man of business and two servants.

Casvellan ignored him. 'Do I have your word?' he thundered at the miners, scanning gaunt haggard faces, seeing relief, a grin, tears.

'Yes!' The answering roar was deafening.

'Bloody heroics,' Pengarrick muttered and stalked away as his servants cleared a path for him through the crowd.

Devlin jumped down and Casvellan followed. At the entrance to the market-house the mayor was busy dispatching various minions to fetch keys and set up tables with scales. Clerks hurried forward with ledgers preparing to take the money.

'You need a glass of cognac,' Devlin said.

'I need to clean up.'

Devlin grinned. 'You're a hero.'

'The blood was useful. Will you stay here and keep an eye on things?'

'I'll come back as soon as I've taken you across to the Angel.'

'I don't need—'

'With every man-jack of them wanting to shake your hand? It will take you an hour to get through. That won't help your headache.'

Casvellan frowned in irritation. 'Who said anything about—?'

'I've got eyes,' Devlin cut in. 'Come on.'

'Remind me why I employed you,' Casvellan glowered.

'It'd take too long. Besides, I'm too modest.'

As his wound throbbed, the ache made worse by the noise of the crowd, he felt his elbow steadied by a large callused hand, a hand rumoured to have killed at least one man, and was glad of the unobtrusive support.

When he had announced his intention of making Devlin Varcoe his bailiff, his mother had promptly succumbed to a fit of vapours. His brother Davy, nine years his junior, had tried without success to mask awe with a shrug. Busy with their mother, Deborah had simply stared at him for a moment, then nodded.

Later she had crossed the drive to the building that housed his Justice room.

49

'Why him, Bran? Surely his reputation—'

'Deb, I'm surprised at you.'

'Don't mock,' she scolded.

'I meant only that if you are judging him on his reputation, then you should take *all* of it into account. Yes, he was a smuggler. Though he was never caught until his own brother betrayed him. Why did I hire him? Because he is one of the bravest men I've ever met, and one of the few I know I can trust. Apart from that, I like him.'

In the three months since that evening Casvellan had never once doubted the wisdom of what to many appeared a quixotic decision.

'Shall I have the doctor brung to 'ee, sir?' the landlord of the Angel hotel enquired, moving aside as his wife bustled in with a steaming basin of water and several towels.

'No, thank you. But I would be obliged if you could find me a clean shirt and neckcloth. I have no wish to alarm my dinner guests.'

'Right away, sir.' Knuckling his forehead the landlord withdrew.

An hour later, his wound bathed, his black hair drying into thick springy waves and arranged to cover the scab, he shrugged his frock coat over the borrowed shirt and checked his appearance in the glass. His head still ached. He wished he could just ride home. But as he was hosting tonight's dinner that wasn't an option. Perhaps he might feel better after a meal.

As the landlord moved round the table refilling glasses with an excellent claret, Casvellan shook his head, his own still half full. Halfway down the table Christopher Frayne drained his glass and pushed it forward for more.

'Smuggling is costing the country thousands in lost revenue,' he stated, glancing around at the other guests. 'It cannot go on. The government needs that money.' His tone demanded agreement.

'If the duty on spirits and tobacco was lowered,' Casvellan said evenly, 'there would be no advantage to smuggling and the trade would stop.'

Frayne's expression reflected belligerence and scorn. 'You can't expect the government to play into the hands of the free traders.'

That wasn't what he had suggested but he knew argument would be pointless. Frayne was drunk. Besides which, as a borough MP in the pay of the government, he was saying what was expected of him. Nor had he finished.

'It has not escaped notice, Casvellan, that when trying these miscreants your punishments tend towards leniency.'

Anger flared, hot and bright, but not a flicker crossed Casvellan's composed features. He held Frayne's gaze, saying nothing, guessing there was more to come.

'In fact, when one looks at the record of your esteemed neighbour,' Frayne raised his glass in salute to Sir Edward Pengarrick who sat opposite, 'one cannot help but wonder whose side you are on.'

Casvellan had had enough. To be chided like a schoolboy by a man who had bought his position using his wife's money was bad enough. But to be told he compared unfavourably to a man as corrupt as Pengarrick was insupportable.

'You are right.' He spoke quietly but his voice had a steely edge. 'Pengarrick and I have little in common. Unlike him, I have no financial interest in smuggling.'

'Casvellan?' Seated at the far end of the table, Oliver Morley-Noles raised his voice. Glad to end the conversation and annoyed with himself for allowing Frayne to irritate him, Casvellan turned away.

'Yes?'

'These French prisoners of war, how many are you willing to take?'

'I could manage twenty but I would prefer fewer. I can find work for fifteen.'

'Doing what?' Frayne enquired.

'I shall employ them on the farm.'

'Casvellan has an astonishing number of newfangled ideas about farming,' the baronet announced scornfully.

'Their worth has been proved.' Casvellan turned the stem of his wineglass. Used to Pengarrick's mockery he ignored it. 'Cornwall has always known poverty. But now people are starving. We need more land under the plough.'

'If they are starving, it's their own fault,' Pengarrick said. 'They are too much attached to drinking. They don't want to work.'

'I cannot agree.' At his flat contradiction the others at the table swivelled their heads in his direction. 'Every community has some who are feckless and idle. But in the villages under my jurisdiction the majority work hard yet still find

52

it difficult to earn enough to feed their families. The price of wheat is now the highest it has been for a hundred years. No man can give his best at work if he's not getting enough to eat. I do not, and never will, condone smuggling. But I understand the desperation that drives men to risk everything for some of those luxuries we take for granted.'

'It's just a game to them,' Frayne declared, swallowing another mouthful of wine. 'They enjoy pitting their wits against the customs men.'

'Risking not just their liberty but their very lives? Those are high stakes indeed,' Casvellan said. 'Yet the government could put a stop to it within twenty-four hours.'

'Oh yes?' Pengarrick sneered. 'How?'

'I've told you. Reduce the duty on wines, spirits, tobacco and tea.' There was a brief silence.

Frayne gave a bark of laughter. 'That's ridiculous.'

'No it isn't. Twelve years ago the government reduced the duty on tea from one hundred and twenty-seven per cent to twelve per cent. That meant it was no longer profitable as contraband and the trade stopped almost overnight.'

'But if you cut the duties,' Frayne demanded, 'how is the government to raise the money it needs to fight the war with France?'

Casvellan shrugged. 'I have suggested how smuggling could be eradicated. Funding the war is a different matter. I am no politician.'

'That's obvious,' Frayne muttered, glancing

round the table seeking support.

'I state the facts as I see them,' Casvellan said, ignoring the interruption.

'I agree,' Oliver Morley-Noles nodded. 'We have unprecedented levels of poverty, and the main cause of this is two years of poor harvest plus shortages due to the war. Britain used to import surplus grain from France. But the French have also suffered bad harvests. Meanwhile any grain from America that gets past the French blockade is sent to English towns and cities where it is most needed.'

'That being the case,' Casvellan said, 'surely it is up to us who have land to make it as productive as possible.'

'How do you propose to do that?' Morley-Noles asked.

'I have already started a four-crop rotation. This will give me winter fodder so I won't need to slaughter half my herd at Michaelmas. Nor will any of my land lie fallow. Once my wheat and barley have been harvested, the fields can be ploughed. I'll plant turnips in the wheat fields, and clover or lucerne where the barley grew. I broke a new area of poor land at the end of last year and sweetened it with ashes, oreweed, pilchard trash and lime. Then I planted potatoes. They'll be ready for lifting at the end of August.'

'Are you ploughing with ox-teams or horses?' Morley-Noles asked, his manner one of genuine interest.

'Both. Oxen are slower, but need less looking after. And though I only get three years' working life out of them, I also get several hundredweight of beef when they are slaughtered. But each ox team needs two men, whereas one man on his own can manage either a single horse or a team of two, and plough an acre a day. Not only are horses faster, their working life of ten to twelve years outweighs the cost of feed and care.'

Frayne drained his glass. 'Talking of horses,' he slurred, squinting as he signalled the landlord. A generous host who gave his guests the best in wine and food, Casvellan did not begrudge Frayne another bottle, but rued the fact that by now the MP was beyond appreciating the claret's discreet bouquet and fine flavour. He nodded imperceptibly and with a brief roll of his eyes the landlord stumped out.

'That stallion of yours, what the devil d'you call him?'

'Raad. It means lightning.'

'You going to sell him?' Frayne asked.

'Possibly.' This was something Casvellan had been thinking about for months without reaching a decision.

'Our host can tell you every detail of his stallion's illustrious lineage,' Pengarrick snorted. 'But ancestry proves nothing. The only way to test the animal's true worth is to race him.' Though his mouth widened in a smile his gaze was bright with malice. 'Unless, of course, Casvellan intends to harness him to a plough.'

Frayne laughed.

Casvellan knew Pengarrick wanted the stallion. And selling Raad would finance new machinery and another team of shires. But with the baronet rumoured to be as brutal to his horses as he was with his punishments, he was reluctant.

'You anticipate me, Pengarrick. I have indeed been thinking about racing him,' he said, and saw bitter envy behind the baronet's sneer.

Carrying the quarter's rent money for the inn in a leather purse, Roz rode across the moor towards Trescowe. The morning sun was warm on her back through the thin shawl tied over her cotton bodice and calico petticoat. A bonnet shaded her face, allowing her a measure of blessed anonymity.

Paying the inn rent was a job Jack Hicks had passed on to her soon after she began working for him. She was grateful, for it showed he trusted her. He didn't trust her mother. Nor did she, and the implied disloyalty made her feel horribly guilty. But nothing about her rekindled relationship with Mary-Blanche was straightforward or easy.

Today she was glad of a brief escape from the heat of the kitchen. In the winter when an east wind drove icy rain it was a miserable journey. All too often she returned to the village soaked through and chilled to the bone, her fingers blue-white and aching.

At least riding shortened the time she was out, and it was less tiring. Asking Jack if he possessed a sidesaddle had been an indication of her artlessness. Even as the words left her lips she had wished them unsaid. He had simply looked at her, his brows climbing. Blushing deeply she had apologized.

'It was a foolish question, Mr Hicks. I–I wasn't thinking.'

'Yes, well, 'tis your choice, maid. You can ride or you can walk.'

Acutely self-conscious, she had begun riding astride. But her embarrassment quickly faded for she rarely saw anyone. The few people she did encounter simply ignored her. Her drab clothes and the fact that she was riding bareback instantly classed her as beneath their notice. She had learned to prefer invisibility.

Though the cob was big and strong he responded readily to her touch on the rein and the pressure of her heels. On the empty moor beneath a wide sky, Roz would give him his head and urge him on, enjoying the sensation of speed and the illusion of freedom as they pounded along narrow tracks amid the bracken and heather.

The contrast between her life with her grandparents and her life now was almost beyond comprehension. Only two years had passed but when she looked back she was amazed at her naïvety and saddened by the manner of its loss. The harsh reality of life with her mother had shattered her idealism. But she would not, *must not*, abandon the belief that things would get better.

Meanwhile, at least when she came to Trescowe to pay the rents she did not have to face Justice Casvellan crippled with shame and embarrassment at her mother's most recent public exhibition. He was rarely in his justice room on rent day. This was all for the best. For what had they to say to one another?

She had told him how grateful she was for Tom's apprenticeship. No doubt he had done similar things for other people. He was that kind of man. She would be foolish to read anything into it other than his desire to prevent her young half-brother plunging from mischief into crime. No, far better that she didn't see him. Yearning for something she could never have was foolish and pointless. She knew that. Yet as she rode down the drive towards the building where Mr Ellacott waited with his ledger, her heart still quickened. *Perhaps ... just a glimpse...*

She climbed the wooden stairs. The door to Mr Casvellan's room was shut, but the clerk's stood open and she saw Devlin Varcoe sitting behind the table with the clerk standing beside him pointing to an entry in one of the ledgers. Hesitating, she cleared her throat.

Devlin looked up. Instantly a smile softened the harsh planes of his face. 'Hello, Roz. Come in. All right, are you?'

She found herself smiling back, warmed by his welcome.

'Yes, thank you. How is Tamara?'

'Keeping well. She was talking about you just last night.'

'I've wanted to visit but—'

He raised a hand. 'It's all right. She understands you've got your hands full. But any time you can get away she'd love to see you.'

'I will try. I miss her.'

The clerk cleared his throat gently.

'All right, George,' Devlin grinned up at him. 'Point made.' He turned to Roz. 'What can we do for you?'

Roz laid the leather purse on the desk. 'The quarter's rent for the Three Mackerel.'

Roz watched Devlin count the money and make entries in the ledger. She wondered why he was doing it and not the clerk.

As if reading her thoughts, he glanced up. 'Mr Ellacott could do this far more quickly. But as Mr Casvellan's agent it's my job to know how the estate operates. I've never asked any man to do something I haven't done myself. Mind you, I'm discovering my limitations. I'm definitely better outdoors.' He grinned briefly at the clerk. 'Mr Ellacott will have no difficult managing without me.'

'Quite so, sir,' the clerk murmured, a smile quivering at the corners of his mouth.

Many men elevated as Devlin Varcoe had been would have become aloof and self-important. But he hadn't changed. Perhaps because he had nothing to prove. His appointment had been the talk of the village for weeks. But the Justice had needed someone to replace Femley Crowle who, having worked for Harry Casvellan, couldn't come to terms with all the changes being made on the farm and estate.

Roz was acquainted with Devlin only through her friendship with his wife Tamara. And her knowledge of the Justice was limited to her visits to his rooms regarding her mother, or glimpses of him at various village functions. Yet she recognized strong similarities between the two men.

As Devlin returned the empty purse and the clerk placed the coins in a small chest, booted feet bounded up the stairs and along the passage.

Even before he appeared, Roz knew who it was. Her heart leapt and a scalding flush swept up her throat to her hairline. Even her ears burned.

'Varcoe? Are you—?' Casvellan stopped short on the threshold. Shock and pleasure were so swiftly masked by his habitual expression of cool detachment she dismissed what she had glimpsed as wishful thinking.

'Miss Trevaskis,' he inclined his head.

'Mr Casvellan.' She bobbed a curtsey. She longed to look up but didn't dare as she edged past him to the door. Her skin felt as if it was on fire. 'Please excuse me.' Her voice was little more than a cracked whisper. She hadn't expected to see him. She wasn't prepared.

'You—' He cleared his throat. 'You will be pleased to know that your brother has settled in and is doing well. Eathorne has high hopes of him.'

Roz's head came up. Relief and delight surged through her. 'Really?' Watching his eyes darken she barely registered the hint of colour along his high cheekbones. 'That is so ... You cannot know how much...' She bit her lip. What a fool he must think her. But she was so very grateful. 'Thank you. I know my mother will—'

'Indeed,' he cut her short. Then with a curt nod of dismissal he looked past her to his agent. Feeling her blush deepen, this time with embarrassment, she bobbed another curtsey. Then dipping her head she slipped quickly past him into the passage. As she hurried to the stairs she heard him telling Devlin to leave Ellacott to his ledgers and accompany him to the stables. He sounded impatient. With so much to do, so many things to think about, he would have forgotten her already. She was no one, just another of his tenants come to pay the rent.

Riding back across the moor she relived the moment he had strode into the room and the pleasure that had softened his features as he saw her. Though it had gone in an instant perhaps she had not imagined it. Seeing him, and the fact that he had taken the time to reassure her about Tom, these were treasures to be hoarded. But like so many treasures they carried a high price.

She should be grateful. She *was*. Thanks to the Justice, Tom had a job and a future. And that meant one less worry for her.

Five

In the four days since her visit to Trescowe, Roz had been so busy she'd barely had time to think. When Annie collapsed, a victim of the summer flu that was sweeping through the village, Nell had asked Roz to work additional hours.

Knowing her mother would make a fuss, and too tired to face it when she arrived home, Roz had waited until the following morning to tell her.

'Why did you say yes?' Mary-Blanche demanded.

'Because Nell can't manage on her own.' Roz kept her voice level and tried to ignore the knots of tension in her stomach.

'What am I supposed to do all day?'

Roz could think of a score of jobs that needed doing in the cottage and garden. 'Well, perhaps you might—'

But her mother wasn't listening. 'Now Tom's gone it's lonely here all by myself.'

Roz tried once more. 'So why don't you—?'

'I bet there's nothing wrong with her,' Mary-Blanche grumbled. 'She's just putting it on.'

'Mama! That's not fair!' Roz's sharpness startled them both. She fought for calm. 'Annie came in yesterday even though it was plain she was ill.

Then she fainted and Nell took her home.'

'Where?' Mary-Blanche demanded.

'What do you mean, where?' Roz said, bewildered. 'You know where Annie lives.'

Mary-Blanche clicked her tongue impatiently. 'No, I meant where did she faint?'

'In the taproom. Fortunately she wasn't carrying—'

'Making an exhibition of herself,' Mary-Blanche sniffed. 'She just wanted attention and people feeling sorry for her.'

Roz turned away. Sometimes she disliked her mother intensely, which made her feel guilty and ashamed. The constant emotional turmoil was exhausting. But though her mother hated being alone, whenever Roz suggested that she look for work of some kind, Mary-Blanche recoiled in horror, babbling a stream of excuses.

It had taken a while for Roz to realize that her mother was afraid. Knowing she was higher-born than most of the villagers and conscious of having sunk lower, she feared their mockery. Unless she was drunk: then she cared nothing for anyone's opinion, least of all Roz's. The rumours about her past and her erratic behaviour meant she was not welcome in the group of ladies dominated by the wives of the local doctor and parish priest. Yet nor did she wish to mix with the fishermen's families, considering them beneath her.

Roz drew a steadying breath. 'I have to go, Mama.'

'Why?' Mary-Blanche wailed. 'Why do you...'

'Mama, we need the money. Paying your

fines...' Roz could have bitten her tongue off.

Flinching as if she had been slapped, Mary-Blanche stared at the floor. 'It's my fault, isn't it. All of this.' Her voice sounded hollow.

'Look,' Roz forced a cheerful smile though she felt like screaming. 'It's just until Annie is better. A few days, that's all. Then we'll be back to normal.' As the word left her lips it occurred to Roz that just two years ago what she now thought of as *normal*, would have appalled her. What a terrible distance she had travelled.

Hunched in a wooden armchair in front of the small pile of glowing embers over which Roz had boiled water and toasted some slices of barley bread, Mary-Blanche turned her head away.

Roz opened the door. 'I'll see you later.' She waited a moment, but her mother didn't reply. 'I'm sorry, Mama. I shouldn't have said—'

'I can't help it, you know,' Mary-Blanche muttered. 'I don't like being like this.'

Then make an effort. Be different. The words echoed in Roz's head, hovered on her tongue, and it took all her resolve to hold them back. Once she might have spoken. Now she knew better. Her mother would dissolve in floods of tears and she would feel wretched for having made things even worse than they were already.

'I'll be home as soon as I can, but it will be late,' she warned, pausing in the doorway. Her mother didn't respond so she walked out leaving the door open to let in sunshine and fresh air, and turned towards the inn.

It was almost two when, at Nell's insistence,

Roz dropped on to a chair at the big kitchen table and ate a plate of stew with some crusty bread and butter. Four hours later Nell brought out a tin caddy containing some carefully hoarded tea and brewed a pot. She poured two cups.

'Here, bird, come and rest your feet a minute,' she ordered. 'Worked like a demon you have. I'd 'ave been in some awful mess without you, and that's the gospel truth.'

Roz looked up from rubbing her aching feet. 'Thank you.' She was both touched and surprised, for Nell worked hard herself and expected no less from her staff.

'I speak as I find.' Nell gave a decisive nod. 'Here, any of that heavy cake left is there? I could just fancy a bit.'

'In the larder, on the second shelf,' Roz pushed her foot back into her shoe. 'Shall I—?'

'You'll stay where you're to,' Nell was brisk. 'I aren't in me dotage yet.'

While they ate they discussed the following day's work. Then as soon as she had drained her cup, Roz returned to her chores.

The evening wore on. Daylight faded to dusk. Toby lit the lanterns in the taproom. The party in the private dining room returned to a trading schooner due to sail on the tide. Roz washed and dried the best wineglasses, china and silverware. Nell was making pastry that would stand overnight in the cool larder ready for the morning. She glanced up as Roz put the last of the cutlery in its box.

''Ere, go and ask Jack if he wants me to keep a dish of beef stew back for'n. Take a tray in

65

with you for the dirty plates. I'll boil up some more water.'

Removing the coarse apron she had tied over one of white cotton loaned to her by Nell, Roz tucked curls that had escaped onto her neck back into her frilled cap. She picked up a tray, flexing her spine and shoulders as she trudged along the short passage to the taproom. She had been on her feet for almost fourteen hours.

She paused in the doorway, automatically checking the number of customers. The evening crowd had thinned. A group of elderly fishermen sat in high-backed settles near the fire, smoking clay pipes and nursing their tankards as they talked. Used plates and dishes littered several empty tables.

Tension tightened the back of her neck as she noticed Will Prowse at a table in the corner. Davy Casvellan was with him. This was the third time she had seen them together. She longed to warn the young man off. But in Davy Casvellan's eyes she was merely a tavern wench. He would call her impudent and tell her to stay out of what did not concern her. He might even complain about her to Jack. The possible repercussions of *that* didn't bear thinking about.

Davy's brother was the justice responsible for renewing the inn's licence. Rather than upset him, Jack might choose the easy way out and dismiss her. Given the trouble her mother had caused, she wouldn't blame him. But then what would she do? How would she manage?

'Want something, girl?' Jack said, wiping up spills on the dark wood counter with a rag.

Trying to banish anxieties that always loomed larger when she was tired, Roz moistened her lips. 'Nell says should she keep some beef stew for you?'

Jack nodded. ''Andsome. I'll come d'rectly. Toby can watch the tap.'

As Davy pushed back his chair and rose unsteadily to his feet, Will called out, 'Roz, here a minute.'

When Roz hesitated, Jack urged softly, 'Go on, maid. 'Tis business.'

Reluctantly she crossed the room, passing Davy Casvellan, who didn't appear to see her as he bumped into a table then stumbled against a chair.

'Look at the state of 'n.' Will shook his head. 'He'd better mind the Justice don't see'n like that. Mr Casvellan wouldn' like his baby brother mixing with the likes of we.' Will's face betrayed evil delight.

At the mention of Casvellan's name, Roz remembered the moment he had erupted into his clerk's office, shock and pleasure crossing his face. Swiftly she shut him out, terrified that Will Prowse might somehow sense her thoughts. Though Will needed her and she, God forgive her, needed the additional money, she knew he had not forgiven her rejection. Nor would he forget it. If an opportunity for revenge arose he would not hesitate.

'Another drink, Mr Prowse?' she enquired, setting her tray down on an adjoining table and loading the dirty plates onto it. Keeping busy enabled her to avoid looking at him. Unshaven, his greasy hair tied back with a bit of cord, everything about him was *grubby*. His jacket and trousers were filthy and the kerchief knotted over his blue checked shirt was spotted with food.

He leaned forward, and as his rank odour reached her, Roz suppressed a shudder. Marry him? *Never*.

'Only if you'll have one with me,' he leered.

'Jack doesn't allow that.' As he knew perfectly well. She lowered her voice. 'He mentioned business?'

Will clasped both hands round his tankard. As he dragged it nearer, Roz smelled the brandy. 'Cargo's coming in tomorrow night,' he hissed. 'I want the string down in Rannys Cove by midnight.'

Her heart tripped on an extra beat, giving a heavy uncomfortable thud. *She didn't want to do it.* But keeping her gaze on the tray as she nodded, she started to move away.

'Hang on, I haven't finished. Which way did you come last time?'

Roz moistened dry lips. 'Drinnick Lane.'

'Use Vounder instead, all right?'

As she gave another quick nod Will picked up his tankard. She should go *now*. Instead she found herself asking, 'What did Davy Casvellan want?'

Swallowing the brandy Will eyed her as he wiped his mouth with the back of his hand, his expression ugly. 'Fancy him, do you?'

'For heaven's sake, he's just a boy.' Her incredulity was genuine.

'Yes, well,' he muttered, hunching one shoulder in a petulant shrug.

Roz pressed on. 'Aren't you taking a risk involving him?'

Will's grin exposed blackened teeth. Roz tried not to breathe. The reek was overpowering. 'Don't you worry your pretty head about that.'

'But if he's caught—'

'My good luck charm he is.' Will's grin widened and the pleasure Roz saw in his eyes deepened her anxiety. 'Boy's desperate for a bit of excitement. He'll do whatever I tell him. If we have a clear run, he'll owe me. If we get caught, his big brother will pay well to avoid any scandal. What do you think of that, then? Can't lose, can I?' He drained his tankard.

Horrified, Roz shook her head. 'Mr Prowse, that's a scheme the devil himself would be proud of.'

After a blink of surprise Will puffed out his chest. 'I aren't no fool.'

He had taken her words as a compliment.

Then his features sharpened into hunger. 'Having second thoughts are you? Wishing you hadn't been quite so hasty turning me down? Lucky for you I'd be willing to—'

'I have to go,' Roz blurted, picking up the loaded tray. On impulse she turned back. 'Instead of paying me for tomorrow night, you keep the money. Then my debt will be cleared and—'

'Whoa, my bird, hold hard.' He sat back, eyeing her through narrowed lids. 'Tell you what, once the cargo is landed and hidden, we'll have a little chat about it. Go on now, Jack's looking over.'

Roz knew she would get nothing more from him. She returned to the kitchen, her thoughts chaotic, desperate. She *had* to get free of Will. She had a bad feeling about tomorrow. So far they had been lucky. But that kind of luck couldn't last.

She should warn the Justice about his brother. But how could she without incriminating herself? Mr Casvellan was a very astute man. He would know that simply *overhearing* such information wasn't possible. Besides, if Davy backed out now Will would know she had talked. That's why he hadn't minded telling her. She was trapped.

Casvellan spent Saturday morning out riding. His father had left management of the estate to Fernley Crowle, a man who clung to the old ways even though they were hopelessly in-efficient. Following his father's death Casvellan had tried to interest the bailiff in the changes he planned. But the response had been totally negative. Getting on in years, Crowle had grown used to doing the minimum necessary, knowing Harry Casvellan had little interest in anything but his horses.

But though he understood, Casvellan refused to condone. Instead he offered Crowle retire-ment and a small pension. The bailiff's accep-tance was a relief to them both. Then the real work had started.

Owner of a considerable estate, and a justice,

meant Casvellan had dealings with a wide variety of Cornishmen. He knew that, provided they believed in what they were doing and were amply rewarded for their efforts, they possessed an infinite capacity for hard work and astonishing endurance. But they could also be petty and incredibly stubborn.

For his plans to have any chance of success he needed his farm workers' willingness to commit to new crops and new ways of growing them. So instead of simply issuing orders and leaving Devlin Varcoe to implement them, which would have resulted in shoddy work and simmering resentment, he had organized meetings complete with ample food and drink. There he had explained the new crop system and set up demonstrations of a new plough, a metal-tined horse-drawn cultivator, and a seed drill.

A few had been reluctant. But year-round crops and the abandonment of the traditional Michaelmas slaughter would mean their jobs were safe. Given the turbulent times this was a powerful argument. Yet many of his peers continued to mock. Some called him a farmer. Others – with greater bitterness – deemed him a traitor to his class. It rankled. But after the first year the results had spoken for themselves.

Arriving to check progress on work preparing the old stable block for the French prisoners of war, he found Devlin dressed in old trousers and a check shirt, his sleeves rolled up, carrying a bucket of cement towards a ladder propped against the wall. Another man sat astride the tiled roof.

Casvellan shaded his eyes. 'The chimney?'

'Cracked right through and half the mortar's gone. Joe said it's be easier to scat it down and build a new one. So that's what we're doing.' He jerked his head towards the newly repaired doors that stood wide open. From inside came the sound of hammering. 'Mark and Santo have done wonders. The tackroom's been lime-washed. They got the old stove working a treat.'

'What are they doing now?'

'Knocking up a couple of cots for the officers. Treat 'em well and they got no reason to make trouble. Men who get decent food and a dry place to sleep always work better.'

As a smile flickered at the corners of his mouth, Casvellan switched his gaze from the mason on the roof to the new wood that replaced the lower edges of doors previously ragged with rot. 'How ever did I manage before you came?' he said dryly.

'I've wondered that myself,' Devlin said with a grin. 'Well, better get on. We're burning daylight here.'

Before Casvellan could reply he heard his name called and turned to see a manservant hurrying towards him.

'Yes, John?'

'Mr Bassett sent me, sir. Said to tell you the Riding Officer's come and would like a word.'

'I've put the Lieutenant in the library, sir,' the butler murmured, meeting him at the front door.

'Thank you, Bassett.'

'Lieutenant Crocker.' Closing the door, Casvellan crossed to a small side table where a silver tray contained two crystal decanters. 'My apologies for keeping you waiting. No doubt you are aware we are expecting a number of French prisoners of war?'

'I am, sir. I hear you intend to put them to work on your land.'

'My, how news travels.'

A faint flush appeared on the officer's cheeks. 'I consider it part of my job to keep abreast of local—'

'Forgive me, lieutenant. My comment was merely an observation, and certainly not intended as a slight. May I offer you a glass of madeira?' As his guest hesitated Casvellan smiled. 'Come, we are allies in this battle, are we not?'

The lieutenant unbent a little. 'Indeed, sir. Sometimes I think you are the only one I have.'

Filling two glasses, Casvellan handed one to the officer and indicated a chair. 'Do sit down. What brings you here this morning?'

Seating himself the Riding Officer crossed one leg over the other, visibly more relaxed.

'A tip-off concerning a cargo of contraband.'

'Due in when?'

'Tonight.'

'Where did this information come from?'

'Forgive me, sir, but I'd rather not say.'

'You're sure this informant is trustworthy? I haven't forgotten the time we sent the dragoons to—'

'I haven't forgotten it either, sir. Nor is it an experience I care to repeat. However, I have complete faith in my informant.'

'And you are telling me because?'

'They are landing in one of the coves on your property. It's not just the cargo I want, Mr Casvellan. We need to get the landsmen and handlers as well.'

Her legs encased in breeches, coarse stockings and boots, her slim figure hidden beneath a flannel shirt and an old dark jacket, Roz had twisted her hair beneath a soft-brimmed felt hat pulled low. Riding bareback and astride, relying on a simple halter and her own skill for control, she guided the butcher's mare down the narrow lane made darker by overhanging trees on either side. They hadn't used this route for some time. Which was probably why Will had chosen it. But though further from the village and risk of discovery, it was much steeper.

Trained to follow the mare, the string of mules and ponies plodded along behind. Leaves shed over countless autumns made a thick carpet so the loudest sound was the animals' breath. They were not roped together. When their owners had brought them to the designated collection point, Roz had spent an hour smearing their coats with grease. Then she had removed their halters. Their manes were already clipped short. These precautions meant that even if the worst happened and the animals were cornered, they would be impossible to hold onto.

Everything was running exactly to plan so there was no reason for the apprehension that weighed on her heart, heavy as a lump of iron.

She tried to shake it off. This was the last time. If Will said she still owed him money then she would find some other way to earn what she needed to pay him back. She'd ask Nell for extra hours or take on another job. She could not do this any more.

The landsmen finished loading the kegs and casks into rope nets slung over the animals' backs. The gig that had ferried the kegs ashore with Davy Casvellan at one of the oars had disappeared around the headland, and darkness had swallowed the cutter that had brought the cargo from Guernsey.

Given the nod by Will, who would return home using a different route, Roz pressed her knees to the mare's side and they started back up the lane. Armed with thick cudgels to deter would-be thieves, the four landsmen spaced themselves out alongside the animals urging them on with a touch when necessary.

Roz's unease deepened, communicating itself to the mare. She stroked the horse's sweating neck. Heavily laden, the animals were blowing hard. The hedges on each side dipped lower and the path widened as she approached the place where it divided. One fork led on up the valley. The other curved round the steep hillside.

Of course she was anxious. She was breaking the law. She pictured Branoc Casvellan's face, his expression as he realized she had thrown all his kindness back in his face. She couldn't bear it.

A horse snorted. Assuming it was one of the pack animals she glanced over her shoulder.

Then she heard the clink of metal. Fear zinged unpleasantly along every nerve. Instinct had warned her something was wrong. She had assumed it was her conscience. That had been bad enough. This was far more dangerous. She was riding into a trap.

Wheeling the mare round, she hissed like a snake at the ponies. They reacted instantly. As those at the rear turned and bolted back down the lane, the silence was shattered by voices bellowing orders and shouting warnings. Horses snorted and whinnied. Urged on by the landsmen several of the string scrambled over the hedge and into the woods beyond.

As dragoons approached from among the trees shots rang out. The pack animals closest to Roz fought to get away. For a moment she was trapped in the melee. Roz pulled the mare round just as a tall figure loomed in front of her, his arm raised.

She was going to die. Then she felt the stinging lash of a whip across her face. Shock and pain made her gasp. Knowing any sound she made would betray her she clamped her teeth onto her lower lip. The flesh spilt and she tasted the warm saltiness of blood. But she didn't cry out.

Crouching low, she wheeled the mare from the valley track. Crashing through the yelling, cursing dragoons, she plunged along the narrow curving path. Several mules and ponies followed, leaving grease-smeared dragoons emptyhanded. But despite her efforts she knew some would be caught.

By the time she pulled the mare to a panting

halt in the copse behind the church her face felt as if it was on fire. During her headlong dash she had wept tears of pure shock. Where they had dried her skin felt swollen and tight. The waiting men emerged from the crypt.

'What happened?'

'Where's the rest?'

Afraid her legs wouldn't support her Roz didn't dismount. She was trembling uncontrollably and though she was sweating her teeth chattered. 'The dragoons were waiting,' she gasped, her heart hammering painfully against her ribs. 'Some of the ponies got away but some will have been caught.'

Swearing and furious they quickly unloaded the casks and carried them into the crypt. One man stopped beside her.

'Bleddy 'ell, maid! What've ee done to your face?'

Roz's hand went to her cheek. It hurt terribly. She touched a long raised weal and clots and runnels of dried blood. She knew who was responsible. And prayed he hadn't recognized her.

'A tree branch. I'd better get the animals back.'

Choosing rarely used tracks added more time to her journey. But it reduced the likelihood of being seen as she returned the animals to their owners.

Once the mare was in her stable Roz quickly wiped her down with a hay-wisp. Then, after checking there was clean water in the bucket, she slipped quietly down the back lane. Skirting the edge of the field she heard rustling in the long grass by the hedge. In the distance a fox barked. An owl swooped across in front of her, pale and silent as a ghost. The shock made her heart race. Eventually she reached the cottage.

Closing the door quietly Roz pulled off her hat and leaned against the wood. Her mother's rhythmic snores didn't falter. Testing the kettle she poured warm water into a bowl. Her hands were shaking so badly she almost dropped it.

Setting it on the table she fetched a muslin rag that could be buried in the embers and carefully bathed her face. Unwilling to wake her mother she didn't dare light a candle. Besides, whatever her face looked like now, she knew it would be worse in the morning.

She had an arnica salve that would prevent bruising. But she couldn't use it on an open wound. Moving carefully she went to the cupboard and took out a small pot. Dipping a finger in she smeared honey along the length of the cut. That would stop infection and help it heal. *But it wouldn't have healed by tomorrow.*

What was she to do? She couldn't stay at home. Nell needed her and she needed her job. But being seen in the tap or dining room with her face like this would invite curiosity and questions. She climbed the narrow stairs to the small space under the roof where she slept. Airless in summer and freezing in winter, it allowed her a small measure of privacy. And because her mother was usually too drunk to attempt the stairs it was up here that she hid what little money she managed to save.

Stripping off her jacket, shirt and breeches, she lifted the mattress and laid the garments out of sight on the wooden slats. Her thoughts flew like sparks. No one must see her. But what if her mother was arrested again? She would have to go to Trescowe. The Justice would ... *Stop*. Blanking her mind she put on her nightgown and got into bed. Aching, exhausted, she closed her eyes. Hot tears slid down her temples. What was she to do?

Six

After a restless night plagued by dreams in which she was fleeing from some nameless horror, Roz woke with a start, eyes wide, heart pounding, and sat up. Lifting her hair from her hot damp neck she looked towards the small window and the pearl grey light of the breaking dawn.

As the memory of her nightmare faded, she became aware of the throbbing ache in her face and tentatively traced the length of the cut with her fingertips. Swollen and clotted with dried blood, it branded her. If Mr Casvellan saw this would he recognize her as the 'boy' who had led the pack animals?

She fought the anxiety quickening her heartbeat, reminding herself it had been dark. Everything had happened very fast. Though the officer and soldiers had shouted, she had not heard the Justice's voice. Nor had she made a sound. So there was no reason for him to suspect her. *Unless he saw her face.* She touched the wound again. She had to remain out of sight until it healed.

Who had betrayed them? How many of the men had been caught? How was she to work looking like this? *How unsightly was it?*

Forcing herself out of bed she crossed the bare planks to the tea chest that served as a stand for her washbasin. Beside her comb lay a hand mirror. Carrying it to the window she closed her eyes for an instant. She knew it was bad. Her fingers and the pain had warned her of that.

Lifting the mirror she looked at her reflection. Shock stopped her breath. A newly formed scab ran diagonally from her forehead, across her nose and down her right cheek. The flesh on either side of the cut was raised and red. Beneath her right eye a crimson and purple bruise lay across her cheekbone.

Roz compressed trembling lips. Staying at home until it healed was simply not possible. She would have to remain in the kitchen, out of public gaze. Even so, there would be questions. Telling the truth might win her sympathy from Nell. But both Jack and Will Prowse would find it hard to believe she hadn't cried out. They'd be anxious, on edge, waiting for the Riding Officer to turn up and ask questions. The more people who knew what had really happened, the more likely it was that someone would inadvertently – or deliberately – give her away.

The Justice couldn't be certain his whip had actually connected. As of this moment, only she knew exactly what had happened. Perhaps this was her punishment. Maybe she deserved it. He had shown her and her family kindness and she had violated his trust.

He had acted in order to try and prevent smugglers from getting away with their illicit cargo. She could not blame him. Nor would she implicate him. She would hold fast to what she had told the men waiting at the church, that in her haste to escape she simply had not seen the tree branch that whipped across her face.

Downstairs her mother coughed. Roz held her breath. *Don't let her wake yet.* A moment later the rhythmic snores resumed. Replacing the mirror Roz went downstairs to light the fire and fill the kettle.

Washed, dressed, her hair combed and twisted up into a neat coil, Roz fetched another bucket of water from the pump, refilled the kettle and set it over the fire. Then, fetching her mirror and moving to the kitchen window for more light, she carefully smeared a little more honey onto the laceration.

'What are you doing?' Mary-Blanche demanded in a voice thick with sleep, making her jump.

Putting the glass face down on the table Roz picked up the knife and cut two thick slices of barley bread. 'Last night was a disaster. The dragoons were waiting.'

'Thank goodness they didn't catch you.' Mary-Blanche struggled upright. 'Did they get the brandy?'

'Half of it. Four ponies stayed with me and we managed to reach the church, but—'

'Four's better than nothing, I suppose.' Heaving herself out of bed, Mary-Blanche pushed her feet into her shoes and slopped across to the door. 'Will Prowse is going to be mad as fire. But at least you'll still get paid.' Her voice sharpened. 'You will, won't you?' As Roz looked up, her hand flew to her mouth. 'Oh dear

God. Whatever have you done to your face? You can't go out like that.' Panic drove her voice higher.

'I don't have any choice,' Roz said. 'If I don't turn up for work I'll be blamed for what happened.'

'What *did* happen?'

'The dragoons had set a trap.'

'Where, on the beach?'

'No. They were in the lane, lying in wait until we were on the way back up with the load. They knew when we'd be there and which route we'd take.' *Who had talked?*

'But your face, how did—'

'A tree. When I realized what was happening I made a dash for the lane. It's very dark where the branches overhang. One caught me.' Each time she said it, she sounded more convincing.

Mary-Blanche moaned, hugging herself as she rocked back and forth. 'What if they come for you? What'll happen to me? How will I manage?'

'They aren't going to come for me, Mama,' Roz reassured. 'If they were, they'd have come last night. No one knows I was involved.'

'Someone does,' Mary-Blanche cried. 'Otherwise the dragoons wouldn't have been waiting.'

'They knew there was a cargo being landed. They don't know the names of—'

'They will though, won't they, if some of the men were caught. What if they tell?'

'They won't,' Roz said with a confidence she didn't feel. But her mother was already in a state. 'Mama, I have to go in a moment. I want

83

to reach the inn without anyone seeing me.' She took her bonnet from the hook on the back of the door and put it on, pulling it forward to hide her face. 'Will you boil up some barley and save the water for me? I'll pick some woundwort and make a compress when I get home tonight.'

Mary-Blanche peered at her, frowning and anxious. 'You're going to have a dreadful scar.'

Thank you, Mama. Biting her tongue, Roz opened the door and slipped quietly out.

In shirtsleeves and breeches, his waistcoat unbuttoned, Jack was seated at the table eating a breakfast of cold beef and bread and butter. A tankard of ale stood by his plate.

'Morning,' he mumbled as Roz took off her bonnet.

'You're some early,' Nell said over her shoulder as she stoked the fire to heat the cloam oven ready for the bread and pies. 'I aren't complaining, mind. Give us a head start it will.'

'C'mon, maid,' Jack was impatient. 'How did it go last night?'

Swallowing her nervousness, Roz turned round. 'Not well. In fact—' She flinched as Jack glanced up. His eyes narrowed then widened.

'Jesus!'

'Jack!' Nell swung round, pointing the poker at him. 'You mind your tongue.' Then she saw Roz's face. 'Oh my dear life! What've 'ee done, my bird? It do look some sore. Here, come and sit down a minute.'

Instead Roz reached for her apron. 'Someone had tipped off the dragoons. They were waiting in the lane. I managed to get away with a few of the ponies and warned the men at the church. But I'm afraid the Riding Officer got the rest.'

Jack cursed under his breath.

'But your face,' Nell persisted. 'What happened?'

'A branch. I was so anxious to get away I just didn't see it.'

'Well, there id'n no way you can go out in the tap looking like that,' Jack said flatly. 'Don't matter if 'twas an accident. It happened last night. There's bound to be questions. We can't be doing with that.'

'I know. I'm sorry.'

'I can't send Keren to wait on tables,' Nell put her hands on her hips. 'She'd never remember the orders. I tell 'ee, that girl 'aven't got the sense she was born with. And Annie's still sick—'

'How don't you do it, Nell?' Jack said. 'You used to like a chat with the customers.'

'That was years ago. We wad'n half so busy then,' Nell objected.

'Well, let Sarah do the tap, and you look after the private rooms,' Jack said.

'I'll manage in here, Nell,' Roz pulled her cap on and tucked a stray curl up into the white cotton. 'Just tell me what you want done.'

At the sound of booted feet on the flagged yard they all looked round. The back door opened and Will Prowse stormed in.

'Bleddy disaster it was. Me and Ben 'ave been out all bleddy night shifting casks out of the crypt to the buyers. Lost at least half the bleddy cargo. If I get my 'ands on—' As he saw Roz's face he stopped dead, visibly startled. Then his mouth curled. 'Well, well, look who's 'ere. How much did they pay you then?'

Roz gaped at him. 'What are you talking about?'

'Somebody gabbed didn't they?'

'It wasn't me!' Roz cried.

'Don't be so daft, Will,' Nell snapped. 'Look at the state of her.'

'That don't mean nothing.' He peered more closely at Roz. 'You got some great bruise coming.' His mouth curled in a sneer. 'Not so pretty now, are you?'

Roz flinched, heat flooding her face as she crossed to the larder and brought out the big bowl of pastry and a stone jar of flour.

'Nor would you be if you'd been hit in the face by a tree,' Nell snapped. 'She could've lost her eye.'

Sprinkling flour on the tabletop, Roz tore off a lump of dough, shaped it into a ball and began rolling it into a circle. 'Who else knew?' she demanded, looking at Will. 'How many other people did you tell?' Had Davy Casvellan known the cargo would be landed on his brother's property? Had he let something slip? But surely Will would never have told him if he didn't believe Davy could be trusted?

'It wasn't you, was it, girl?' Jack spoke quietly.

Roz turned, holding his gaze, her head high. 'No, it wasn't. On my honour it wasn't. You and Nell have been so kind to me. I'm more grateful than I can— I would *never* do anything to cause you trouble.'

After gazing at her for a long moment, Jack gave an abrupt nod. Relief that he believed her, that he trusted her word, brought a lump to Roz's throat. Swallowing hard she turned to Will again, overwhelmed by fury. The force of it made her hands shake.

'How dare you accuse me! You have neither right nor reason. I needed this cargo just as much as you did. Maybe more. My fee would have paid off what I owe you.'

'Don't you come all high and mighty with me, Miss! Cost me good money this have. Bleddy cock-up, all of it. Anyhow, seeing the Riding Officer and his bleddy dragoons got half the kegs, no way am I paying you—'

'But that wasn't my fault!' Roz cried. 'I led the string down to the cove and even after the trap was sprung I still got a third of them to the church. It was *your* idea to use Vounder.'

'That's enough!' Jack crashed his fist down on the table making the cutlery rattle. Roz and Nell both jumped. 'Will, go on home. Way you are now you're no good to man nor beast. Come back tonight when you've had some sleep. We'll talk then. Meantime, leave Roz be. You hear me?'

Will sidled towards the door. 'Can I talk to her a minute?'

'No,' Roz said quickly. 'I've too much to do.'

Will's gaze was on Jack. 'I won't keep her long.'

Roz shot the landlord a pleading look, but he waved her towards the door. 'Go on, maid. Leave 'n say sorry. 'Tis as rare as teats on a bull so you'd best make the most of it.'

Dusting the flour from her hands, Roz followed Will. She stopped in the doorway.

He tried to take hold of her arm but she pulled it away. 'Don't be like that,' he whined. 'All right, I shouldn've said what I did. But what with losing that cargo and no sleep—'

'You aren't the only one affected. Now you'll have to excuse me. Annie's ill, and I have to—'

'Hark a minute. If Jack don't mind, you no need to. Anyhow, what I wanted to say: how don't us forget all about this bit of trouble, and the money you owe. If you was nice to me – I know you turned me down, but there id'n no law says you can't change your mind. And if you did, I'd give you whatever you want: pretty clothes, stuff like that.'

Listening with mounting horror, Roz struggled to keep her feelings from showing as she saw naked desire on his unshaven face. His clothes were filthy and he reeked of old cooking and stale sweat.

Not if he were the last man alive. But Will Prowse had a lot of friends in the village whereas even after two years she was still an outsider. She needed to tread warily. 'I–I–this is not the time or place for such a conversation. My face is so sore I can hardly think straight.'

Jack appeared behind her. 'All right, maid, that's long enough. Get to work. And when Toby come in, tell'n to get on with the cellar work. I'm gone over the brewhouse.'

'I'll see you dreckly,' Will called after her as she fled back inside.

Nell looked up from the bread dough she was kneading. 'Mind you stay in here,' she warned. 'If anyone was to see your face, 't would be round the village quicker'n duckshit. Begging your pardon.'

'I'm sorry, Nell.'

'Tid'n your fault, my bird. But what with Annie away – and Keren's neither use nor ornament. Oh, she id'n bad really. But you got to keep after her all the time.' She sighed. 'It never rain but it do bleddy pour. Still, 'tis only till Annie get back. Right,' she looked up at Roz. 'Soon as I got the bread in, I'll scald the milk. You finish they pies then cut up the veg for the stew. When it get busy, you'll have to help Keren with the washing-up. If I leave it to she, we'll be stacked up from here to Thursday.'

Roz had thought the previous day busy, but this one was harder. Her face ached and throbbed, and perspiration made the raw flesh sting painfully. Even with the kitchen door and window open the air was stifling. At first the aromas of fresh-baked bread, rabbit pie, beef stew, rhubarb crumble and raspberry tart were appetising. But after many hours in the hot kitchen Roz felt slightly queasy.

'All right, my bird,' Nell said eventually. ''Tis after ten. You get on 'ome.'

Removing her apron and cap, Roz unhooked her bonnet from the peg. Inside it a small kerchief contained the woundwort flowers she had gathered that morning. Her back ached, her feet ached and she was so tired she could have wept. As she started towards the door, Nell pushed a cloth-wrapped parcel into her hands.

'Tid'n much, just a slice of rabbit pie and half a raspberry tart. Save you cooking for your mother when you get in.'

'Oh Nell, that's so kind.'

'Get on.' Pink-faced, Nell gripped Roz's forearm. 'I tell 'ee what, my bird, there id'n many would work like you done today, not after what you been through. And I know this life id'n what you're used to. But I'm some glad you're here, and that's the truth.'

Roz's eyes burned with sudden tears. Deeply touched, she bent and kissed Nell's plump cheek. 'I'll see you in the morning.'

After the heat of the kitchen the night air was cool and fresh. She looked up. Turquoise in the west, the sky darkened overhead to sapphire. As her eyes adjusted she saw pinpoints of light as bright and sharp as the diamonds in her grandmother's necklace.

She pushed the thought away. She could not afford such memories. The sound of male voices floated back to her from the street. Fearful of being seen, and suddenly anxious in case Will Prowse might be lurking nearby, she crossed quickly to the shadows and hurried down the lane.

As soon as she opened the door she smelled it. She stood on the threshold. What if she didn't go in? What if she simply turned around and walked away? *And go where?*

'Where have you been?' her mother demanded from her chair by the hearth.

Stepping inside, Roz closed the door and slid

the wooden bar through the slots to lock it. 'You know where I've been. At work.'

'Till this hour?' Her mother's tone was querulous, her speech slurred.

Placing the cloth-wrapped bundle on the table, Roz untied her bonnet. 'Where did you get it, Mama? And don't ask what,' she added as her mother drew an indignant breath. 'We both know you've been drinking.'

'So what if I have? It's lonely here all by myself.'

'Where did you get it?' Roz repeated.

Mary-Blanche waved a careless hand. 'I have friends,' she replied.

Too tired to press further, Roz turned away and hung up her bonnet. 'Nell sent some food for you.'

'I don't need her charity!'

'Then don't eat it.' She crossed to the hearth. 'Where's the barley water?'

'What? Oh.' Mary-Blanche pulled a face then shrugged. 'I forgot.'

Roz said nothing, for what was there to say? She picked up the kettle. It was empty. Fetching a small saucepan she carried it to the fresh water bucket. That was barely a quarter full. Unable to face walking to the pump now, Roz scooped half a pint into the pan and carried it back to the fire, set it on the three-legged iron stand and poked the embers into a blaze.

'Why don't you say something?' Mary-Blanche shrilled.

'I'm tired, Mama. I want to make a poultice for my face, then I'm going to bed.'

'I'm not like you. I don't have your strength. Do you think I *enjoy* being the way I am?'

'I don't know, Mama. Do you?' Roz opened her small kerchief and tipped the wilted wound-wort flowers into the pan.

'No! I hate it!'

'Then stop.'

'I want to. I *do*,' she shouted, though Roz had not said anything. 'But when I try I feel so – you've cannot imagine – the shame, the guilt – I can't bear it. Brandy takes the pain away.'

While the pan boiled, Roz tore a strip from an old frayed muslin kerchief. Lifting the pan off the stand she poured the liquid into a basin. With a spoon she scooped up the flowers onto the muslin and folded it over.

'Goodnight, Mama.' Leaving her shoes at the bottom of the stairs, she climbed up to her tiny room. Setting the pad beside her basin, she took off everything but her shift and unpinned her hair. Then picking up the pad she lay down, placed it on her face, and closed her eyes.

She could hear her mother mumbling as she shuffled around in the room below.

'You don't understand,' Mary-Blanche cried. 'If you had accepted Will Prowse we wouldn't have to live like this.'

Roz heard several loud creaks as her mother got into bed still muttering. How much longer could she go on?

Seven

Casvellan looked at the two handcuffed men standing in front of his desk. He had questioned them, but with little expectation. Both had remained stubbornly silent. Knowing the kind of retribution that befell those who informed on their friends, they preferred to take their chances with him. He sighed inwardly.

'I am minded to send you both to gaol.' He saw one flinch. The other bent his head. This gave him hope.

'However, as you are both family men it is your wives and children who would suffer.' Among the papers on his desk was a letter from the parish overseers warning that the workhouse could take no more.

'This is the first time either of you has appeared before me.' His voice hardened. 'I advise you to make it the last. You will both receive twenty lashes and be bound over to be of good behaviour. If you refuse to be bound over, or if you commit another offence, you will go to gaol. Do you understand?'

Swallowing audibly both men nodded.

'And do you agree to be bound over?'

'Yes, sir.'

'Aye, sir.'

'Take them down, Constable. My clerk will be with you directly to witness the punishment.'

As the door closed on Colenso and his two prisoners, Casvellan rose from his chair and paced to the window. 'The whole thing was a shambles, George. Crocker had too many men in the lane. They got in each other's way.' He pushed an impatient hand through his black mane. Already rumpled and untidy, it betrayed his agitation. 'Before you ask, I had no say in it. The lieutenant invited me as a courtesy. He would have been grossly offended had I presumed to advise him on the deployment of his men.' He flexed shoulders tense from too many demands and too little time.

'I tried to stop the lad in charge of the string. But he simply whirled the animal round and bolted with four of the ponies. To be fair, no one would have expected him to go the way he did. I had no idea that path existed. It's barely visible and there's a sheer drop on one side. He is either very brave or extremely reckless.' He shook his head. 'We should have caught more of them.'

'At least the lieutenant retrieved half the cargo,' the clerk offered.

'It's not enough, George.' Casvellan turned. 'I'm keeping you from your work.'

'For what it's worth, sir, you have my sympathy. You were anticipating a very different outcome.' Pausing by the door he cleared his throat. 'Mr Varcoe asked me to remind you about the French prisoners.'

Casvellan looked up. He had forgotten. 'When are they expected?'

'This afternoon, sir.'

'Tell him to come and fetch me when they arrive.' He frowned at the paper cluttering the surface of his desk. 'I swear this stuff breeds.'

It was after three when a wagon pulled by four horses rumbled up the drive. Quickly putting on his coat, Casvellan settled it more comfortably as he clattered down the wooden stairs and strode across the gravel to join his agent.

'Nine in the back,' Devlin murmured. 'And the officer riding next to the driver.'

'What are your plans?' Casvellan asked, interested in how Devlin intended to deal with the prisoners.

'Feed 'em, then set 'em to work.'

'Today?'

'Why not? We need that hay cut, dried, turned and gathered in before the weather breaks.' He raised his brows. 'Unless you—'

'No. I was simply curious. It's an excellent idea.' Casvellan waited for the wagon to stop. The driver climbed down and went to the back to unlock the shackles chaining the prisoners together. Meanwhile the officer sat a moment longer, looking about him and taking stock of his surroundings.

'In your own time,' Devlin muttered under his breath.

At last the officer jumped down and strode forward. Stopping a few feet away he removed his hat and made a stiff bow. *'Armand Phillippe, capitaine de le corsaire* Levrier.'

Casvellan inclined his head. 'Do you speak English, Captain?'

'Of course.'

Looking into cool grey eyes, Casvellan weighed up the man facing him, aware that he too was being assessed. 'Then you will have no difficulty translating Mr Varcoe's orders for your crew. Do I have your parole?'

At this reminder, that his freedom to remain unshackled was conditional upon his promise not to try to escape, the captain's lips thinned. 'Yes.'

'And you answer for your men?'

'Yes.'

'Good. Mr Varcoe is my agent. He acts for me in all matters pertaining to the estate. You will obey him as you would me. While in my custody, you and your men will live in warm dry quarters and be properly fed. In a few minutes, after you have eaten, Mr Varcoe will take you around the farm. And before you tell me that you are not obliged to work, I should inform you that anyone who refuses, unless he is ill or disabled, will be removed to a barred cell. If any of your men causes trouble I expect you to ensure he is suitably punished. Your time here will be as easy or as difficult as you choose to make it. Do I make myself clear?'

There was new respect in the captain's gaze as he bowed. *'Bien-sûr.* Indeed you do.'

After returning the bow Casvellan turned to Devlin and murmured, 'They're all yours.'

Having spent much of the day writing letters and reading reports, and reluctant to return to yet more, he decided to walk over to the stables. Horses were the only interest he and his father had shared. As he approached the yard he saw two of his thoroughbred fillies racing around one of the paddocks. Stopping to watch, he felt the tension in his shoulders begin to loosen as the stresses of the day dissolved.

Sarab was the same pewter-grey as Raad, her half-brother. Her Arabian ancestry showed in the shape of her head, her fine muzzle and expressive eyes. Agile and beautiful, she carried her tail high and her neck proudly arched. Flight stood taller with long legs and a glossy chestnut coat. Watching her long, low stride, it was clear that she and the colt, Arrow, would make excellent cavalry horses.

Dan Eathorne, the head groom, emerged from the harness room and knuckled his forehead. 'Af'noon, sir.'

'Good afternoon, Daniel.'

'Riding out are 'ee?'

Casvellan was tempted. But he had promised himself he would clear his desk. 'Not today. How's the swelling on Damis's leg?'

Dan shook his head. 'I wanted to see 'ee about that. I put a paste of fuller's earth and vinegar on un. Now normally I'd expect to see'n gone in a couple of days.'

'And it hasn't?'

Dan shook his head. 'I'm wondering if he might have a soft splint. When I was over to Helston last week I got talking to a farrier there. He've treated soft splints using plantain leaves. Said they worked a treat. See, when the leg sweat it do draw the goodness out of the leaves and into the skin.'

'This farrier—'

'Works for a military man, sir, a Captain Visick. Been with'n years. Travelled all over, he have. Captain's family is well-to-do by all accounts, and the captain have just come back from—'

'Yes, thank you, Daniel,' Casvellan broke in gently. 'You've been very thorough.'

'So I should hope. I aren't one to ever take a risk with our horses, sir.'

Biting the inside of his lip to hold back a smile at being so firmly put in his place, Casvellan nodded. 'Indeed. By all means try the plantain leaves.' About to leave, he hesitated. 'About young Trevaskis—' he got no further.

'Tom?' The groom's weathered face wrinkled like a raisin as he grinned. 'Boy's a natural. You'd think he'd been here years. Keen as mustard he is. I never have to chase un, not like some we've had. Wear me out with all his questions, he do. But I only have to tell un the once.'

Casvellan had never seen the groom so enthused. 'Good. That's good.' Taking the boy on had been an act of impulse. He was not normally given to impulsive acts. He knew why he'd done it. It was because of the boy's sister, Roz. She was making such valiant efforts. Giving the boy to a trade and removing him from bad company simply meant he was less likely to end up in trouble. Once the idea had occurred, naturally he had made inquiries. He was glad – relieved – it had worked out so well. He might instruct Ellacott to write ... No, better not.

'Has the boy been home since he started here?'

Dan blinked. 'Not that I know of.'

'Let him go on Sunday for two hours. His mother will want to see—'

'Begging your pardon, sir, but I doubt his mother even know he've gone. 'Tis Roz who look after 'em all, dear of her. 'Tis she the boy do talk about. I reckon he miss her more'n he miss his ma. Jimmy got to take Miss Deborah's mare to be shod. He can tell Roz when he's in the village. Send the boy home over dinnertime, shall I, sir? We're quiet then.'

'As you wish.' The matter had been dealt with and could be put from his mind. *If only it were so easy.* 'Well, Daniel, if there's nothing else—'

'Only the smallpox. But I 'spect you heard already.'

Casvellan froze. 'Smallpox? Where?'

'Helston. Mrs Hambley said about it this morning when I went up for my breakfast. One of the deliverymen told her. Come in with a crewman off one of the boats, it did. Now there's two dead and half a score took sick.'

'No, I hadn't heard. Thank you.' Instead of returning to the work on his desk, Casvellan went directly to the house. It was seven years since the last outbreak. That had been in Falmouth, a much busier port. But as he knew only too well, the effects had spread like ripples and been felt even here.

He wasn't worried for himself. Dr Avers had told him that the cowpox he'd contracted as a child had given him immunity to the deadlier disease. But with the outbreak only a few miles distant, his mother, Deb and Davy would be at risk.

Learning from Bassett that the ladies were taking afternoon tea in his mother's upstairs sitting room, he went up to join them. He opened the door to a room filled with sunshine that streamed in through the long windows. Deborah's needlework lay abandoned on the green and gold brocade sofa. In front of her, beside a tray of tea things on a low rosewood table, were plates of bread and butter, a small glass dish of raspberry jam, sliced fruitcake and strawberry tartlets. His stomach gurgled and it occurred to him that he hadn't eaten since breakfast.

'Branoc!' His mother beamed as he walked in. 'What a lovely surprise! I cannot remember when last you graced us with your presence in the afternoon. I find it quite astonishing that we can live in the same house yet see each other so seldom.'

'Mama,' Deborah chided gently. 'You know how busy Bran is.'

'Oh indeed.' Lisette Casvellan's tone verged on petulant as she adjusted the froth of gauze that filled the neckline of her green and crimson striped silk gown. 'Men lead such full lives. They have no idea how lonely it is for us—'

'He is here now, Mama. So let us enjoy his company. I'll ring for another cup.'

'No, Deb. I cannot stay long.'

'You never do.' His mother frowned at him. 'My dear boy, you must eat. You will make yourself ill.'

Had his mother been a warm or demonstrative

100

woman, he would have kissed her: partly in reassurance, but also because she had given him the perfect opening. 'Actually, Mama, that's why I've come.'

Lisette Casvellan's hand flew to her bosom and her eyes widened. 'You're ill? There you are, didn't I warn you? Haven't I always said—'

'No, Mama, I'm fine,' he interrupted before she could work herself into a state. Sitting down, he reached for a strawberry tartlet and swallowed it in two bites. 'But I've just learned there is smallpox in Helston. I must insist that this time you, Deb and Davy are innoculated.'

It took the two of them half an hour to calm their mother down. After Deb had fetched hartshorn and water, and Casvellan had waved his mother's vinaigrette beneath her nose, she finally stopped shuddering and sat up in her chair.

'But are you sure it's safe?'

'Dr Avers has great faith in it. Surely what's most important is that it will protect you against a disease which, even if it does not kill, causes dreadful disfigurement.' He caught his sister's eye and knew she too was remembering.

'So if Ellen had been inoculated she wouldn't have died?' Lisette dabbed her eyes. 'Poor Ellen, such a sweet girl.' She looked up at her son, her eyes brimming with tears. 'When I think of the losses all three of us have suffered—'

'Now, Mama,' Deborah broke in gently. 'Do not make yourself unhappy. I think Bran's suggestion is an excellent idea. It is a terrible disease, and if there is something we can do to ensure we are protected, then it would be very foolish to refuse.'

Throwing her a look of gratitude, Casvellan stood up. 'I'll send a note asking Dr Avers to call. In fact, as the outbreak is so close, I think it wise for all the household staff and the estate workers to be inoculated as well.'

Bone-weary from the extra-long days she had been working all week, Roz forced herself out of bed soon after daybreak on Sunday morning. The cottage was in desperate need of cleaning and she wanted to get that done and the meal in the oven before she got herself washed and ready. If Tom had not been coming she would have done the laundry as well.

All this work on the Sabbath contravened everything her grandparents had taught her. Flouting their rules gave her no pleasure. But clothes and bed linen needed to be washed and Sunday was the only day she was there to do it. Her grandfather, a clergyman in the Church of England, did not approve of John Wesley's Methodism. However, she had heard him concede Wesley's claim that neatness of apparel was a duty not a sin, and cleanliness was indeed next to godliness.

Though her current circumstances bore little resemblance to the life she had left behind, she was trying her best to maintain the standards with which she had been brought up. Keeping herself and the cottage clean allowed her to feel that she had some control over her life. But in reality she was clinging on by her fingernails.

Quickly putting on a calico bodice, an old woollen petticoat and a pair of worn-out slippers, she rekindled the fire, then brushed ash and cinders from the hearth onto a small shovel and emptied it into a bucket. Later she would take it up the garden to the earth privy where the ashes helped deaden the smell.

She had assumed her mother's lack of interest in Tom's visit was due to her headache. But that had been three days ago. Now she was refusing to get out of bed.

'I'm tired,' Mary-Blanche complained. 'You've been coming in all hours, then waking me early. I need my rest. Anyway, I don't know why you're making such a fuss. The boy has only been gone five minutes.'

'It's almost a month, Mama. This is his first job and his first visit home. Surely you're looking forward to seeing him?'

Mary-Blanche snorted. 'So he can tell us about Mr Casvellan's horses, and Mr Casvellan's stables, and how the sun shines out of Mr Casvellan's backside?'

Roz turned away. Even after two years there were still times when her mother's coarseness shocked her. Filling the kettle she hung it over the fire.

'I don't know what you're so uppity about,' Mary-Blanche goaded. 'He's cost you enough.'

'I never minded that. Tom's only a child.'

'Not Tom, you ninny. I'm talking about the Justice, Mr high-and-mighty Casvellan.'

Roz crouched to roll up the threadbare rug. *Yes, it has cost me. I've paid fine after fine. I used all my savings and put myself in debt to a man I detest and am frightened of. I did it because if I hadn't you would have gone to gaol. And you said if I let that happen you would kill yourself.*

'Cat got your tongue?' Mary-Blanche taunted.

'I'm going to shake the rug.' Roz carried it outside.

When she came back in, her mother was lying on her side, her back to the room. So Roz got on with her chores. She swept the floor, added more furze to the fire, washed and dried the dishes piled in the basin, then wiped the table.

After peeling and dicing carrots and parsnips into an earthenware pot, she jointed the rabbit Eddy Winnen had given her the previous evening. He had skinned it, knowing that was a job she hated. The gift was his thanks for the pot of coltsfoot, mallow and comfrey ointment she had given him for his boils.

Coating the meat in barley flour, she melted a knob of butter in an iron pan and seared the joints on both sides, then scooped them into the pot on top of the vegetables. Adding a little water and some herbs from her patch in the garden she put the pot into the cloam oven.

Next she chopped five sticks of rhubarb, drizzled honey over the fruit and put that in the oven as well. She would serve it with the dish of clotted cream Nell had given her. With the meal prepared and cooking, she put the peelings into the slop bucket for the butcher's pigs, wiped the table again and set out three plates and cutlery.

Then filling a large pitcher with hot water she

took it up to her room. Shutting out memories of deep baths and scented soap, rosewater hair-wash and soft towels, she stripped off all her clothes and washed herself from head to toe using a sliver of hard yellow soap and a cotton rag.

Refreshed, she put on a clean shift, brushed her hair thoroughly, then twisted it into the usual coil. Her chemise gown of pale yellow dotted muslin was faded and worn. But though five years old and hopelessly out of fashion, at least it still fitted. After tying the sash around her waist, Roz pushed the three-quarter sleeves up to her elbows. Picking up a clean kerchief of white muslin she crossed it in front of the gown's low neckline and knotted the ends behind her back. Then, and only then, did she reach for her looking glass.

The scab had finally fallen off. And thanks to the honey and woundwort, the scar was only slightly pinker than the rest of her face. She knew it would fade with time. But to Roz it screamed guilt.

Replacing the mirror she took a deep breath to steady herself. Emptying the basin into the pitcher, she carried it downstairs. Her mother hadn't moved. Just for an instant she thought she caught a whiff of brandy. But when she sniffed all she could smell was the appetizing aroma of meat and herbs. Her mouth watered. Taking the pitcher outside she emptied the water onto her herb patch.

Back in the kitchen she opened the old chest in which her mother kept her clothes and flinched at the sour and musty odour.

'What are you doing?'

Roz looked round.

Her mother was sitting up, bleary-eyed, hair a wild tangle, glaring at her. 'There's nothing of yours in there. You've no business rummaging.'

'Mama, why do you put things back that need washing? I told you I'd do it. I wasn't prying. I just wanted to find you something to wear.'

'I can do that for myself. I don't need your help.'

'As you wish.' Anxious not to provoke yet another row, Roz kept her voice calm and level. 'Are you ready to get up now? Tom will be here soon.'

'Oh all right, if I must. Anything to stop your nagging.' Pushing back the bedclothes, Mary-Blanche swung her legs over the side. But as she tried to stand up, she staggered and fell back. The wooden bed frame creaked ominously. 'Whoops!' She giggled.

Roz stared at her mother. Surely not. She *couldn't* be. She was, but how? 'You're drunk.'

Mary-Blanche's gaze slid away. She bridled as if about to deny the accusation. Then clearly realizing she wouldn't be believed decided to brazen it out. 'What if I am?'

Roz wanted to scream. Instead she fisted her hands and struggled to keep her voice down. *'Why*, Mama? You knew Tom was coming. You knew I wanted this to be a special day for him, for the three of us—'

'For God's sake, stop making such a fuss! All right, I've had a drop of brandy. Why shouldn't

I? I'm stuck in this awful place day after day—'

'Where did you get it?'

'None of your business. And before you start on at me about money, it didn't cost anything. I told you, I've got friends.'

'How could you?' Roz was trembling with rage, hurt and disappointment. Picking up a pad of sacking to protect her hands, she reached into the oven for the pot containing the rabbit. An aching stiffness in her throat threatened to choke her. She swallowed hard, glad of the heat that dried her tears before they could fall. *She would not cry.*

'Don't you use that tone with me!' Mary-Blanche shouted. 'You sound exactly like your grandmother. Everything was always *my* fault. *Mary-Blanche, how could you?*' she mimicked savagely and lurched to her feet, swaying. 'You don't know what it's like!'

Roz set the pot on the table. Reaching into the drawer for a ladle, she glanced briefly at her mother's contorted face.

'Don't look at me like that!' Mary-Blanche yelled.

Roz turned away, catching the soft flesh of her bottom lip between her teeth. Whatever she said would only make things worse. Silence was safer. She lifted the rhubarb from the oven and set the dish on the table. As she tested the fruit with a spoon to make sure it was soft her hands shook uncontrollably.

'You think you're better than me.'

'No, I don't—' Roz tried, but her mother was beyond listening.

'Well, you're not. You're bossy and interfering. Always spying on me and telling me what to do.'

Roz flinched as if the words had been blows. 'That's not fair!'

'Fair?' her mother shrieked. 'You think what happened to me was *fair*? Abandoned by the man I loved—'

'Mama, please—'

'Go away! Go on, go back where you came from and let me be. I never asked you to—'

'Stop it! Stop it!'

Roz whirled round to see Tom standing in the doorway.

'Tom!' Mary-Blanche's mood and expression changed in an instant. She smiled widely at her son. 'How's my little man? Come and— Ow!' As her foot caught in the ragged hem of her shift she stumbled against the table. It rocked on the uneven floor and before Roz could move, tipped onto its side. Plates, cutlery, and the two pots tumbled to the floor, spilling meat, gravy, vegetables and rhubarb all over the rug.

'Oh dear!' Mary-Blanche giggled.

With a sob, Tom bolted. Tearing off her apron and ignoring her mother's plaintive wail, Roz ran after him.

Eight

'Tom, wait!' Though he was quick, she was quicker. She caught his shoulder. 'Please don't run away. I've looked forward so much to seeing you.'

He stopped, head bent as he knuckled his eyes.

Looking at the nape of his neck, so thin and vulnerable, Roz's heart contracted. She crouched, turned him towards her and forced cheerfulness into her voice. 'I've had an idea. Why don't we go and see Jack and Nell. They've been asking me how you're getting on.'

Tom raised his eyes to hers. The lids were red. Roz could imagine the effort it was costing him not to cry, to shrug it off and pretend it didn't matter. The past two years had been hard enough for her, and she was an adult. Tom was just a child. Could her mother not see how badly her behaviour hurt the boy? Or did she simply not care?

'Will they give us something to eat?' he asked hopefully. 'I'm hungry.'

'I'm sure they will,' she said with far more confidence than she felt.

The inn was closed on Sundays. Though he had grumbled bitterly about losing business by having to shut on the Sabbath, Jack valued his licence too much to risk losing it by defying the order.

Roz guided Tom round to the back. Though there were no customers to feed, Nell would still have cooked dinner for Jack and herself. Delicious savoury smells drifted from the open doorway. Her stomach cramping from the effects of stress and hunger, Roz knocked.

'Hello?' she called, and as her eyes grew accustomed to the darker kitchen after the bright sunshine, she heard the scrape of a chair on the flagged floor.

'Roz?' Nell bustled towards her. 'What's wrong? Why, here's Tom. Dear life, boy, growing like a fern, you are. Come in. Come in. Jack,' she called over her shoulder, 'Roz 'ave brought Tom to say 'ullo. Go on, my 'andsome.' As he trotted into the big kitchen, she turned to Roz. 'Trouble?' she whispered.

Roz nodded.

'I thought you was cooking the rabbit Eddy Winnen give 'ee,' Nell's forehead puckered.

'I did. Only,' her breath caught on a dry sob, 'I'd just taken dinner out of the oven. Mama knocked the table over and it all went on the floor.' Roz felt the tremble in her chest and caught her lower lip between her teeth, torn between hysterical laughter and tears of despair; afraid if she gave way to either she wouldn't be able to stop.

Nell gripped her arm. 'All right, bird. Hush now.'

'I'm so sorry.' Roz gestured helplessly. 'Only Tom's hungry and I didn't know where else—'

110

'You done right.' Ushering Roz ahead of her, she smiled at Tom. 'I hope you brung your appetite, boy. Like roast lamb, do you?' As he nodded, she gave Roz a gentle push. 'Sit down.'

'Let me help—'

'Nothing to do.' Within moments she had set plates containing slices of succulent meat, mashed potatoes, cabbage and gravy before each of them.'There now, don't leave it go cold.' She resumed her own place. 'Nice to have a bit of company, id'n it, Jack?'

The landlord's sharp gaze shifted from his wife to Roz and then to Tom. 'It is too.' He nodded. 'Now, boy, how don't you tell us what you been doing?'

That was all the encouragement Tom needed. Over the next hour they learned about the tasks he'd been set, which of the horses he liked best, his opinion of the other grooms and Mr Eathorne, where he slept, and the food at Trescowe. ''Tis all right, but not so nice as this,' he grinned at Nell, who beamed back.

'He's no fool,' Jack said dryly. 'Got room for another strawberry tart, boy?'

Tom nodded. 'Lovely, they are.' Then, swallowing a mouthful, he turned to Roz. 'What you done to your face?'

There was a moment's total silence. Then Roz touched her scar lightly. 'This? I wasn't looking where I was going and a branch caught me.'

'Did it hurt?'

'A bit, at first. But not any more.' She forced herself to ask, leering to making a joke of it and hide her anxiety, 'Does it look horrible?'

111

Tom screwed up his eyes and peered at her. Then he shook his head. 'Nah. You can't hardly see it. Tid'n nothing like Jimmy. He got kicked and now his cheek is all scrunched up.' He crammed the rest of the tart into his mouth.

Jack looked at his watch. 'What time you s'posed to be back, boy?'

'Three.'

'Best be on your way then.'

As Tom scrambled down from his chair, Roz stood up and looked from Jack to Nell. 'Thank you both so much. Tom, what do you say?'

'Lovely it was.' Grinning, the boy patted his stomach. 'I'm full as a tick.'

'Tom!' Roz was mortified, but Nell burst out laughing.

'Don't take on, my bird. He don't mean no harm.'

Jack reached for his pipe. 'Boy's doing all right. Best thing for'n, being over Trescowe.'

'Dan Eathorne's a good man,' Nell said as she walked with Roz to the door.

So is Justice Casvellan. The apprenticeship was his doing. But Roz kept the thought to herself.

'Lost both his boys to the measles, Dan did,' Nell went on. 'It broke Sal's heart. Within a twelvemonth she was gone as well. Must be ten years since. I reckon 't was the horses kept him going. Dan love they animals like they was his own. He've got a sharp tongue and he won't stand no nonsense. But it look to me like he've taken a shine to young Tom.' She patted Roz's arm. ''Tis plain the boy's happy. Let'n go, and stop worrying.' She dropped her voice. '' T wasn't no life for 'n here.'

'I know,' Roz whispered.

'Better make haste.' Nell stood in the doorway to wave them off.

'I'll see you in the morning,' Roz called over her shoulder.

'You don't have to come,' Tom said as Roz reached his side and they headed up the dusty stony track onto the moor. 'I can walk by my-self.'

'I know you can,' Roz agreed. 'You're a big boy now and you have a job. But as it's such a lovely afternoon perhaps I could come halfway with you? I've been working in Nell's kitchen all week and it's been very hot so I'd enjoy some fresh air.' She could see he was torn between proving his independence and the daunting pros-pect of a long, lonely walk. She yearned to hug him, but instead she linked her fingers, waiting while he considered.

Eventually he sighed. 'All right then.' His expression suggested he was conferring a huge favour. Then it became suspicious. 'What are you smiling at?'

Roz shrugged. 'I'm happy. It's a beautiful day, I've been looking forward to seeing you, and here you are. Now, tell me more about the horses. What are their names?' Then she asked him what colours they were, what they ate, how often they were groomed: anything to keep his thoughts cheerful and away from the scene he had witnessed on his arrival at the cottage.

They reached the top of the moor. Beneath a

clear blue sky dotted with white puffs of cloud lay the patchwork of fields belonging to the estate farm. Beyond them, trees lined the drive and framed the manor house. Roz tore her gaze and her thoughts from it as Tom stopped. Kicking the toe of his boot against a big stone he glanced sideways at her.

'You better go back now.'

Roz looked around, deliberately widening her eyes. 'Goodness, I had no idea I'd come so far.' She crouched so her eyes were level with his. Her arms ached to hug him. 'It's been lovely seeing you, Tom. And hearing everything you've been doing. Off you go then. Mind you do your best for Mr Eathorne. Just one more thing.'

'What?'

Laughing, she grabbed him and planted a deliberately noisy kiss on his cheek. 'I'm so proud of you.'

'Ugh!' Screwing up his face, he rubbed it with his sleeve then backed away, grinning widely. 'Bye.' He gave a quick wave. Then, arms whirling like windmills, he began to skip and run.

Roz watched him until he disappeared around the curve in the track. She wondered if he might look back. But he didn't. She told herself that was a good sign. Nell was right. He was happy. She had Mr Casvellan to thank for that. Perhaps she might write him a note expressing her gratitude.

But where would she find paper, pen and ink? She couldn't afford to buy them. If she asked Jack or Nell she'd feel bound to explain why.

Anyway Tom was her half-brother, not her son. Properly it should be her mother who thanked the Justice, though there was little chance of that.

Refusing to allow thoughts of her mother to intrude and spoil her walk, Roz turned off the rutted cart track and followed a narrow path that wound between dense cushions of purple heather and furze bushes thick with yellow blossom that smelled of melted butter. On the uplands weathered outcrops of granite patched with orange and silver-green lichen were surrounded by vivid green bracken.

Having fled the cottage in desperate haste to catch Tom she was without either cap or bonnet. The sun, now halfway down the western sky, was still hot on her head and back. It was too late now to worry about her complexion. She raised one hand to the scar on her face. It had been too late long before that.

With the moor on her left, she joined the coastal footpath that would eventually take her back to the village. Following the undulations of the hillside, the path climbed and dipped. High and precipitous in some places, the cliff edge was shallower, less steep in others. Where the slope was gentle, twisting rocky paths led down to hidden coves and beaches. The sea was calm and a glittering sapphire-blue.

Roz paused, gazing down onto a stretch of beach bounded by two craggy headlands. At the water's edge small waves curled and broke. The tide was ebbing. Below the fringe of dark sea-weed marking high water, wet sand smoothed flat by the receding tide glistened gold and bronze.

She was about to move on when a horse and rider appeared, moving down the beach towards the water. Wearing only breeches and a full-sleeved loose white shirt, the dark-haired rider rode bareback. Roz's heart kicked painfully and she gasped, her hand flying to her mouth. Even from this distance she recognized him. How could she not? He was her last thought before she slept, and her first when she woke.

The horse pranced, jinking sideways. Gun-metal grey, big and powerful, it had to be Raad. Tom had spoken the stallion's name with awe and told her none of the junior grooms was allowed near him. Watching the animal's antics, Roz hoped fervently that Tom wouldn't be tempted to disobey.

As they splashed into the water, man and horse appeared totally at ease. Then, turning the stallion parallel to the sea, the rider leaned forward. The horse broke instantly into a gallop, a long flat stride that ate up the distance. They hurtled through the shallows kicking up clouds of spray that plastered the rider's shirt to his body and dampened his hair into wild black curls. As they approached the rocks at the far end, Casvellan straightened up and drew in the reins. The horse slowed, dancing sideways and tossing his head. Patting and stroking the arched neck, Casvellan wheeled the animal round and once again the horse took off like an arrow back the way they had come.

Perfectly in tune, horse and rider moved as one

116

in a demonstration of speed, power and control that left Roz dry-mouthed with awe. Thrilled to have witnessed something she guessed few had ever seen she was nonetheless conscious of intruding on his privacy.

Reluctantly she turned away and continued her walk. He had chosen this isolated spot seeking solitude. Given the demands of his life, pressures she could only imagine, where else would he find it? But the startling image of man and horse racing along the water's edge was one she would treasure always, not least for its stark contrast to his usual appearance: immaculately dressed, formal, austere, *burdened*.

Raising a hand she touched her scar. It was healing well. And Tom's response had reassured her. But as well as marking her face Justice Casvellan's whip had scored her soul. Had she still been living with her grandparents, she might perhaps have met him in a social setting. Though that was unlikely, for the stigma of her illegitimate birth set her apart. A few of her grandparents' friends were sufficiently enlightened, or kind, to include her in their invitations. But many more were not.

It was a cruel irony that during the past two years she had in fact met Mr Casvellan on several occasions. But in almost every case it had been to plead for her mother following yet another arrest. Now she too was a criminal.

Since the dramatic reunion with her mother in Penzance, everything she had done had been with the best of intentions. How had it all gone so terribly wrong?

She thought about the dinner she had prepared, and the mess on the floor. Would her mother have left it there for her to clean up? Thank God for Nell and Jack. Tom had enjoyed his visit. That was what really mattered. As for the rest, she would cope as best she could. After all, what choice did she have?

'Good morning, Deb,' Casvellan greeted his sister.

'Good morning, Bran.' Cool and fresh in pale blue figured muslin, she was seated at the table, a cup of hot chocolate and a slice of bread and butter in front of her.

'How is our mother this morning?' Spooning scrambled eggs from a chafing dish onto his plate, he carried it to his place and sat down. Then he looked more closely at her. 'Deb?' Concern tightened his features. 'Oh no, don't say—'

'No, no, she's perfectly well. I had to send Preece out with a note yesterday afternoon, asking Dr Avers to call at the house before he left.'

'Again? How many times is that?'

'Three. She has asked to see him every day since her inoculation. I'm just relieved he was already here.'

'He won't be after today. He finished with our own people yesterday. Today he'll treat those of the French prisoners who require the inoculation. Two of them have already had the disease judging by their scars, poor devils.'

'Well, he came, and he was very forbearing.'

'So I should expect. I pay him enough.' Pouring steaming coffee from the silver pot into his cup, he glanced up. 'I'm sorry. Go on.'

'Oh, Bran. Is it costing a very great deal of money?'

He could have kicked himself. Coping with their mother was burden enough for Deb. The financial concerns of the estate were his responsibility.

'No more than I anticipated,' he said easily. 'I meant simply that as she is such a very *loyal* patient, he must surely know by now how best to treat her. So what happened?' Setting his cup on the table he pulled out his chair and sat down.

'He explained yet again that the mark on her arm was simply the inoculation scratch healing, and everything was just as it should be. He said it was a pleasure to see her in such excellent health.'

'How did she take that?' Casvellan asked dryly, shaking the folds from the starched napkin and laying it across his lap.

The corners of Deborah's mouth lifted. 'This time she was actually relieved. I confess that before he went in I asked him to reassure her, and to suggest that a walk in the fresh air would be of greater benefit than remaining in bed.'

'Deb, you minx!'

'I know. I suppose I was wrong really. But I'm sure she would be able to sleep better if she took some exercise. She's been waking up during the night. When that happens she calls for me. If I don't go to her she worries herself into a state.'

'This is ridiculous,' Casvellan snapped. 'If she wants something it's her maid's job to fetch it, not yours.'

119

'Dear Bran. You're missing the point. It's not a soothing drink or her vinaigrette that Mama wants, it's reassurance. Anyway,' she smiled at him, 'the worst is over. She is herself again.'

He held her gaze, wishing there were something he could do, some way in which he could make her life easier. Then he realized with a shock that though he was looking at his sister, it was Roz Trevaskis he was thinking of.

Dipping her head, Deborah set her cup down gently, patted her mouth with her napkin and rose from her chair. 'Will you excuse me? I want to call on Mrs Varcoe this morning.'

'Is she well?'

Deborah's smile was wistful. 'She's positively glowing. Her energy puts me to shame. You know how neglected that garden was? Well, she has cleared a small patch and planted all sorts of different herbs. She uses some for cooking and with others she makes tisanes and tinctures. Apparently she has a friend, Roz Trevaskis, who knows about such things and taught her.'

Rising abruptly, Casvellan carried his plate to the sideboard, struggling with his reaction to the sound of her name on his sister's lips. He glanced over his shoulder. 'Have you seen Davy this morning?'

'Briefly. He was just finishing his breakfast when I came in. I think he's riding out. He said something about wanting his horses fully fit before hunting starts after the harvest.'

Pausing in the yard a short distance from the inn's back door, Annie set down her pitcher and gripped Roz's chin, turning her face first one way then the other. 'I dunno what you're fretting about. 'Tis no more'n a faint line. I tell 'ee what, girl, you was some lucky. My granfer near lost his eye to one of they springy branches. Last winter it was, during one of they bad gales.' Releasing Roz's chin, she patted her cheek. 'If Will Prowse hadn't 'ave said about it, I wouldn't 've known. I can see it now, but only 'cos I'm looking for it. If you wasn't standing in direct sun I'd never—'

'What are you pair doing of out here?' Nell shouted from the doorway. 'Annie, get over stairs and clear the table. Roz, c'mon with that pitcher. If Keren do lean on that sink much longer she'll go sleep. Soon as you filled the kettle,' she added as Roz passed her, 'go and ask Jack if he want pie or stew.'

Roz jerked round, panic clutching her throat. 'Couldn't—?'

'No,' Nell cut her short. 'You can't hide in here for ever, and I can't be two places at once. Dear life, girl, stop fretting. You're still pretty as a picture.'

'Nell! You surely can't think that's what I'm worried about.'

'Course I don't,' Nell patted Roz's arm. 'Now get on and do what you're told. And take a tray,' she called over her shoulder.

Straightening her apron, Roz pulled her frilled cap a little further forward. Picking up the tray she took a deep breath and left the kitchen.

Nine

Pausing in the doorway, Roz glanced quickly round. Seeing no sign of Will Prowse she released the breath she had been holding.

It was now well after two and the dinnertime crowd had thinned, leaving the usual debris of dirty plates and empty tankards. After glancing towards the bar where Jack was busy, Roz crossed to the nearest table. She was acutely aware that the group of elderly fishermen who always sat in the corner by the window smoking their pipes and nursing their ale had all looked up.

'All right, maid?' one called. 'Missed you we 'ave.'

Roz smiled. 'That's nice to hear.' As she leaned forward to collect more tankards, she felt the sun's warmth on the unmarked side of her face.

One man nudged his neighbour. 'Been away, 'ave she?'

'No,' he was told. 'Nell been teaching 'er to cook.'

Another winked at her. 'Make someone a lovely wife, you will.'

'Why, thank you, Mr Laity,' Roz forced a cheerful smile to hide her shudder at the memory of Will Prowse's proposal. 'Isn't this weather beautiful?'

One ancient, his face leathery and creased by wind and sun, sucked air between his teeth. ''Tis 'andsome now, but we'll pay,' he warned. 'You wait,' he eyed her, 'there'll be some great storm—'

'Ais, and we'll 'ave snow afore Christmas,' Laity interrupted, clicking his tongue. 'Bleddy 'ell, Janner. Proper Jonah you are.'

They began to bicker amongst themselves and Roz knew she had been forgotten. Relieved, grateful to be ignored, she concentrated on stacking plates onto her tray. When it was full she picked it up carefully and turned towards the kitchen.

It was then that she noticed Davy Casvellan sitting alone, his head in his hands, his tankard still half-full.

Anger flared and Roz wanted to shake him. He had so much. He was young, strong, and blessed with every advantage. What was he doing slumped half-senseless in a taproom in the middle of the day? *It was none of her business*.

She paused by the bar to give Jack his wife's message.

'What kind of pie?' he asked, wiping spilled ale from the scarred wood.

'Rabbit, or mutton with apple and onion.'

His face brightened. 'I'll have the mutton.'

Back in the kitchen she passed on Jack's request, unloaded the dishes, then returned to the taproom feeling much more confident. The old men didn't even glance in her direction: too busy arguing about which seine had achieved the best pilchard catch of the season.

She had just loaded her tray for the second time and was about to pick it up when there was a crash behind her. Startled, she whirled round. Davy Casvellan had knocked over the table and now lay sprawled on the floor.

As the old men stared in silence, Jack came out from behind the bar. After an instant's hesitation, Roz moved towards Davy who was trying to push himself up. His forehead was bleeding and beneath the cut a pink and purple swelling had begun to form.

As she reached him, Roz saw he was trembling. His gaze was glassy and a brick-coloured flush stained his cheekbones.

'Hurts,' he muttered.

'What's on?' Jack said, righting the table. 'He've only had the one and it look like most of that's on the floor.'

Uncertain, but moved to do *something*, Roz touched the back of her hand to the young man's face and forehead. Shocked, she looked up at Jack. 'I think he has a fever. He's burning hot.' Slipping an arm around the young man she helped him up, staggering as he swayed and she took his full weight. She eased him onto a settle and crouched so she could see his face. Something was very wrong. 'Mr Casvellan? Where does it hurt?'

He raised a trembling hand to the bump on his forehead. 'Back.' He grimaced, baring his teeth. 'Dreadful pains.'

'If he's ill, best get'n home.' Jack kept his voice low. 'If word get out he was took sick in here, it won't do my trade no good at all. Look, prop 'n so he don't fall off that settle. Soon as Toby have harnessed up the cart you drive the boy back to Trescowe.'

'Me?' Roz blurted.

'Yes, you,' Jack was terse. 'I haven't had no dinner yet. Toby can't go. I need'n here to look after the tap. Anyway, you been up-long so many times you could do it with your eyes shut.'

Wincing at this reminder of her numerous appearances before the Justice, Roz turned her head away. But Jack's blunt statement was no more than the truth. She knew the route only too well.

'Go on, maid. I got me licence to think of. Who else is there?' Flicking his gaze towards the group of old men Jack arched his brows.

How could she refuse? She owed him more than just her job. 'All right. I'll take him.' She started to untie her apron.

Catching her arm he brought his head close to hers. 'No need to say the boy was took bad in here,' he whispered. 'I don't want no trouble.'

'I'd better tell Nell where I'm going.' But should she say what she suspected? She could be wrong. She hoped she was. Why worry them unnecessarily?

'Quick as you can.' Jack turned back to the bar. 'Toby!'

'Have you anything for him to lie on?' Roz asked. 'The track is badly rutted. He'll be dreadfully uncomfortable.'

'There's some empty sacks in the brewhouse.'

Twenty minutes later Jack and Toby had

125

hoisted the young man onto the canvas and hessian spread out to pad the bare boards. He lay on his side, semiconscious and groaning.

As Roz climbed onto the cart and picked up the reins, Nell bustled out clutching one of the old cushions from her kitchen chair. Shaking and punching it into shape she thrust it at Toby.

'Put's under his head. Poor boy's mazed already. Can't leave un go banging about all the way from here to Trescowe.'

Toby jumped down, Nell stepped back.

'Make haste now,' Jack urged, releasing his hold on the horse's bridle.

Nell slapped his arm. 'Don't be so daft!' She looked up at Roz. 'You go careful, my bird. Justice won't thank 'ee for rushing and making the boy worse.'

The Justice. As she tried to maintain a steady pace while avoiding the deepest ruts, Roz's emotions were in turmoil. Guilty pleasure at the prospect of seeing him again warred with apprehension. Despite Annie's reassurance and the old men's lack of reaction she was still self-conscious about her face.

Surely the Justice would be too worried about his brother to notice the fine pale line across her nose and cheek? But she knew it was there. Nor could she forget the circumstances in which it had been inflicted. Yet her anxiety seemed selfish when she considered the enormity of what she might be bringing him.

She tried to empty her mind and concentrate solely on her driving. But as Davy Casvellan's groans grew more frequent and anguished, her disquiet increased. He was obviously in agony. It suddenly occurred to her that someone should have sent a message to Dr Avers. Would Jack have done so? It was unlikely. He was more concerned with protecting his inn's reputation. Yet who could blame him when the Three Mackerel provided work for nearly a dozen people.

In any case, the doctor would respond far more quickly to a summons from the Justice. But first she must get his brother home. The leather reins were slippery in her hands and she ached all over from tension and the bouncing, jarring ride. If it was uncomfortable for her, it must be far worse for the young man in the back. Hearing him retch Roz glanced over her shoulder and saw he'd been sick. Despite the afternoon heat a cold shiver feathered down her spine.

At last they reached the stone pillars marking the gateway to the estate. Once on the well-tended drive she clicked her tongue and slapped the reins, urging the brown cob into a spanking trot. Ignoring the sign for the tradesmen's entrance she drove straight on.

Her heart lurched as she saw Casvellan standing on the gravelled circle outside the front door. He looked immaculate in a holly-green coat, buff breeches and polished topboots. His hair gleamed in the sunshine like a raven's wing, the thick waves combed loosely back from his forehead to curve on his collar. For an instant Roz saw him as she had glimpsed him on the beach astride the dark grey stallion: barefoot, clad only in shirt and breeches, spray-drenched, windblown and briefly free of responsibilities.

She blinked, the image dissolved, and she saw the Justice, ever formal and controlled, talking to his agent. As befitted his new role, Devlin, too, was smart in brown coat and fawn breeches. His brother Thomas had dressed like a dandy. But Devlin had always preferred a seaman's garb of blue check shirt, red kerchief, canvas trousers and high leather boots.

Both men looked round as the cart approached at a fast trot. She could not read Mr Casvellan's expression. But she saw him freeze, utterly still. Then as she pulled hard on the reins, forcing the cob to a halt he started across the gravel. Devlin was barely a step behind him.

'No, don't!' Roz blurted, raising her hand to stop him. 'Stay back! Don't come any closer.'

The two men exchanged a glance.

'What?' Devlin frowned. 'Why?'

'Please, for the sake of your wife and child.' As he stopped dead, Roz swallowed hard then addressed the Justice.

'Mr Casvellan, your brother is unwell. He collapsed and Jack – Mr Hicks – told me to bring him home.' She jumped down, stumbled on trembling legs, and would have fallen but for Casvellan's instant reaction. As he caught her arm and steadied her, her heart gave another violent leap.

'Ill? Not cast away?'

'No, sir. He has a high fever. He spoke of severe pains in his back and on the way here he was sick.' She clasped her hands tightly. 'Sir, I'm afraid – I hope I'm wrong but—'

'What?' he rapped. 'Just tell me.'

She swallowed again. 'Sir, has your brother recently been in Helston? Only there is small-pox—'

'Oh dear God,' he said before she could finish. The blood had drained from his face leaving him ashen. 'Wait here,' he ordered. 'Don't move.' He turned to Devlin. 'Go and find my sister. Tell her to open up rooms in the west wing close to the back stairs. Davy must be isolated. And Varcoe, if Deb is with my mother—'

'Don't worry, I'll take her aside.' Devlin turn-ed and ran towards the house.

As the Justice swung back to her, Roz flinched at the anguish in his gaze. 'How do you know?' he demanded.

'I don't, not for certain. But I've seen the disease. A relative—' she stopped. 'Fever, back pains and vomiting are all signs.'

'He was at the inn?'

After an instant's hesitation she nodded. 'But he'd drunk very little.' She would not lie until she had no choice, and that time would come all too soon.

His blue gaze was unreadable as it held hers. 'You suspected smallpox and yet you brought him home?'

Shock widened Roz's eyes. 'Where else would I have taken him?'

'No, I mean why *you*? Why did *you* bring him?'

She shrugged helplessly. 'Jack couldn't leave the inn and Toby was busy. Besides, I was the best person to do it because I had cowpox as a child so—'

'You're safe.' A muscle jumped in Casvellan's jaw. 'What about Jack and Nell Hicks? Do they know?'

Roz shook her head quickly. 'I didn't tell them. I did not want to worry them without good reason. Dr Avers—'

'Will be sent for. Meanwhile, regardless of what ails my brother, he will need a nurse.'

Roz shrugged helplessly. 'I'm sorry, I don't know anyone.'

'You,' he was brusque. 'You must stay. My mother is not suited to such a task. Indeed, she...' He made a brief dismissive gesture. 'Nor can I expose my sister to risk.'

'Me?' Roz's head spun as shock and yearning to agree battled powerful reasons to refuse. Now Annie was back, Nell would not have to cope with only Keren to help. But once word reached Will Prowse that she was staying at Trescowe to help the Justice, he would never trust her again. *If she were here she would not have to see him.*

'I can't. My job – I need—'

'Whatever Hicks is paying you, I'll triple it.'

Her head jerked up, but just as quickly she turned away, terrified of betraying herself.

He knew – who better – that she needed money, and his offer was generous. Grief pierced her at the thought that accepting would make her one more servant in his household. *How could it be otherwise?* She would be mad to refuse when the money would settle her debt to Will Prowse and she'd be free of him at last.

What about her mother? Drunk, abusive,

accusing her of bossy interference, Mary-Blanche had claimed she could manage perfectly well by herself.

'You must stay.' Strain roughened his voice, but his tone forbade argument. 'I've no time to look elsewhere. Davy needs you now. Nor do I want a stranger. I need someone I can trust.'

As guilt swamped her with a scalding flush from hairline to toes, she recalled his forbearance with her mother and his kindness to Tom. Turning to the cart so he should not see her shame, she nodded. 'As you wish, sir.'

'I am in your debt.'

Roz let down the tailboard. Beside her Casvellan reached in to draw the sacks towards him.

'Careful, sir. He was sick. Your coat—'

'Is of no account.' As Roz gently removed the vomit-stained cushion he leaned over, gathered his brother into his arms, and lifted him out.

Davy groaned, his face contorting in pain. 'Aaaggh...' His eyes fluttered open. 'Bran? I hurt.'

'We'll get you inside,' Casvellan spoke softly. 'You'll soon be more comfortable.' His face was set as he strode towards the front door. Roz saw it open and the butler started forward.

'Stay back,' Casvellan commanded.

'Sir—'

'That's an order, Bassett.' He glanced at Roz. 'Up the stairs, Miss Trevaskis. Turn left then right. Go ahead of me. I need you to open the doors.'

Running up the broad curving staircase

131

carpeted in crimson and gold, Roz saw a maid dash along the landing and heard faint shrieks.

'Deb?' Casvellan called.

'Bran?'

Seeing a fair head emerge from an open doorway in the narrow passage, Roz stepped back and let Casvellan pass.

'Oh, the poor boy. Bring him in.'

Following behind, Roz inhaled the dank, slightly musty smell of a room long unused. The shutters had been hastily folded back revealing walls painted a faded pastel green. The floorboards were bare of carpet or rugs. The room contained a bed missing its curtains and canopy. Next to it was a small table and on the far side, a nightstand on which stood a decorated china basin and matching jug. A side table stood between the two deep windows, and in the corner was a walnut armchair upholstered in faded crimson velvet. The fireplace was empty, so were the two candleholders on the marble mantelpiece.

As the Justice gently laid his brother down, Roz heard the creak and bang of shutters being opened in the adjoining room and through the connecting door she glimpsed the pale blue gown and white apron of a maid.

Deborah Casvellan started toward the bed. Her fair hair curled softly at her temples and the nape of her neck. One glance at the fashionably high-waisted gown of lavender muslin made Roz horribly aware of her own shabby appearance.

'No, Deb,' Casvellan said sharply. 'Don't touch him.'

Starting at his abrupt command she folded her hands over the ruffled chemisette that filled the low neckline of her gown. 'What happened? What's wrong?'

'Didn't Varcoe...?'

'He said only that Davy had been taken ill and I was to open up rooms in this wing so he could be isolated. That seems very extreme, Bran. Is it really necessary?'

Roz saw him take a breath then meet his sister's gaze. 'Deb, he might have smallpox.'

Gasping, Deborah shook her head, shock and disbelief stark on her face. 'No, he can't. It's not possible. The inoculation...'

'If I'd thought for one moment—' he cut himself short. 'Send for Avers, will you? I hope to God we're wrong, but until we're sure, the fewer people in contact with him the better.' As he turned to beckon her forward, Roz saw how drawn his face was. 'Deb, this is Miss Trevaskis. She brought Davy home and I have persuaded her to stay and nurse him.'

Sympathizing with the surprise, doubt and bewilderment that chased each other across the young woman's face, Roz bobbed a curtsey.

'Miss Trevaskis,' Deborah replied automatically and turned once more to her brother, her pretty features clouded with concern, 'Bran—'

'In a moment, Deb.' He crossed to the adjoining room and addressed the maid. 'Leave that. Go downstairs and fetch—' he turned to Roz. 'What do you need?'

'Pitchers of hot and cold water, soap and towels,' she said quickly. 'Kindling and coal for the fire.' At his frown she explained. 'The windows must be left open day and night for fresh air. A fire will keep the room comfortable and drive off any damp.'

'Leave everything at the bottom of the servants' staircase,' Casvellan instructed the maid, who bobbed nervously. 'Have Preece fetch paper, pens and ink from my study and leave them with the other things. From this moment on, no one except Miss Trevaskis and myself is to use that staircase. Food and other necessities are to be left at the bottom. We will collect them from there. Do you understand?'

The maid nodded frantically. 'Yes, sir.'

'When you have done that, no doubt Miss Deborah will have errands for you.'

'Please, sir, what about mistress?' the maid babbled. 'Beside herself she is.'

Deborah waved the maid out. 'Go and do as you're bid, Sally. If you see Daisy, tell her I will come to my mother in a few minutes.'

'No, Deb. Go now,' Casvellan said.

'But—'

'Deborah,' he cut her short. 'If it is smallpox I don't want anyone else put at risk.'

As Deborah's gaze switched to her Roz spoke quickly. 'I'll take no harm, ma'am. Having had cowpox as a child I am safe. I'll do all in my power to make your brother comfortable.' She saw the astonishment and curiosity Deborah tried and failed to hide. But the elegant young woman simply inclined her head.

'Thank you, Miss Trevaskis. But you cannot possibly manage alone.'

'I would not expect it,' Casvellan cut in. 'I will assist.'

'Bran, my dear.' Deborah's gaze brimmed with a sympathy Roz didn't understand. 'You know nothing of nursing.'

'Then I will learn,' he said fiercely and, grasping his sister's arm, he led her to the door. 'Deb, if you wish to help, send at once for Dr Avers then take care of our mother.'

'Sir,' Roz blurted. 'The cart...'

'Don't worry, Miss Trevaskis,' Deborah said. 'One of the grooms will return it. Where should he—?'

'To Jack Hicks, ma'am. Landlord of the Three Mackerel.'

Deborah nodded. 'As you are remaining here, Miss Trevaskis, is there anyone you wish to be informed?'

Though grateful for Deborah's tact, Roz turned instinctively to Casvellan. He better than anyone knew what awaited her at home. She would not miss her mother's difficult behaviour. But Jack and Nell would be seriously inconvenienced by her absence.

He gave an imperceptible nod and turned once more to his sister. 'Have the horse fed and watered, Deb. That will allow Miss Trevaskis time to write a note.'

Once again Roz saw the flicker of surprise in Deborah Casvellan's eyes. *Given her shabby clothes and her job at the Three Mackerel no one would expect her to be able to read and write.*

'Of course.'

As Deborah turned to the door, Roz followed

135

her. 'Miss Casvellan, please would you ask your cook to make a large quantity of barley water and flavour it with lemon and sugar? The fever will give your brother a terrible thirst.'

'I'll see to it at once.'

As the door closed the Justice gazed down at his brother then swung round. 'For God's sake, tell me what to do.'

The anguish in his voice dried her throat. Crossing to the windows to open them from the top allowed her to keep her back to him. She spoke over her shoulder. 'If you will remove his clothes, sir, I'll go and fetch the water and towels.'

He raked his hair. 'A nightshirt, I should have thought—'

'He will be more comfortable without.' She walked quickly to the door. 'And it will be easier to sponge him down.' Before she had finished he was already shaking his head.

'That is not a job for you.'

Impatience bubbled. 'Sir, you insisted I stay because you need a nurse. You know I have experience.' How many times had he seen her mother in desperate straits after a surfeit of brandy? 'Nor can you have forgotten that I have a younger brother of my own. Until he took up his new position it was my task every week to get him into a tub and scrub him clean.'

He glared at her. 'Miss Trevaskis, *my* brother is not ten years old.'

'No, he's not,' she acknowledged, desperately hoping he was too preoccupied to notice fiery colour burning her cheeks. She could feel

136

perspiration prickling her upper lip and temples. 'But he's sick and feverish, and frequent sponge baths with cool water are the only way to bring him any comfort.'

'Then we will share the task.' Stripping off his elegant coat, Casvellan tossed it onto the old armchair and began rolling up his shirt-sleeves.

When Roz returned a third time from the back stairs with aching legs and her arms full, Davy's clothes lay in a heap on the floor, his boots tossed nearby. Covered from the waist down by a sheet, he moved restlessly, groaning, his features pinched with pain.

Casvellan had dragged the small table closer and placed the basin on top of it. Sitting on the side of the bed, he dipped a muslin cloth in the water, squeezed out the excess, then gently bathed his brother's bruised and fever-flushed face.

As she crossed the room he spoke without looking up. 'Write your notes.'

Pulling the walnut armchair around in front of the dressing table, Roz sat and quickly penned a few lines, first to Jack and Nell, then with more difficulty to her mother. When she had finished, she folded and addressed them, scooped up the discarded clothes and boots, and took everything down the back stairs, leaving the notes on top of the pile.

Picking up the bundle of candles and the two additional holders Deborah had thoughtfully provided, she returned to the bedroom, where the Justice was drying one of his brother's arms with a clumsy tenderness that tugged at her heart.

She recalled her recent summons to his rooms, hearing his weary irritation at his clerk's mention of Davy's latest scrape. But when she had confided her fear that Davy might be suffering from smallpox, his habitually guarded expression had shattered, betraying shock then disbelief and finally utter dismay.

She understood his insistence on a nurse for his brother, but she had never expected him to share the work himself. What it was like to be loved that much?

She had grown up with every material comfort: good food and a suitable wardrobe for each season. If her clothes were sometimes made over from her aunts' discards no one would have guessed. Having taken her into the family, her grandparents' pride and sense of what was right would not permit treating her differently from her two aunts, something they bitterly resented and never missed an opportunity to make plain.

Catching herself, she thrust the memory into the past where it belonged. Yet perhaps it was a timely reminder. For though he had insisted she remain in his house to nurse his brother, it wasn't just what she had done that put her beyond hope of Branoc Casvellan's interest, it was who she was: a bastard, forever tainted by her mother's sin.

She turned away, studying the candles: a mixed bundle of beeswax and spermaceti; the best money could buy. They would burn bright and clear, without the dreadful reek of the tallow dips that too often were all she could afford in the cottage.

Setting them on the mantelpiece, Roz laid and lit the fire, hoping fervently that this chimney had been swept along with the others and was not blocked by a bird's nest. A tapping on the door made her look round.

Deborah's head appeared and she beckoned Roz across, handing her a small bundle. 'I hope you will find these useful. The barley water will be ready shortly. Is there anything else you need?'

Roz had been thinking. 'Perhaps a small hand bell that we could leave at the bottom of the stairs?'

'An excellent idea. Then you or the servants can let each other know when there is something to be collected.' Deborah's brief smile was warm. 'I will arrange it at once. Miss Trevaskis, we are all most grateful to you.' Backing out she closed the door quietly.

Roz opened the bundle and saw a clean night-gown, a hair-brush, a cake of soap, a wash cloth, toothbrush and a tin of tooth powder. The kind-ness brought a lump to her throat.

The soap's sweet scent reminded her of her grandmother's boudoir. The clear and close bond between the Casvellans made her ache for something she had never known. She walked quickly into the adjoining room, breathing deeply to regain control.

The room was the same size and similarly furnished. Setting her bundle down on a chair upholstered in worn brocade, the pink and ivory stripes barely discernible, she opened the window then turned to the bed. The sheets and blankets, still folded, sat in a neat pile on the bare mattress.

Which of them was to sleep here? Suddenly her head was filled with images: the Justice formal behind his desk, unexpectedly striding in as she paid the rent, alone on the beach with his horse. She saw his face: the penetrating blue gaze that saw much and revealed little, that could be icy one moment and oddly shy the next.

Swamped by a hopeless yearning, Roz covered her face with both hands. She had to pull herself together. She *had* to. He needed her. She straightened her shoulders. She would not let him down.

Moving the bedding to the chair she concentrated on shaking out the sheets and tucking in the blankets. With the bed made, she fetched the leftover kindling, coal scuttle and tinderbox, and lit the fire. Then she tried the door to the passage to see if the next room had been opened up. But the door was locked and there was no key.

Returning to the sickroom she saw the Justice standing at the window gazing out. Telling herself it was a perfectly reasonable question and she needed to know about the third room, she crouched and added more coal to the fire. Already the room smelled fresher and the dankness had gone.

Straightening, she wiped her palms down her petticoat. She drew a breath, about to speak, and saw him stiffen.

'At last,' he said. 'Avers is come.'

Ten

'I'll leave you to be private with the doctor,' Roz said as she emptied the basin and folded the towel, then added some coals to the fire.

'Yes,' he said absently, studying his brother.

Rising to her feet she smoothed down her apron and retreated into the adjoining room.

'Don't close the door,' he called. 'I imagine Avers will wish to speak to you.'

Leaving the door ajar Roz tended the fire then adjusted the sash window. She heard the doctor arrive, and the two men talking. Then there was a short silence. She moved towards the door, waiting to be summoned.

'It's smallpox, no doubt about it,' she heard Dr Avers say.

'How could it have happened?' Casvellan demanded.

'I wish I could tell you. I've heard of other cases where people have received the inoculation then gone on to develop the disease. However, the two events are not necessarily connected.'

Roz bit the inside of her lip. No wonder the Justice had been so shaken when she told him what she suspected was wrong with his brother. If he had arranged for the family to be inoculated in the belief that he was protecting them, he would feel personally responsible for his brother's illness.

'It was suggested to me that Davy might have been in contact with a sufferer and therefore was already incubating the illness when he was inoculated. Is this possible?'

'Perfectly possible. Indeed, it is more than likely. Casvellan, your decision to protect your family was correct. Had you not done so, I might now be attending at more than one patient in your household. As it is, Davy is young and strong. His chances of recovery are high. But he will need careful nursing.'

'As I have immunity, I shall—'

'My dear Casvellan, I applaud your compassion, but you cannot possibly—'

'Not on my own, Avers,' the Justice interrupted dryly. 'I know my limitations.' He pushed open the door behind which Roz waited. 'Come in please.' As she emerged he turned to the doctor. 'Miss Trevaskis is—'

'An excellent choice,' Dr Avers said, nodding at Roz who felt a quick glow of pleasure and bobbed a curtsey.

'I was about to say that Miss Trevaskis contracted cowpox as a child and so—'

'Is not at risk,' Avers finished. 'Capital. You couldn't have done better, Casvellan. Miss Trevaskis was of great help and comfort to the villagers who suffered injuries during that terrible storm we had in the spring.'

'You are very kind, sir,' Roz murmured.

'Not a bit of it. Praise where it's due.' He looked around and she saw his gaze linger on the fire and the open window. 'Your idea, Miss Tre-vaskis?'

'Yes, sir.'

'Well done. Now, this young man's fever will make him very thirsty, so he will require soothing drinks: spring water, fruit juice. Milk will nourish him and soothe his throat, and he may have beef tea if he desires something more savoury. Sponge baths might help cool him, though I doubt there is much that will make him comfortable. Pay particular attention to his eyes. They should be irrigated several times a day with cool boiled water.'

Roz sensed Casvellan's quick glance, but kept her gaze on the doctor and nodded.

'All surfaces including the floor must be disinfected every day.'

'Yes, sir,' Roz said again.

'I recommend a solution of chloride of lime. A small amount of the liquid placed in dishes around the room should help overcome the noxious smells that will develop as the illness progresses. I think you may expect to see the rash erupt in three or four days. When it does, it will burn and ache. Barley water added to a hip bath might offer some relief.'

'Is there nothing more you can do?'

Hearing the anger in Casvellan's voice, Roz knew it was born of anxiety and frustration. Clearly the doctor understood, for he took no offence and his expression was sympathetic.

'I wish there were. Unfortunately the disease must take its course. But as I'm here I'll bleed the boy. It might reduce his fever a little.'

Seeing unease flicker across Casvellan's face and noting the tension in his jaw, Roz stepped forward.

'Shall I hold the basin for you, Dr Avers?' She glanced up at Casvellan. 'With your permission, sir?'

Gesturing acquiescence he turned away, but not before she had glimpsed a flash of gratitude.

While the crimson stream dripped from Davy's arm into the white basin, the doctor continued. 'You must both maintain strict separation from the rest of the household. The young man's bed linen should be changed every day, sprinkled with a little of the disinfecting solution and boiled separately. Wash your hands after contact with him or anything that has touched him.' He looked down at the blood in the basin. 'That should be sufficient.'

Pressing a gauze pad over the incision he swiftly loosened the leather tie he had fastened around Davy's arm to swell the vein and folded it into his bag. While Roz bound the pad in place with a strip of muslin, he rose to his feet. 'And now I must go.'

'How long?' Casvellan's voice was rough.

'Provided there are no complications perhaps two, maybe three weeks.'

Roz kept her head averted as she straightened the sheet over the comatose youth. *Two weeks alone with the man she admired above all others, a man she thought about and dreamed of. The man who believed well of her because he did not know the truth.*

'I'll see myself out. Good day to you both.'

While Casvellan accompanied the doctor into the passage and directed him to the main staircase, Roz emptied the blood into the slop bucket, replaced the lid and quickly rinsed the basin. It was fortunate that she had a strong stomach. Without it she would never have survived the past two years.

Taking bucket and coal scuttle down the back stairs she rang the bell, then picked up the two large copper cans, one of hot and one of cold water, that were waiting. When she returned to the sickroom, Casvellan was replacing the wet cloth on his brotherforehead. He cleared his throat.

'I'm obliged to you. I'm not familiar with the business of sickrooms.'

'It's no trouble, sir. That's why I'm here.' Crossing to the washstand she poured clean water into the basin then soaped, rinsed and dried her hands. Replacing the towel she smoothed the skirt of her apron and moistened her lips. 'Sir, I've made up the bed next door, and lit the fire. But where am I to sleep?'

He glanced at her, the groove between his brows deepening. Then he rose and walked out into the passage. Roz followed. He tried the locked door, then moved on to the next one, glancing at her with mild impatience when it opened. The shutters were closed so the room was dark. But there was enough light from the big window above the stairs for Roz to see that it was full of tables, chairs and other pieces of furniture stacked precariously on top of each other.

'Ah,' was all he said. Closing the door he returned to the sickroom. Roz followed. He indicated the adjoining room. 'You will sleep in there. I shall remain in here. The chair will suffice. When next you go down, kindly ask for a few blankets and a pillow.'

He could not possibly spend the next two or three weeks sleeping in a chair. But as she opened her mouth to tell him so, the bell rang again.

'Now would appear to be an opportune moment. I have letters to write.' Crossing to the dressing table he sat down with his back to her, drew a sheet of paper forward, and picked up the pen.

In the passage at the bottom of the stairs a small table had been placed against the wall. On it were two trays, one holding covered dishes, the other plates, cutlery, napkins, a carafe of wine, a jug of barley water, two tumblers and a wine glass. The savoury aromas made her stomach gurgle and she realized how hungry she was. Ringing the bell, she waited, then heard a voice growing louder as someone approached from the kitchen.

Seeing Roz, the maid's hand flew to her chest. 'Dear life, gived me some start you did.'

'Mr Casvellan would like some extra blankets and pillows, and an additional ewer and basin. Also could I have the slop pail back as soon as possible?'

'Right,' the maid nodded and turned away.

Roz picked up the first tray and carried it upstairs.

146

'Excuse me, sir? Where would you like me to put this?'

Still writing, he spoke without looking round. 'What is it?'

'I believe it's dinner, sir.'

'Take it next door. Have whatever you wish. I'm not hungry.'

Roz took a breath. 'Sir, if you don't eat, I cannot. And if neither of us takes proper nourishment our own health will suffer. How will that help your brother?'

He swivelled round on the chair, and she had to bite her lip as his astonishment darkened to a haughty glare. 'I beg your pardon?'

'Sir, I understand your concern—'

He rose so quickly the chair scraped along the floorboards making her flinch.

'No, you don't,' he snapped and pointed to his brother. 'That is my doing. If I hadn't insisted—'

'You cannot blame yourself,' Roz cried, forgetting both her manners and her position. 'Your mother and sister also had the inoculation and they are perfectly well.'

He glowered at her, and as blood rushed to her face she dropped her gaze, realizing just how far she had overstepped the bounds of what was proper.

'You defend me, Miss Trevaskis?'

She gave a helpless shrug. 'Sir, you must eat. Your brother needs you.'

'Your point is made. Is there a table in the other room?'

Roz moistened her dry lips. 'Yes, sir.'

'Then I suggest you set the tray down in there. In his current state I doubt my brother would appreciate the sight or smell of food.'

In the adjoining room Roz set the tray down, rolled her aching shoulders, and returned to the sickroom door.

'Where are you going?'

'To fetch the other tray.'

He came towards her holding two letters. 'Kindly take these down with you.'

Glancing at the bold scrawl on the folded papers as she hurried along the passage, Roz saw one was addressed to Devlin Varcoe and the other to Mr Ellacott. Sir Edward Pengarrick and Mr Morley-Noles were the Justices nearest to Porthinnis and Trescowe. Though he had no alternative, she knew Casvellan would hate having to transfer his work. He'd especially loathe being forced to rely on Sir Edward whose attitude and beliefs were so different from his own. At least Devlin could be relied upon to keep the estate running smoothly. And though he would not have sought it, he'd relish the challenge.

As she re-entered the sickroom, Casvellan took the tray from her.

'Go and sit down. You shame me with your bustling.'

The weary humour in his voice warmed her. She dropped a neat curtsey.

'Certainly, sir. While you have your dinner I will write a list of items we shall need tomorrow.'

'You really are...' He broke off, shaking his

head. 'Never mind.' He disappeared into the adjoining room and Roz, very aware of the heat in her cheeks, sat down and picked up the pen.

After they had both eaten, she carried the trays down, fetched more water, clean towels and a rolled bundle that contained a clean shirt and folded neckcloth wrapped around a hairbrush and shaving gear.

'For you, sir. From your valet.' She handed him the bundle, aware as she did so that after the day's heat and hard work her own garments were none too fresh. 'Sir, if any of your people are going into the village tomorrow I wonder if I might send a note to my mother? I will need more clothes.'

'I'll—' But whatever he intended to say was interrupted by a pain-filled groan from the bed.

After Davy had been sponged down once more and Roz had bathed his eyes, dusk was falling. Bone-weary and with a headache gnawing at the base of her skull, she carried the slop bucket and damp towels downstairs. As she climbed back up for what felt like the hundredth time with more hot water, dizziness swamped her like a breaking wave. She wanted to sit down, but feared being unable to get up again. Sucking in a deep breath, she forced her shaking legs to move.

Casvellan was standing by the fire. He had lit the candles on the mantelpiece and another burned on the table by Davy's bed. He turned towards her as she walked in. Whatever he saw as the light fell across her face made his brows gather.

'Are you all right?'

If she told him the truth – that she was tired – he would think her weak, unable to cope. He might send her home. *She didn't want to go.*

'Yes.' She forced a smile but it felt more like a grimace so she nodded. 'Of course,' she added. 'Perfectly.'

'Indeed,' his tone was dust-dry. 'You have done more than enough for one day, Miss Trevaskis.' His voice softened into a kindness that warmed her and made the back of her eyes hot. 'Get some sleep. That is an order,' he added as she opened her mouth.

She dropped a curtsey. 'If you should need me—' It wasn't until she had spoken that she realized what she'd said. Heat rushed to her face. 'I–I mean if your brother—'

'I know what you meant. And should I require your assistance I know where you are. Now go.' He waved her away.

Closing the door, Roz poured steaming water into the basin. After a thorough wash, she pulled the clean cotton nightgown over her head. It felt deliciously cool and fresh. She brushed her hair and loosely braided it into a single plait. Then slipping between the sheets she bit back a moan of relief and let her aching body relax.

It was hard to believe that this morning she had been working in the Three Mackerel. Now, only hours later, she was lying in bed at Trescowe. And Mr Casvellan was in the next room. Shame prickled her skin. *He was with his desperately ill brother: the sole reason for her being here.*

150

The prospect of remaining, of helping the Justice to nurse his brother, filled her with both joy and trepidation. The longer she stayed, the more time they spent in each other's company, the greater the risk of discovery. Being alone with him was the realization of a secret dream and exquisite torture. But she could not desert him. He needed her and she owed him so much. She would just have to ... but it was so hard to focus ... she needed to think...

She woke with a start and stared at the faint outline of a room she did not recognize. Where was she? As it all flooded back she sat up, sucking in air while she waited for her galloping heartbeat to slow. Pushing back the covers she got out of bed, wincing at the ache in her calf muscles as she stood up. It wasn't the physical work. She was used to that. It was the back stairs. They were steep and narrow and she must have been up and down at least a score of times carrying buckets or heavy cans of water.

Opening the shutters she looked out onto the soft pastel shades of the July dawn. *Dawn.* Shock zinged through her. *She had slept through the night.* He should have woken her. They were supposed to be dividing Davy's care.

Whirling from the window her gaze fell on a bundle just inside the door. He must have put it there. She had not heard a thing. Her bare feet silent on the floorboards, she picked it up, catching her breath as it unrolled and a note fell out. Wrapped in a clean white apron were two short-sleeved muslin gowns, one pale blue and one apricot, a large square shawl of fine wool, two shifts, two pairs of fine cotton stockings, a pair of kid slippers and another apron of coarse dowlas the colour of sacking. She picked up the note.

Dear Miss Trevaskis,
As you arrived here unprepared I hope you will find these of use. Please send your own garments down for laundering. Should you need anything else you have only to ask.
Yours sincerely,
Deborah Casvellan.

Moved by a kindness she had not expected and certainly wasn't used to, questions clamoured in Roz's head as she washed quickly, then put on one of the shifts and the pale blue gown. Though it was slightly large for her slender figure, she experienced a moment's pure pleasure at having something pretty and fashionable to wear. Laying everything else across the chair with the cream coloured shawl on top, she folded her own grubby clothes into the faded calico petticoat.

After twisting her hair into a neat coil she tied on the white apron, plumped up the pillow, and remade the bed. She emptied and rinsed the basin and chamberpot, picked up the slop bucket and, pausing to straighten her shoulders, took a deep breath and opened the door.

Casvellan was sound asleep, sprawled awkwardly in a chair facing the bed. Setting the bucket down beside the passage door, Roz crossed the room and opened the shutters. Pearly light spilled over his face and she felt a sharp tug in her heart at the tousled hair falling across his forehead, the purple shadows beneath his eyes and dark stubble bearding his jaw.

His eyes opened and he bolted upright.

'Sir.' Roz kept her voice low, moving so he could see her. 'You should have woken me.'

He rubbed his face. 'You were exhausted.' He rose stiffly to his feet, discomfort tightening his features as he flexed broad shoulders under a crumpled shirt.

If he thought she couldn't cope he might send her away, hire someone else. 'Sir, it's still very early. Will you not go and sleep a while longer?'

'I have slept.'

'Not properly. You need to lie down. I will take care of your brother.'

He stretched, shaking his head and smothering a yawn. 'I'm perfectly—'

'With respect, sir, without sufficient rest you'll fall ill yourself.'

He glared at her. 'Miss Trevaskis, I don't need you to—'

'Sir, please, you cannot do this alone.'

'God's blood, girl,' he muttered with a suppressed violence that made her stomach clench. 'You'd outflank Wellington himself. All right, I'll go. But you are to call me immediately if—'

'Yes, sir. Of course.'

'For the love of God, stop sir-ing me,' he snarled over his shoulder and closed the door with a snap.

Above the pounding in her ears she heard a croaking cough. Setting her tangled emotions aside, she moved swiftly to the disordered bed and laid her palm gently on Davy's forehead. Fever burned beneath his skin and glittered in his heavy-lidded eyes. 'Are you thirsty?'

He moaned and tried to swallow. 'Sore,' he rasped.

Pouring lemon-flavoured barley water into a glass, Roz supported his head and held the glass to his cracked lips.

Sitting on the edge of the bed, Casvellan tugged off his boots then raked his hair with both hands. His brother had stirred every half-hour throughout the night, demanding a drink to soothe his parched throat, or a damp cloth to cool his fevered skin and aching head.

He had sent the girl to bed because she was clearly exhausted and he had needed solitude. He had not woken her because he kept seeing her face. She had arrived on the cart pink and glowing. Eight hours later she had worked herself to a pallor that was almost transparent. Immersed in his own concerns and anxious about Davy he'd barely given her a thought, except to issue orders or argue.

But damn it, she was right about sleep. Though he knew himself physically strong and mentally resilient, the coming weeks would make demands and impose stresses he was only just beginning to comprehend.

He stretched out with a growl of relief at lying flat on a soft mattress. His eyes closed. Avers had said she was a good nurse. She knew what to do. And despite her shabby clothes she was always clean and neat. Turning on his side he inhaled the faint fragrance of the soap she had used and buried his face in the pillow to muffle his groan. He imagined the sheets still warm from her slim body and tumbled into blackness.

Eleven

Roz sponged Davy's face, chest and arms. Yesterday, she had washed and dried as far as the sheet at his waist. Then, as shyness made her hesitate while determination to prove herself equal to any task urged her on, Casvellan had motioned her away.

'My brother is helpless. When the fever clouds his mind I doubt he's even aware of us. But he's not a child and deserves a measure of privacy, don't you think?'

She had looked up quickly, feeling her colour rise as she took his meaning. 'I didn't intend ... meant only to...'

'Make him comfortable while demonstrating your capability. I need no proof, Miss Trevaskis. I do not doubt you.'

His remark – and the trust and confidence it implied – should have thrilled her. Later, when she had time to remember and think about it, it probably would. However, at that moment all she felt was mortification.

'I'm sorry. I should have realized...'

'And now you have. You take care of him above the sheet. I will preserve his dignity by attending to the rest.'

Lifting Davy's head on a folded towel she

156

bathed his eyes, talking softly to reassure him. The bed linen needed changing but she couldn't do that without Casvellan's help, and he was still asleep. So instead she switched aprons. Wrapping coarse dowlas over pretty blue muslin she took down the slops and collected the earthenware pot of powdered chloride of lime, several rough cloths, a dustpan, brush, and the ash bucket.

After cleaning out the grate and lighting the fire she carried the ashes down. Then she dissolved the recommended spoonful of powder in a large basin of warm water. The acrid smell caught in her throat and stung the back of her nose as she wiped every surface, then knelt to do the floor. By the time she had finished her knees ached and her hands were red and sore.

She washed her hands carefully with soap but she could still smell the powerful disinfectant on them. She carried the slop pail downstairs, collected the waiting copper cans, and re-entered the sickroom just as the door to the adjoining room opened.

Her heart kicked as Casvellan emerged rumpled and heavy-eyed.

'Your water, sir.'

He nodded briefly, took the cans, then frowned. 'What's that smell?'

'Chloride of lime, sir. I've just washed the floor.'

'Surely it doesn't have to be so strong? We won't be able to breathe in here.'

'I did wonder, sir. The doctor suggested the amount, but—'

'Clearly he had no idea what it would do to your hands.'

Ashamed of their redness she quickly hid them behind her back, pretending to tighten the ties of her apron. How could the doctor not be aware? He must know. But he would be more concerned with preventing the spread of infection.

'Use half the amount tomorrow. That will be quite powerful enough.' Turning away, he spoke over his shoulder. 'Order breakfast, will you? I'll be twenty minutes.'

'Yes, sir.'

As she went down the back stairs for the fifth time that morning she rubbed her wrinkled fingertips with a thumb. The skin felt dry and rough, work-worn. They were the hands of a maid, not those of a lady. Deborah Casvellan's were soft and white.

Roz knew it didn't matter that her grandfather was a gentleman, or that until she had rescued her mother from the streets of Penzance and came to Porthinnis her own life had been blameless. It didn't matter that she was educated, well mannered and had been schooled in the social graces. The circumstances of her birth, an event entirely beyond her control, branded her an outcast, pitied by those who knew her, ignored by everyone else. Never would she be considered a lady. So who cared if her hands suffered?

But Casvellan had noticed. She realized she no longer thought of him as the Justice, a title and position signifying his separation from the community he administered. She had admired him, felt drawn to him, even when he had appeared as remote as the moon. But having now seen him shy, absorbed, worried and furious, she had glimpsed the man.

When he re-appeared, freshly shaved, he was wearing a clean shirt and neck-cloth. His black hair, neatly brushed, fell in thick glossy waves over his collar, and as he passed her she caught the faint fragrance of soap.

'I'll take this down.' He indicated the lidded pail. 'I need shoes and clean stockings. A sick-room is no place for boots.'

While he was away Roz changed her apron, paused to check on Davy who seemed to be asleep, then went into the other room. Pushing up the bottom sash to air the room, she turned to the bed and saw the dent in the pillow. She picked it up to shake it into shape and, driven by an irresistible impulse, pressed it to her face and breathed him in.

Hearing his footsteps in the passage she dropped it and swiftly re-made the bed, her cheeks fiery. She was on her way to the door when he entered carrying a laden tray.

'Sir, I would have—'

'I'm not helpless and you were busy.' He set the tray down on the dressing table. 'Sit down and have some breakfast.'

Knowing better now than to argue, she sat. The hot chocolate slid down her throat like nectar, soothing her tense stomach. She buttered a soft sweet roll.

Taking his coffee he moved away to stand by the open door so he could see his brother. 'What can I do?' he asked quietly. 'Give me something to do or I shall...' Compressing his lips he shook his head.

'Your brother needs fresh bed linen. He won't welcome the disturbance, but...'

'I know, it must be done,' Casvellan nodded.

By midday he had completed Davy's sponge bath, the linen had been changed and he had fetched furniture from the room along the passage. The additional armchair he set by the fire, and placed another table against the wall to hold the ewer and basin reserved for their use. While Roz wiped everything down to remove the dust and ensure it was disinfected, he took down buckets, fetched coal and tended the fires.

Every two hours they shared the task of giving Davy a sponge bath. Then he supported his brother's head, while she attended to his eyes.

After only twenty-four hours they were working as a team. But while lightening her load, this sharing of duties made Roz ever more conscious of him. Terrified of betraying this awareness and its effect on her, she carefully avoided his gaze.

That evening after they had eaten dinner she took the tray down. When she returned carrying a fresh jug of barley water he looked up from replacing a wet cloth on his brother's forehead.

'It's been a long day. You must be tired.'

About to shake her head, Roz saw one eyebrow lift, and knew denial would be pointless. 'I am a little,' she admitted. 'It's the stairs. I'll get used to them,' she added quickly, anxious he should not think she was complaining.

'I won't,' he grimaced, washing and drying his hands. 'Please sit down.' Indicating the nearest chair he took the one on the far side of the hearth. As she sat, so did he, stretching his legs out as he frowned at the dancing flames. 'I've been pondering how to divide the night so my brother always has one of us on hand. If I sit with him from nine until midnight, you may take over from midnight to four, then I'll return from four until eight a.m.'

Roz swallowed. 'Sir, with respect, apart from the fact that only gives you four hours' rest, I cannot sleep until eight. I would lose two hours' working time. Perhaps instead...' she hesitated.

'Go on.'

'If you take the early watch from nine until midnight, I will sit with your brother from midnight until three, then you return from three until six. I can start work at six while you sleep until eight. Though you do not have to rise then.'

'I could sleep on as long as I wish?' he suggested dryly. He gave an abrupt nod. 'Yours is the better idea, Miss Trevaskis.'

'Then if you will excuse me, sir.' To her astonishment he started to get up. 'No,' she blurted, backing away. 'Please, there is no need.'

He relaxed back into the chair. 'Goodnight, Miss Trevaskis.'

'Goodnight, Mr Casvellan.' Reaching the door she paused. 'Sir, you won't forget to wake me, will you?'

Though his smile was weary, his eyes gleamed in the firelight. 'I wouldn't dare.'

The following day Davy's condition worsened. He shook with chills, burned with a high fever,

161

and complained of a grinding headache and intense pains in his back.

'For pity's sake,' Casvellan grated, prowling the room like a caged animal, 'there must be something we can do to ease his distress?'

Roz shrugged helplessly. 'I don't know what else we can do.' Then it struck her. 'Except...'

'What?' he demanded.

'Perhaps a bath? A proper bath?'

Two servants were sent to bring the hip bath from Davy's dressing room to the end of the passage. Roz helped Casvellan carry it into the sickroom. While she hurried up and down the back stairs fetching cans of hot water, he helped his brother to sit up and knotted a towel at his waist for modesty.

As he supported Davy the few steps to the waiting bath, Roz draped a linen towel over the sloping back and down into the water.

'The fever will make his skin painfully sensitive,' she explained. 'He'll be more comfortable leaning against the towel than the cold surface.'

Casvellan nodded then lowered his brother gently into the water. Davy groaned and trembled. But as he lay against the sloping back, his eyes closed and the suffering that had tightened his face eased a little.

'I'll leave you.' Roz turned away.

'Where are you going?' Casvellan demanded, and beneath his frown she saw gnawing anxiety.

'Only to re-make your brother's bed so it will be fresh and comfortable.' When she had finished she heard him shout.

'Roz?'

The urgency in his cry brought her heart into her throat. As she ran through the door she saw Davy was out of the bath but his legs had buckled. His head fell back as Casvellan caught him and picked him up. Grabbing a folded towel she shook it loose and laid it on the bottom sheet.

'Lie him flat,' Roz said, and quickly covered the youth with another large towel then pulled the sheet over him. 'Will you remove the wet towel? He'll be more comfortable without it. And when he opens his eyes see if he will take a drink.'

'Yes, but what—'

'He fainted.'

'I know that. I saw it happen,' he snapped. 'Is it serious?'

Why was he asking her? How should she know? Helpless, she shrugged. 'He's very weak. It may be due to the fever. Or perhaps because he hasn't eaten anything for two days. There,' she said as Davy sighed and his lashes fluttered. 'I think he's coming round.' She turned away.

'For God's sake, where are you going now?' he hissed.

She swung back to face him. The exhaustion of the past few days on top of two years of ever-increasing strain made his furious demand the final straw. 'To empty the bath,' she whispered fiercely. 'Which means carrying buckets up and down those stairs five more times. And as I only have one pair of hands it will take about twenty minutes.'

He straightened to his full height, his expression closed and cold. 'You forget yourself.'

'As do you, sir,' she retorted instantly. Bravado tilted her chin. 'I am here at your request. Indeed, at your *insistence*. But I am not your servant, and do not deserve to be spoken to thus!'

His features remained set and temper flared in his eyes. He glared at her and she glared back, her heart pounding fast and painful against her ribs. She felt hollow and shaky inside. She'd gone too far. *What had possessed her?* He would send her away, back to the inn where Will Prowse would be waiting to demand an explanation. Why couldn't she have kept silent? God knew she had spent the last two years biting her tongue so hard and so often she had almost chewed it off. And for what? Her breath hitched.

She would not cry. She bent to pick up the wet towel from the curved top of the bath, wrung out the water and turned away to fetch the slop pail. He blocked her path, moving so quickly that she flinched.

Her vision blurred and splintered. Her aunts had used tears to manipulate, browbeat or blackmail. Now her mother did the same. She considered such tricks despicable, and kept her head bent so he could not see her wet eyes.

Why should it matter what he thought? *But it did.* Blinking hard she heard him clear his throat and felt every muscle tense as she waited for the words of dismissal that would strike as hard as any blow. A dismissal she had brought on herself.

'Apologies do not come easily to me. A man in my position rarely has occasion to make them.

Be that as it may, I am offering one now. I could claim any number of excuses for my behaviour. But they would be just that, excuses. And none an adequate reason. I sincerely beg your pardon. Were you to leave, I—' he broke off, silent for a moment. 'I hope you will not.'

Swallowing hard to shift a fist-sized lump in her throat, she coughed to disguise the thickness in her voice. He would never know how much his words meant to her. 'Thank you, sir.'

Behind them Davy groaned.

'Excuse me.' Casvellan turned towards the bed and Roz picked up the pail.

It wasn't until she was carrying the second bucketful down that she suddenly remembered. *He had called her Roz.* It meant nothing. It had simply been quicker than using her full name.

The evening of the following day after they had eaten dinner and Davy twitched in restless sleep, Casvellan carried both armchairs to the window.

'Come and sit down. You've been busy all day.'

'That's why you hired me, sir,' Roz said, more to remind herself than him.

'Indeed.' He regarded her thoughtfully. 'However we have both done all we can for the moment. There isn't anything else requiring your immediate attention is there?'

'No.'

'Then sit down.'

She sat straight-backed, her hands folded in her lap.

'That won't do at all,' he sighed, sinking into

the chair opposite. He flicked his fingers, waving her back. 'I can't possibly talk to you while you're perched on the edge like a bird about to take flight.' His frown deepened the furrow between his brows. But as he gazed at her one corner of his mouth lifted. 'As your current employer I am giving you an order. As someone much in your debt, I would ask that you consider it a request.'

Roz felt her heart turn over. Biting her lip she inclined her head. 'In that case, sir, of course.' She eased herself further back and was instantly more comfortable supported by the padded velvet. She turned her head and looked out of the window.

'Take a deep breath,' he invited. 'What do you smell?'

Roz inhaled. The evening air was warm and heady with fragrance. She smiled. 'Roses and honeysuckle.'

He crossed one leg over the other and rested his elbows on the padded arms of the chair, his fingers loosely linked across his flat stomach. 'What brought you to Porthinnis?'

Momentarily panicked, Roz lowered her gaze. 'It can be of little interest to you, sir.'

'On the contrary. My family would tell you that I have no time and even less patience for idle conversation. I ask *because* I'm interested.'

She raised her eyes. 'Why?'

He tilted his head. 'You and I have met on several occasions, though in circumstances neither of us would have chosen. Yet I know little more of you now than I did at our first encounter. I confess to being intrigued. So I ask again, why did you come to Porthinnis? You have no relatives here.'

She should make some excuse and retire to bed. If she did, she wouldn't be able to sleep. No one had ever professed interest in her. Curiosity, yes, but never genuine interest.

'I needed work. My mother was acquainted with Mr Hicks and he kindly offered me employment.'

'I have no doubt you are an asset to the inn. But why did you need work? You were not born to the life you are leading.'

A sigh shuddered up from deep inside her. 'It's a long story.' One she wasn't sure she wanted to tell.

He shrugged. 'We are prisoners of circumstance, Miss Trevaskis. Neither of us is going anywhere. My brother is asleep. Time is the least of our concerns.'

Not entirely sure what he meant, Roz took a deep breath. The kindness he had shown her family deserved some recompense. She owed him more than she could ever repay. 'I was raised by my grandparents. I was told only that my mother had disgraced herself and the family. As I grew up I learned not to ask questions. One day just over two years ago I was in Penzance with my grandparents. This – person – made herself known to us. It was my mother. She was in desperate straits. I begged my grandparents to help her but they felt unable to do so. At the time I could not understand their refusal and thought very badly of them.' She looked down at her hands.

'Please go on,' he said quietly.

She shrugged. 'I was full of anger and indignation. I decided that if they would not help her, then I must.'

'And you told your grandfather this?'

'Not to his face. We had already exchanged harsh words. I packed a bag and took my savings – a pitifully small amount, but I was very young and naïve – and left a letter. I told him of my intention to take responsibility for my mother and make a home for the two of us. I thanked him for all he and my grandmother had done for me, and hoped that my decision would reflect credit on the principles by which they had raised me. I didn't know about Tom. I only learned of him after I arrived back in Penzance and found my mother.'

His brows climbed. 'To suddenly acquire a half-brother must have come as something of a shock.'

She nodded. 'It did. Yet somehow it made us more of a family.' Her smile held painful self-mockery. 'I was so sure I could cope. I convinced myself that once we had found somewhere to live and I obtained work, my mother would stop drinking. I truly believed that now we were reunited she would no longer need it.' Anger had tightened his face. But this time she knew it was not directed at her.

'As I say, I was younger then, and I realize now, very naïve.'

'So where were you brought up?'

She hesitated, telling herself it didn't matter

what he thought of her. But it did. And once he knew the truth everything would change. He would change. But if she didn't tell him, sooner or later someone else would. Better that he learned it from her. *Better that her foolish dreams dissolved to dust and scattered on the wind.*

'In Lanisley. My grandfather is vicar of the parish.'

As he studied her his eyes narrowed. 'The Reverend Dr John Trevaskis?' She nodded. 'He's a Justice.' She dipped her head once more. 'I seem to recall meeting him at Bodmin Quarter Sessions. You have not mentioned your father.'

Roz looked at her tightly clasped hands then forced herself to meet his gaze. 'That is because I don't know him.' She forced the words out. 'My parents were not married.'

'A difficult situation for you,' he observed quietly. 'But neither your fault nor your responsibility.'

She smiled briefly, her throat stiff with years of unshed tears. 'In my experience, few people see it that way.'

'Indeed?'

'Oh yes.'

'Tell me,' he insisted.

'I would not have you think...' She stopped, cleared her throat, started again. 'My grandparents did their best. It cannot have been easy for them having a babe in arms abandoned to their care. Though they were strict they were never deliberately unkind. Nor were my aunts while I was small and amusing. But as I grew up things changed. They claimed I cost them friends, and that I was responsible for more than one promising romantic attachment coming to grief.'

'How so?'

'Isn't it obvious?' she demanded as the hurt and shame she had tried so hard and so long to bury erupted once more. 'According to a young man Aunt Chlorenda had hopes of, my mother's actions indicated bad blood in the family. Apparently his parents insisted he cease his visits as no one with a care for their good name could afford any connection with the Trevaskis girls.'

'It occurs to me your aunt had a lucky escape.'

'Perhaps. But for her it was a devastating blow. From that moment both my aunts held me responsible for blighting their lives.'

'Did they indeed?' He spoke softly, but something in his voice made the hair on the back of her neck stand up. 'How did your grandfather respond to their behaviour?'

Roz shrugged. 'He never knew.'

His frown deepened. 'What?'

'They were always careful never to say or do anything unpleasant while he was around.'

'But surely you told him?'

She met his gaze. 'To what end? Even if he had believed me it would only have made matters worse.' Looking away she rose to her feet. 'If you'll excuse me—'

He was on his feet in an instant. 'Miss Trevaskis, I—'

Not daring to look up she waited. But his next words took her completely by surprise.

'What happened to your face?'

Shock surged through her, a hot wave that flooded her face with colour as her right hand flew up, her fingers touching the fine scar. *She shouldn't have stayed, shouldn't have sat with him, should never have dropped her guard. If she had kept her distance he might not have noticed. But now he had. And it was too late.* Her mouth was dry and she heard herself swallow.

'An accident.' She forced the lie between quivering lips. 'A tree branch. I must ... please excuse me.' Before he could move she fled into the bedroom. Closing the door she leaned against it, swallowing the sobs that made her chest heave.

The money she earned here would pay off her debt to Will Prowse. But she would never be free. For Will knew what she had done and would hold it over her. The only way to remove that threat was for her to tell Casvellan herself.

But as she pictured his disappointment and disgust she couldn't face it. Besides, what would it achieve? The circumstances of her birth, her responsibility for her mother, and her involvement in smuggling had all put her on the far side of an unbridgeable chasm. He was a Justice, she a felon.

Once his brother's illness reached its conclusion he would have no further need of her. She would leave Trescowe with memories too painful to remember but too precious to forget.

Twelve

Roz jerked bolt upright and pulled her night-gown away from clammy skin. Still caught in a dream where she was forcing her way through a throng of stony-faced people while searching desperately for – she didn't know, couldn't remember – she stared into the darkness, her heart racing. A sharp rap on the door made her start.

Kicking free of the tangled sheet she scrambled out of bed. She swung her shawl around her shoulders. Though the nightgown covered her from throat to ankles, the shawl made her feel less vulnerable. She held it close as she ran barefoot to the door and opened it.

Casvellan loomed tall and momentarily forbidding in the candlelight.

'What is it?' Roz croaked, her throat dry.

'I'm not sure,' Casvellan whispered. 'But something has changed. He's sweating heavily.'

She crossed to the bed and laid her hand on Davy's forehead. 'The fever has broken.'

'Perhaps he is over the worst?' Casvellan stood close: so close she could feel the warmth radiating from his body and smell the soap they shared. 'What do you think?'

Glancing up she saw how desperately he wanted to believe it. 'He is certainly more peaceful,' she said. 'Will you excuse me for a moment?'

'Why?'

'I must get dressed.' She cleared her throat. 'Then your brother should be bathed and his linen changed. Damp like this, he is vulnerable to a chill. The maids won't be up yet, but there may still be some warm water in the boiler.'

He gave an abrupt nod. 'I'll go and see.'

But as she pinned up her hair then quickly tied the strings of her white apron she knew his hope was premature and there was worse to come.

An hour later a rash erupted on Davy's face. By mid-morning the palms of his hands and soles of his feet were covered with hard red spots. Complaining that they ached and burned, Davy tossed restlessly. At noon they started to appear inside his nose and mouth.

As they completed one set of tasks and began the next, Roz could see Casvellan's anger building.

'This is insupportable,' he hissed at her. 'On the estate, in my justice work, people come to me with problems and I solve them. But this—' He gestured towards Davy's bed. 'I'm helpless, and—' Breaking off he raked his hair in frustration.

'You hate it.' But she didn't offer words of comfort for there were none. And platitudes would demean them both. He did not need her to tell him what he already knew: that all they could do was watch and wait, and in the meantime try to relieve Davy's discomfort.

Once again the hip bath was filled. But this

time he helped carry the copper cans. While Davy lay in soothing barley water, Roz drew Casvellan aside.

'Compresses of woundwort might ease the pain in his hands and feet.'

'Woundwort?'

'It's a herb. It often grows wild by river banks or in damp ditches.'

'Then go and find some.'

'But—'

'Don't argue. You know what to look for. Besides, you need fresh air. You're too pale. If you fall ill...'

'I won't,' she promised. It was the only re-assurance she could give him, and not what he sought. Looking into his face she saw new lines etched by strain at the outer corners of his eyes. Beneath them purple smudges betrayed his weariness. Only when he fell briefly asleep in one of the armchairs did the groove between his brows relax. He needed exercise and fresh air even more than she did, but he refused to leave his brother.

'I'll be as quick as I can.'

'Just find the herb. Turn left at the bottom of the stairs. The door at the end of the passage leads into the yard.'

Following his directions Roz left the house without meeting any of the servants. Once out-side she paused for a moment to get her bearings and drew a deep breath, filling her lungs with the sweet fragrance of summer flowers. A gusty wind caught her skirts and blew warm against her face. The air felt close.

Casvellan hurried towards the front door.

Visibly torn, Deborah looked from her mother's retreating figure to Roz. Her gown of jonquil muslin suited her fair hair and creamy skin but there were violet shadows beneath her eyes.

'As you see, Miss Trevaskis, my mother is deeply anxious. What can I tell her that might ease her fears?'

'I am no doctor, Miss Casvellan. It is not my place.'

'Please. Tell me something – anything. I must stop her fretting. She cannot sleep without the aid of laudanum. I fear for her health if ... Forgive me,' she forced a smile, and now that the blush had faded, Roz could see how drawn and weary she looked. 'You already have enough concerns.'

Roz lifted one shoulder. 'All I can tell you is that the illness is progressing exactly as the doctor predicted. Your brother's youth and strength are very much in his favour. In the meantime' – feeling a tide of warmth climb her throat and flood her cheeks Roz prayed it did not show – 'Mr Casvellan and I are obeying all Dr Avers' instructions. Please try not to worry.'

'You are very kind, Miss Trevaskis. If you were not here I don't know how...' She bent her head, visibly fighting for control.

'But I am here, and will remain for as long as I'm needed. I've had no opportunity to thank you.'

Deborah looked up, clearly bewildered. 'For what?'

'The dresses and—'

'Please, say no more. It was the very least I could do. Is there anything else you need? Anything at all?'

For Davy, Roz reminded herself. She nodded. 'Two small bowls, a can of boiling water and lengths of muslin or cheesecloth to make the compresses.'

'I will see to it immediately. How is my elder brother coping? He is a man of many talents, yet I find it impossible to imagine him of use in a sickroom.'

'With respect, Miss Casvellan, you do him an injustice. Naturally he has found the situation difficult. Any man would. And believing that he was responsible made the burden even greater.'

'But Dr Avers told my mother and me that Davy contracting the disease had nothing to do with the inoculation. Surely he made that clear?'

Roz nodded. 'Yes, he did. So did I, though I'm not sure Mr Casvellan believed us. In the end I think he decided that *how* it happened was less important than making sure Davy received the level of care that would give him the best possible chance of recovery.'

'With no servants to take care of the cleaning and fires there must be a great deal of work.'

Roz nodded again. 'There is. And he shares all of it. No task is beneath his dignity. If determination were all that's necessary to see your younger brother well again—' She broke off. 'I wish with all my heart it could be so.'

Reaching out, Deborah gripped the hand in which Roz held the gathered hem of her apron.

'Miss Trevaskis, you have described to me a side of my brother's character I did not know and cannot help but admire. I am most grateful to you.'

'The privilege is mine, ma'am.' Roz dropped a curtsey. 'Forgive me, but I really should get back.'

'Of course. I'll keep you no longer. Good afternoon, and thank you.'

'What took you so long?' Casvellan demanded as she walked in holding the full apron.

'Your mother and sister were taking the air and wanted to know how your brother is.' Holding the gathered cloth in one hand and supporting the weight of the leaves and flowers with the other, she turned her back. 'Please could you undo the ties? I'll keep the leaves in my apron while I go down and fetch—'

'I'll do it.' Starting towards the door he glanced back at her. 'What am I going for?'

After Roz had repeated the list she had given Deborah, she stood for a moment, listening to his footsteps clatter down the stairs. Here in this room, away from the stress and squalor of what she had come to accept as normal life, she mattered. Here, a man like Branoc Casvellan treated her with respect, as an equal.

But even as a small and unexpected glow of self-esteem warmed her, she recalled his mother's cold gaze and sharp tone. Both were understandable. They had not expected to see her. And though Deborah knew who she was, her mother clearly did not. Even so, Mrs Casvellan's critical glance had left Roz in no doubt that while her presence might be necessary it was not welcome. Deborah had shown her nothing but courtesy and kindness. Mrs Casvellan clearly considered she deserved neither. That stung. But the truth was she didn't belong here. Once she had served her purpose she would return to her job at the inn. *And the cramped cottage. And her mother.* This was an interlude. To dream of anything more was foolish. Such yearnings could bring only grief.

She heard his returning footsteps and, realizing her cheeks were wet, wiped them quickly with her palms. Taking a steadying breath she crouched to gather up the apron and its contents. In one basin she steeped half the herb in boiling water then she shredded two handfuls of the remaining leaves and flowers and dropped them into the other bowl. After bruising them with the back of a spoon she added a little hot water then spread the paste between two pieces of gauze and bound them around Davy's hands and feet. Every hour for the rest of the afternoon and into the evening she alternated bandages soaked in the infusion with compresses of leaf paste.

As days passed the spots became blisters then large pustules. Even the powerful disinfectant was not strong enough to disguise the putrid smell. Davy retreated into himself, shutting his eyes and refusing to talk.

One morning she had just finished washing the floor when Casvellan came out of the bedroom rolling back the sleeves of his clean shirt. 'I'll fetch the breakfast tray.'

She simply nodded, and turned to empty the

180

pungent water into the slop pail. She understood that the continuing hot weather, the necessary fires and the physical demands of caring for Davy would make even a waistcoat uncomfortable. But to see him clad only in shirt and breeches, a state normally shared with no one but his valet, took her breath away. Though proud, confident, and imposing, he wasn't vain. She doubted he had any idea how devastatingly attractive he was.

Washing and drying her hands, she went into the bedroom. She changed her coarse disinfectant-splashed apron for the clean white one, then threw back the covers and picked up the pillow. Hugging it for comfort, she crossed to the window. Today she could see deer in the park. Some cropped the grass while others sought shade beneath the wide branches of an oak.

Not even during the worst days with her mother had she felt so tired. Though she would not wish to be anywhere else, it was a struggle to cope with broken nights and long days of demanding physical work. She wasn't doing it alone. But to have Branoc Casvellan sharing the burden was both pleasure and torment.

The sound of the sickroom door closing made her jump and she spun round. Quickly tossing the pillow onto the bed, she bent to tuck in the bottom sheet as he walked in carrying the tray.

'The smell is appalling,' he whispered. 'Even the disinfectant is not sufficient to mask it. Surely there must be something...?'

She straightened up. 'I was wondering if perhaps lavender bags might help. They could be added to his bath water and placed around the room.' She kept her voice deliberately low, anxious not to add to Davy's misery.

'Anything is worth trying.' He set the tray down on the table near the window. 'Send a message to my sister for whatever you need.'

'Sir, why don't you go? You haven't left this room since—'

'Me?' The frown between his black brows deepened as he eyed her. 'Go down into the garden and pick flowers?' His tone said *Are you mad?*

Had she not been so tired she would never have reacted so *unsuitably*. But the contrast between his words and expression conjured a picture so vivid that laughter swelled her chest and bubbled into her throat. She pressed her lips together, then bit them hard in a desperate effort to hold it back. He'd be furious. He would think her impertinent and frivolous and—

Hearing a snort she sneaked a glance and saw that he had one arm across his stomach while the other hand covered his mouth. His shoulders were shaking. Their eyes met in a moment of shared understanding. Then like a lightning bolt, awareness arced between them. As the smile died on her lips, his hands dropped and he turned away.

At the door he stopped. 'Leave that,' he gestured towards the bed without actually looking at it. 'Have your breakfast. I'll eat when you've finished.' Then he strode out.

An hour later, hearing the bell, she went downstairs and found a huge sheaf of lavender in a shallow basket, needle, cotton and scissors, and a letter addressed to Casvellan who was sitting on the bed, talking quietly to his brother. Davy's eyes remained closed.

Recognizing Mr Ellacott's handwriting, she left the letter on the faded velvet armchair where Casvellan was bound to see it, and placed the basket on the floor by the chair nearest the window. Making herself comfortable she began sewing sachets from remnants of gauze and muslin.

Casvellan rose from the bed, rubbing the back of his neck where knotted muscles were iron-hard. Frustration sat like a weight at the base of his skull and pain throbbed behind his eyes. Crossing to the armchair he picked up the letter. After a brief glance at Roz, whose head was bent over her sewing, he sat down to read it. When she didn't look up he was torn between relief and regret.

Unfolding the paper, he skimmed his clerk's elegant copperplate which regretted having to inform him that two miners living on the out-skirts of Porthinnis had been caught with six freshly killed rabbits by one of Sir Edward Pengarrick's gamekeepers.

Both men had large families and had been involved in the march on Helston, but neither was a troublemaker. Both had sworn to Constable Colenso – sent by Ellacott to discover the truth of the situation – that they had not set foot on the baronet's property. Which meant, Casvellan realized, the rabbits had been trapped on Trescowe land.

Air hissed between his teeth as fury burned through him. As far as the law was concerned ownership of the land on which they had trespassed was irrelevant. What counted was the irrefutable evidence that they had been poaching.

If he did nothing Pengarrick would send the men to prison. Their families would be forced into the workhouse, mothers and children separated from each other. Cursing Pengarrick and the miners for putting him in this position he bolted from the chair, crushing the letter in his fist. Roz flinched as she pricked her finger.

'I beg your pardon. I didn't mean to startle you.' Formality was a long-established habit. Normally the more turbulent his emotions, the cooler and more distant his manner. Having adopted this mask to conceal his shame at his father's behaviour, he had found it invaluable in his dealings as a Justice. But here, now, needing detachment more than ever before, he was finding it increasingly difficult to achieve.

As Roz raised her head he saw sympathy in her eyes. Unable to contain himself he brandished the crumpled letter. 'Pengarrick.'

She didn't ask. She simply nodded. The baronet's reputation was well known in the village. His frustration dissolved, leaving clarity and determination. Crossing to the table he sat down, pulled a sheet of paper towards him and dipped the pen. After a moment to organize his thoughts he began writing.

The two men, he told the baronet, had been hunting on his land with his permission, trapping rabbits that were attacking his crops. No crime had been committed and he requested their immediate release. He signed it then penned a quick note to his clerk telling him to make certain the men realized that if ever they were caught again they could expect no mercy.

Folding the two sheets, he stood up. 'Is there anything you need while I'm downstairs?'

She shook her head. 'No, thank you.'

He started towards the door.

'Mr Casvellan?'

He glanced back.

'Sir, I don't mean to be impertinent, but for your own wellbeing will you not spend an hour or two outside? When Tom came home he spoke with awe of your stallion and said you allow no one else to ride him. That being so, will he not be in need of exercise?'

About to shake his head he hesitated. Confinement was certainly making him edgy. *Would that confinement were his only problem.* And without work Raad would become not merely difficult but dangerous. He looked across to the bed and the still figure of his brother.

'He's asleep,' she said quietly. 'Should he wake and need anything I'm here.'

'You're sure?'

'Yes.'

Taking the letters down he rang the bell, gave the maid a message for his head groom, asked for his beaver hat to be left on the table, then bounded back upstairs. In the bedroom he put on a clean neckcloth, striped muslin waistcoat, his green frock-coat of fine-faced cloth and his

185

boots. As he reached the door he saw her look up from her sewing.

'Enjoy your ride, sir.'

Relief, guilt and gratitude he knew to be unnecessary and inappropriate left him tongue-tied. Reminding himself that he was paying her to be there he nodded abruptly and ran down the stairs.

His first twenty minutes astride the stallion were a battle of wills and strength. But once up on the sloping hillside he gave Raad his head, relishing the animal's power and speed as they thundered along faint tracks through heather and bracken. Reaching the top of the moor he reined in. They had both needed that wild headlong dash.

From up here he could see the entire estate: the lawns and wooded walks, the old stables now housing the French prisoners, and the expanse of paddocks neatly divided by post-and-rail fences behind the new stable block.

Between Trescowe house and the home farm a crescent-shaped lake glittered blue and silver in the afternoon sun. Separated from the lake by a large well-stocked kitchen garden, the sheds, stores and pigsties clustered across the yard from the farmhouse. The sties were quiet now while the pigs roamed fenced areas of the woods. Between late autumn and Christmas a score would be slaughtered and once more every family on his estate would have fresh pork and sausages on the table, and hams hanging in the smokehouse.

Fields surrounded the house on three sides: a

patchwork of varying shapes and sizes bounded by hedges of grey stone. Narrowing his gaze against the hazy afternoon sun he saw yellow barley nearly ripe. Oats, so pale they were almost white, rippled like water in the breeze. The wheat fields – a greater number this year since he had broken new ground – were rich golden-brown and dotted with scarlet poppies. In one of the clover fields now shorn of its crop a man was ploughing with a pair of heavy horses. A team of oxen worked another field.

His gaze skimmed over tiny figures planting another crop of turnips. Others were cutting grass for hay, while more turned or raked fields scythed earlier that week. A laden cart trundled along the sanding road. The salt sand would be mixed with lime and seaweed to enrich and sweeten the poor soil.

Raad tossed his head, jingling the bit. Casvellan guided the stallion along the hilltop, through heather and butter-yellow gorse that smelled like coconut. He glimpsed a score of black short-horned cattle turned loose during the summer months to forage on the moor. Reassured that despite his absence all was as it should be, he turned and headed down.

The air was hot and heavy. Small grey clouds edged with silver moved slowly across a milky sky. He wished he might have dispensed with both hat and coat. But it would not do. Standards must be maintained, expectations met. Even up here someone would be watching him.

His decision to hire a known smuggler and suspected murderer had proved to some that his wits had gone begging. But he knew better than most how appearances could deceive. Convinced by nothing more than instinct to trust Devlin Varcoe he had not regretted it.

If only his current problem might as easily be resolved. Occupying every waking moment it was driving him to distraction. He knew his duty. Had he not grown up with an excellent example of how *not* to behave? Since adulthood all his actions and choices had been governed by the need to live down the scandal, repair the damage and restore the family name. He had done so willingly, confident in his abilities, judgement and authority. Then Roz Trevaskis had walked into his life and his beliefs – once so solid – had shivered into quicksand.

Doing the right thing had been easy when the alternatives inspired only irritation or distaste. He hated this new uncertainty. Yet suspicion that this upheaval was not altogether a bad thing was even more unsettling.

How much of the past ten years had he spent doing what others required of him? He had become a Justice because his uncle, who had inherited the role from his grandfather, had been forced by ill health to retire and his father had flatly refused.

'Too much paper. Besides, I've got the horses. Anyway it would interfere with hunting. Branoc can take it on.'

So he had become a Justice by default, out of a sense of duty rather than vocation. But having accepted it he determined to do it properly. There had been much to learn. He would have found the task far harder without the quiet and unstinting help of his clerk who had proved a true friend, though he would never presume to call himself that. Usually the most reticent of men, Ellacott had betrayed a warmth and sympathy for Roz Trevaskis that had surprised him.

Was what *he* felt for her real? Or was he fooling himself in an attempt to justify the very behaviour he had so bitterly condemned in his father?

Damn it, he hadn't *done* anything. But he wanted to. Dear God, how he wanted to. Lying between sheets still warm from her body and redolent of her scent, he sweated as he fought to banish the images that plagued him. He pictured her hair loosely braided in a single plait falling over her shoulder, the curve of her hip as she bent over his brother, the swell of her breasts, her slender naked body shrouded in that voluminous nightgown.

The desire to touch, to hold her in his arms and feel her heart beat against his, to discover every curve and hollow, to learn the texture of her skin and taste her soft lips was a nightly torture. He wanted all that and more, far more. And wanting made sleep elusive. When exhaustion finally claimed him she haunted his dreams.

Had she truly been a tavern wench he could have tumbled her without a moment's concern, paid her well for her trouble and walked away without a backward glance. Such behaviour was perfectly acceptable for men of his rank who might take their pleasure where they chose among the lower classes. Honour demanded only that provision be made for any resulting offspring. Most gentlemen sought their amusements some distance from home, a courtesy that enabled sensible wives to pretend ignorance.

His father had cared nothing for such considerations. No housemaid had been safe. But he had disclaimed any responsibility. How could girls who behaved in such a manner possibly know who had fathered their bastards? And without proof, why should he pay? It was this ill-bred and despicable behaviour even more than his indiscriminate seductions among the household staff that had besmirched the Casvellan name.

The stallion's whinny jolted him out of his reverie with a bitter taste in his mouth. One of the mares responded: the sound faint and wavering in the afternoon heat. Patting Raad's muscular neck he pressed booted heels to the animal's side.

As soon as Davy was better he would pay Roz Trevaskis as promised and send her home. She had proved an excellent nurse. Everything about her was better than he'd expected. But none of that changed anything. He was who he was. He had responsibilities, a position to uphold. And she, she had care of her mother.

Out here, away from the pressures and confines of the sickroom, he could see the situation for what it was: an exaggerated response to an exceptionally demanding event. But surely Davy was over the worst? In another week, two at most, he'd be convalescing. As soon as the risk of infection was past, the maids would take over, Roz would leave, and he would put all this behind him.

His mother was right. It was time he married. He could rely on Deb to steer her away from girls who would drive him mad with their twittering, or expect him to fawn and fuss.

A man of his standing required a well-brought-up and sensible young woman of good family. Someone properly trained and competent to manage a house and staff. Someone he could like. He neither sought nor expected more. Someone with interests of her own for he would not want her hanging on his coat tails. After she had given him a son, an heir for Trescowe, he would not question her friendships provided she was discreet.

He passed a hand across his face. If he repeated this to his mother, she would beam with delight and praise his good sense. Deb would think he'd gone mad. And if Roz Trevaskis heard it she would regard him with the contempt he deserved.

Entering the house the same way he had left it, Casvellan looked into the kitchen where the cook and kitchen maid were busy at the large scrubbed table.

'I'd like a can of hot water. Ring the bell when it's ready.'

'Sir.' Blushing furiously, the maid bobbed a curtsey.

Closing the door behind him he climbed the wooden stairs. As he approached the sickroom door he heard Davy shouting, Roz's voice placating, then the crash of breaking glass.

'Go away. I don't want your help,' Davy's hoarse cry was clearly audible. 'Where's my brother?'

Opening the door Casvellan saw Roz kneeling between the door and the bed carefully sweeping shards of shattered glass into a dustpan.

'Where have you been?' Davy demanded. His spotted face was flushed, his eyes overbright. 'Why weren't you here? Why did you go off and leave me with—?'

'Be quiet!' Casvellan snapped. He shifted his gaze to Roz whose head was bent over her task. 'What happened?'

'She—' Davy began.

'Are you deaf as well as ill-mannered?' Casvellan demanded icily.

Roz glanced up. Pink-cheeked and clearly upset, she was trying hard to hide it. 'It was an accident.'

'Have you all the pieces?'

She nodded. 'I think so.'

'Then I'd be obliged if you would excuse us for a few minutes. Leave the dustpan on the hearth.'

Thirteen

Fighting tears of shock, hurt and exhaustion, Roz walked into the bedroom, closed the door and stood where she was, rubbing her bare arms. She couldn't hear his actual words but Casvellan's tone was unmistakable. The cold, quiet ferocity of his anger dried her throat. She had seen him irritated, even annoyed. But never had she seen him lose his temper. She wished she hadn't been the cause of it, or of ill feeling between the brothers.

Crossing to the window she stared blindly out, her folded arms pressed against a stomach knotted with tension. She was tired. That was why Davy telling her to go away and leave him alone had hurt.

No, that wasn't the real cause. What cut deep was the disgust and loathing on his face as he smashed the glass from her hand. She didn't deserve that. *He thought she did.* He was ill. *But not delirious. He had known what he was saying.*

She started at the brisk knock. Not trusting her voice she didn't answer. As she swallowed hard and dragged in an unsteady breath, the door opened and she heard boots on the bare floorboards.

193

'Miss Trevaskis?'

She kept her back to him. She didn't want him to see she had been crying. He would think her weak and silly and she was neither. She was just *tired*.

He came closer. 'There is no excuse for my brother's behaviour as I have made perfectly clear to him. It was totally unacceptable, and you may be sure it will not be repeated. I won't ask your forgiveness. That is for him to do. However, I suspect – in fact I am certain – his outburst was driven by horror at what the disease is doing to his body. I have never known him ill in his life. His present weakness and dependence on us both has shattered his confidence.' His voice dropped. 'Roz, he's terrified.'

Her heart jumped at his use of her name. She nodded but still didn't move. His gaze was sharp and she feared what he might see. But now he had explained, she *did* understand. Her mouth was dry and she had to lick her lips. 'If – if your brother escaped all the usual childhood ailments and grew up taking good health for granted, then to be so severely ill must indeed be unnerving.'

His hand rested lightly on her shoulder and she caught her breath as the pressure increased. 'Were it not for you – first recognizing the disease then bringing him home and staying to nurse him...' As he turned her to face him she bent her head.

'You have every right to be angry. No one knows better than I how demanding recent days have been.' When she still did not look up he tilted her chin with his fingertips. 'I could not have—' Air hissed between his teeth. 'Damn it, he made you cry.'

'No – it's – I—' She shrugged, forced a smile, felt it wobble. 'I'm just tired, that's all.'

The warm weight of his hand on her shoulder was comforting. But he had never touched her before and her galloping heartbeat made her breathless and dizzy. A fiery blush scalded her face and throat. Unable to meet his gaze she tensed as he lifted a loose curl that clung to her damp forehead and tucked it behind her ear.

'Roz—' he stopped. Releasing her he stepped back. 'Forgive me. I fear I smell of the stables.' He had withdrawn into formality. Though his nearness had been deeply unsettling she mourned its loss. He turned to go then glanced over his shoulder. 'You were right. Raad and I *both* needed the exercise.'

She started forward. 'You will want hot water.'

'I'll get it.' He opened the door. 'Did you have time while I was out to prepare any lavender bags?' His tone indicated no more than polite interest. But she knew what he really meant and shared his desire for relief from the dreadful stench.

She nodded and spoke softly. 'Enough for his bath. I will make more this evening.'

Later, when the hip-bath had been filled, Roz removed herself to the bedroom, leaving the door ajar on Casvellan's instructions. She heard Davy, at first scornful and petulant, admit that the combination of barley water and lavender was soothing. Forgetting she was there and could hear, he confided his fear of dying. Then, as if ashamed, he tried to laugh it off. Realizing how frightened he was, Roz's heart ached for him and forgiveness was easy.

Davy might momentarily have forgotten her, but Casvellan had not. He pitched his voice to carry as he reminded his brother that it was to her he owed the compresses, the nourishing drinks, in fact everything that was contributing to his relief and comfort.

Once Davy was back in bed Roz bound fresh compresses onto his hands and feet, while Casvellan emptied the bath.

'I–I owe you an apology,' Davy muttered, a flush darkening his mottled face. 'I should never have said – and the glass...' He shook his head.

'Let us both forget it,' she cut him short, glancing up from the bandages, with a brief smile. 'I cannot even begin to imagine the frustration you must feel, being confined in here like this.'

His gaze met hers, and she saw him gathering his courage. 'Am I going to—?'

'Get well?' She would not let him mention dying. Once spoken the word could not be retracted and would linger, shadowing his thoughts and tainting all their efforts. 'How can you doubt it?' She smiled at him again, resolutely ignoring the knowledge that of those who contracted smallpox fewer than half recovered. 'But it may be another week or two before you are able to leave your bed, and a while longer before you are fully fit again. I understand from Mr Casvellan that you have not suffered a day's illness in your life. That is greatly in your favour, you know. Few people are blessed with such a strong constitution.' She finished tying the gauze and stood up.

'Thank you,' he mumbled. 'I'm very much obliged to you.'

She nodded and moved away to the table, blinking hard as she tried to compose herself before returning to bathe his eyes.

After darkness had fallen and she had completed a further dozen small bags and filled them with lavender, she rose from her chair by the window. Casvellan was sitting on the bed reading to his brother. She went downstairs, rang the bell and waited while one of the maids fetched hot water.

''Ow's young master coming on?' Sally puffed, carrying the heavy copper can with both hands. 'Be all right will 'e? Missus is in some state. Running poor Miss Deborah ragged, she is. Lord knows what she'll do if Master Davy—'

'He is still very weak,' Roz admitted. 'But there are definite signs of improvement.' She chose her words carefully, knowing they would spread swiftly among the staff and lose nothing in the telling. 'I believe Mr Casvellan has good reason to hope his brother will be spared any complications.'

'Been some brave job for you,' Sally clucked sympathetically, but Roz wasn't fooled. Her isolation upstairs with the Justice and his brother was providing endless opportunities for gossip and speculation.

'I'm glad to have been able to help.'

'Still, must be some worry. But you can't be

'ere *and* back 'ome. Best not fret about it, eh? You done your best. No one can say diff'rent. There's some you just can't 'elp.'

'Goodnight.' Roz lifted the can and started up the stairs as Sally closed the door behind her. *Her mother. It had to be her mother.* Guilt made her feel sick and ashamed. What was she doing here nursing a virtual stranger, when her reason for leaving her grandparents was to look after her mother?

Though she regularly claimed she didn't need anyone, and screamed at Roz to go back where she came from and leave her alone, Roz knew her mother dreaded solitude. Desperate for company, and brandy to deaden her guilt and shame, she would pay any price asked. But money was rarely involved. All this Roz had learned over painful, heart-wrenching, stomach-churning months.

Though the money promised by Casvellan had been a poweful incentive, two or three weeks respite from her mother's vicious verbal attacks and increasingly wayward behaviour was a gift she had been unable to turn down.

Perhaps if she had been at home ... It would not have made the slightest difference. For two years she had tried. But her attempts to encourage, sympathize or warn simply infuriated her mother who ended any argument by shrieking, 'You can't possibly understand! You have no idea what I've suffered.'

Roz knew the details of whatever her mother had done would reach her soon enough. Meanwhile, Sally's words were a timely though bitter reminder. There was nothing for her here.

Pausing for an instant outside the sickroom she drew a deep breath then opened the door. Casvellan glanced up, his eyes gleaming in the candlelight.

Her eyes pricking, Roz bobbed a brief curtsey. 'Goodnight.'

'Goodnight.'

She went into the bedroom and closed the door. Working the soap into lather she washed her face, inhaling the floral scent to try and banish the sickroom's foul smell from her nostrils. Cool and refreshed she put on a clean nightgown, folded her discarded clothes for laundering, and laid out a clean shift and the apricot gown for the morning. Unpinning her hair she brushed it thoroughly and drew it over one shoulder to braid it loosely.

Thunder rumbled in the distance as she slipped between the sheets. Stretching out on her back she winced as her aching muscles began to relax. Occasional lightning flashed bright on her eyelids. She reached for sleep, desperately needing both rest and escape. But it eluded her.

After tossing and turning for what seemed like hours she sat up, sure she had heard something. A cough? A cry? Thunder cracked then rolled long and deep, rattling the windows. Lightning flickered, illuminated the room with fierce brilliance. Pushing the covers back, Roz swung her feet out of bed and felt for her slippers. She draped the shawl around her shoulders and quietly opened the door.

Candles burned on the mantelpiece and the

table alongside Davy's bed. Moving restlessly on the pillow he moaned softly. Roz glanced at the chair by the fire where Casvellan sprawled deeply asleep, his long legs stretched out and crossed at the ankles, his head on one side.

Though it was his turn to watch over his brother she felt no anger, only sympathy. He was not used to this. Whereas, since living with her mother, she had become all too familiar with broken nights and interrupted sleep. Her slippers were silent on the floorboards as she crossed to the bed.

'Are you thirsty?' she whispered. 'Would you like a drink?'

Opening puffy eyes he nodded. 'Throat hurts.' His voice was a dry rasp.

'Don't try to talk,' Roz murmured, pouring lemon-flavoured barley water from the jug into a glass. Sitting beside him she slipped her arm beneath his head and held the glass to his lips. 'Just sips,' she warned, 'until your mouth and throat are wet. Then you won't cough. There, now you can take more if you wish.'

When he'd had enough she set the glass down and eased her arm free.

'Don't go,' he whispered.

'I can't sleep either,' she smiled at him. 'I expect the storm is keeping a lot of people awake.'

'My head aches.' Disgust twisted his face. 'God, I stink.'

'Not you,' she held his gaze. 'It's the poison in the rash. That's what smells.'

'How much longer? Shouldn't I be getting better?'

Roz sat on the side of the bed so he could more easily see her in the candlelight. 'You *are* getting better. You had a very high fever. That has gone now.'

'But my hands and feet – the spots are so many and so foul.'

'And painful I know. But you are very brave. Everything is taking its course just as Dr Avers promised. Tomorrow I will make more compresses for your hands and feet.'

'They look ridiculous.'

'Perhaps,' she agreed. Experience with Tom had taught her that boys preferred honesty to lies intended as comfort. 'But do they ease the discomfort?'

He gave a reluctant nod.

'And who is to see? Only your brother, and he would wear them himself if doing so would make you well again.' She stood up.

'Where are you going? Don't go.'

'I would not think of it,' she murmured. 'Now let's see what we can do to ease your headache.' Pouring cool water from the can into the basin, she added a lavender bag, swirling and squeezing it to release the scent. Then she dipped a cloth in the scented water, wrung it out and lay it across his forehead. 'Is that better?'

'Mmm.' Davy's swollen eyelids fluttered closed. 'Talk to me.'

For an instant Roz's mind was blank. Then, as she removed the cloth to soak it, she recalled the difference in Casvellan when he returned from his ride. His expression was no longer strained and the tension had gone from his shoulders.

201

'On my way here I saw horses in the paddocks and in the field behind the stable block. Are any of them yours?'

'Three.' His voice was faint and his eyes remained closed. 'Thoroughbreds. A mare called Malak and two geldings. Damis, that means dark, and Balal, hero.'

'What wonderful names. If they are yours and you have trained them, you will know each one well: their particular colour and markings. If you sat blindfolded on their backs you would know at once which it was. You'd know Malak by the way she moves, how she responds to your touch on the rein or your leg against her side. You'd know Damis from his stride and how he jumps. You'd know whether Balal prefers a carrot or an apple, whether he is calm or skittish.'

As she changed the cloth again she saw the lines of suffering in his face had softened. She kept her voice low and soothing. 'As soon as you are well you will ride again. Imagine the pleasure you will have deciding which of them to ride, and where you will go. There are so many choices, so many different paths and tracks. Perhaps you will ride onto the moor where you can see for miles. It's so quiet up there. All you hear is the sighing wind, or the sound of birdsong. The sky seems vast and if you look up you can watch buzzards slowly circling and hear their mewing cries as they call to each other.'

His breathing had slowed, deepened. Moving quietly she soaked and replaced the cloth once more. 'Maybe another day you will ride through

202

the woods, or across the cliffs. Perhaps you may even go down to the beach and gallop along the hard sand at the water's edge.' She fell silent: her eyes closed at the vivid memory of Casvellan raising clouds of spray as he hurtled through the shallows astride his silver stallion.

Pulling herself back she looked at Davy. He was fast asleep. Getting up carefully so as not to disturb him, she gathered the shawl around her. She started as a long flicker of lightning revealed Casvellan rising from his chair. *How long had he been watching her? Had he heard what she was saying?* Instinctively she drew the shawl closer, moving away from the bed so she would not disturb Davy.

'I couldn't sleep,' she explained in a whisper. 'The thunder ... I–I heard your brother call. He was thirsty and restless and asked me to stay.' She bit the inside of her lip. She was babbling.

'I'm sorry.' He raked his hair with both hands, then arched his back. 'Raad was full of himself and we had quite a battle. But that's no excuse. It was my turn.'

'It's all right, truly. You're getting less sleep than I am. I was awake anyway, so—' Lightning flashed and a thunderclap made her jump.

'I was listening to you,' he murmured. 'You were – are – very kind. If it were me lying there—'

'Don't,' she blurted. 'I cannot bear...' *to think of him hovering, as Davy had been – might yet be – between recovery and death.* Realizing how very near she had come to revealing feelings that could only embarrass them both she shook her

203

head. 'Please excuse me.' She started towards the bedroom.

But he moved to block her path.

She could feel herself trembling and didn't dare look up. Could he hear the drumbeat of her heart? What did he want? What did *she* want?

With gentle hands he cupped her face and tilted it up.

She looked into his face. It was all hard planes and shadows. She saw the furrow between his dark brows and longed to smooth it away. No good could come of this. And yet – and yet—

Was she mad? Had living with her mother taught her nothing? Was she not witness every day to the disastrous repercussions of intemperate behaviour and emotional indulgence? *Branoc Casvellan was different.* He was a man. Men could behave as they wished.

Lowering his head he brushed her cheek with his lips. Her breath hitched on a sound that was half gasp, half sigh. Her eyes closed and heat surged through her body. It meant nothing: a token of thanks, a gesture of gratitude in exceptional circumstances.

Now he would move away. He must, for she could not. But he remained, his breath quickening, standing so close she could feel warmth radiating from him as she inhaled his scent.

Uttering a sound from deep in his throat, he rested his forehead against hers. Unable to stop herself, her eyes still closed, she raised her chin a fraction. She heard his in-drawn breath then his mouth sought hers, covered it. His lips were warm, the kiss tender. But beneath it she sensed

204

more powerful emotions held in check by an iron control. She swayed, and to steady herself rested her hands on the front of his shoulders, feeling the heat of his skin through the fine fabric and the play of muscle as he moved.

Cradling her head, he circled her waist with his other arm, drawing her against him. As her body fit to his, his tongue gently parted her lips, igniting a yearning so profound, so hopeless, that tears slid between her lashes and down her temples.

His mouth moved from hers to press kisses to her cheek, her eyelids. He lifted his head. 'No,' he murmured hoarsely. 'Please ... Don't cry. I didn't mean – I would not have you fear ... Dear God.' His breath hissed as he dropped his hands to her shoulders, his fingers strong, hurting as he deliberately moved her back, away from him. Suddenly she felt cold, so cold.

'I am not my father,' he said through gritted teeth.

Her head jerked up, and she looked directly into his eyes. 'No one who knows you would ever think that.' Her voice was a ragged whisper as she dashed the tears away with the fingers of one hand and the heel of the other. It would be easy, more comfortable, to let him take full responsibility for what had occurred. But it would not be honest.

'Do not reproach yourself.' She felt suddenly shy, but her sense of fairness demanded the truth. 'I don't. Nor can I regret.'

He laid one strong hand gently along her cheek, wiping it dry with his thumb. 'While under my roof you'll come to no harm.'

Her gaze never left his as he drew the shawl around her.

She moistened her lips with the tip of her tongue and, tasting him, felt a deep liquid pull at her core. 'Had I thought otherwise I would not have stayed.' She saw surprise in the quick lift of his brows.

'I offered you a lot of money.'

'You did,' she acknowledged. 'It would have grieved me to turn it down. Though as I didn't, such a claim is meaningless.'

'Why did you stay?' he asked quietly.

'You were kind to Tom. And though my mother does not deserve your forbearance, you have shown it just the same.'

'Are those your only reasons?'

She could say yes. That was what she *should* say. He would accept it at face value, and the last few minutes could be disregarded as if they had never happened.

'No.' She hugged the shawl closer.

'Then why?'

Surely it was obvious? 'You needed me.'

He gazed at her a moment longer then moved aside and gestured her into the bedroom. 'Go. Please.' An underlying strain in his voice kept her silent. Walking past him into the bedroom she gently closed the door, tossed the shawl aside and slid between the sheets. After what had happened – *it was just a kiss* – she did not expect to sleep. But despite the growling thunder and flickering lightning her eyelids were suddenly leaden. She closed them.

It seemed only moments later that she opened them to daylight.

Hearing movement in the adjoining room she glanced toward the closed door and saw a copper can of hot water. Only one person could have put it there. *He had done that for her.*

She sat up and relived the events of the previous night. Though she longed to see him her heart ached. The kiss had been her first, and from a man she admired above all others. She would treasure the memory, knowing that it would never have occurred but for his brother's illness and their enforced isolation. He had kissed her. A boundary had been crossed. *And her mother was in trouble again.*

Pushing back the bedcovers, she crossed to the window and opened it wide. The sultry closeness had gone. The morning air was cool on her face, fresh and sweetly scented.

Washed and dressed, her hair neat, her gown covered by the dowlas apron she picked up the pail and walked to the door. She pressed one palm to her stomach to try and still nerves that fluttered like a trapped bird.

A new bond of understanding? Or a momentary aberration best forgotten? One glance from those deep blue eyes and she would know. Taking a deep breath she opened the door and started as Casvellan entered from the passage carrying another copper can.

'Good morning.' The greeting was formal, his smile fleeting. But his gaze met hers, held it, and glimpsing reflections of her own confusion her heart turned over. 'You slept well?'

She nodded. 'Thank you, yes. The hot water – it was very kind.'

'It was no trouble.' Shadows like dark thumb-prints under his eyes told their own story.

'How is your brother?'

'Asleep.' Standing close, they were speaking in whispers.

'As you should be. Please,' she urged, 'go and rest.'

A harsh wordless sound too bitter for laughter escaped him and he raked his hair. 'Forgive me. You're right. Is there any hot water left?'

'Yes.'

'Take this.' He offered her the can he was holding. 'It will spare you one journey.'

'Thank—'

But he had already closed the bedroom door.

Fourteen

Three hours later the floors and surfaces were dry though the acrid smell of disinfectant still lingered. Roz tended both fires while Casvellan completed his brother's toilet then pulled one of the armchairs closer and helped him across to it so Roz could change the bed linen.

Now, clad in a clean nightshirt, his damp hair neatly combed, Davy lay propped on pillows, his exposed hands and feet resting on rags that would be burned later.

While Roz applied fresh compresses, Davy kept his head turned towards the window unwilling, or unable, to look at the suppurating sores.

How did she do it? Casvellan wondered. He had a strong stomach, but the sickly stench had driven him downstairs with the slop pails. Guilt had brought him swiftly back. Glancing at Roz he saw the tension in her shoulders and realized her reassuring calm was a mask hiding reactions which, if she let them show, would make his brother feel even worse.

She talked quietly to Davy while tending him, checking that the compress was not too hot nor the bandages too tight, and listened gravely to his complaints about the barley water.

'You are right, it is very boring. If you have a fancy for something savoury, I will ask for beef tea for your breakfast. But though it is tasty it has little substance. So to build your strength I suggest a thin gruel made from oatmeal.'

'Ugh!'

'True, on its own it has little to recommend it. Yet flavoured with mace, lemon peel, cloves, ginger, sugar and a little wine it is delicious.' As one of his bandaged hands strayed nervously upward, she added, 'And the very thing when a sore throat makes swallowing difficult. It will certainly make a welcome change from the bland drinks that were all you could manage when you were more seriously ill.' She stood up. 'I'll go directly and ask for it to be prepared. You should have it within the hour.'

Seeing anxiety drain from his brother's expression despite a careless shrug, Casvellan marvelled at Roz's tact. His gaze followed her into the passage. Her slenderness hinted at fragility but was misleading. Indeed her stamina would put many men of his acquaintance to shame.

But what touched him most was her kindness. The unhappiness in her background and her worsening difficulties with her mother made her kindness to Davy all the more remarkable. He knew she was loyal, and that she possessed strength of character. Yet last night she had still managed to astonish him with her candour. Though unexpected it was very welcome, for it had confirmed his suspicions. She was not indifferent to him.

Of course she wasn't. He was unmarried and owner of a large estate. Were he ugly as sin with a hump on his back he would still be smiled at and sought after, and by young women with far more to recommend them than she.

Crossing to the window he gazed out. What in God's name was he thinking? One kiss: of what significance was that? He had been granted far greater liberties, and by women whose willingness to risk their reputations had surprised and amused him. Yet the fire her lips had ignited burned still. Most would have laid all responsibility on him. She hadn't. She was different.

Indeed she was. Her illegitimacy and her mother were drawbacks enough to make any man of sense run hard and fast in the opposite direction. And he knew himself possessed of more than ordinary intelligence. So what was he doing?

Why, instead of taking the event to its natural conclusion, had conscience and memories of his father demanded he release her? If it meant nothing, why did it feel like hope, a promise? And why, when he could ride into Helston and have his every desire catered for at any one of half a dozen establishments, did he have such a powerful desire to repeat it only with her?

When she brought Davy home he had asked, insisted, *demanded* she stay. Even then he had trusted her. Having spent two weeks virtually alone with her he knew his instincts had been right. Without her common sense, her organization of a routine, her way of simply doing whatever needed to be done, he would have been lost.

So might Davy.

He had not expected to find her such easy company. Still more surprising was the realization that as the days had passed their difference in rank, while not forgotten, had lost its importance. She was unfailingly polite but when her ideas or opinions differed from his she said so. Used to women agreeing with him regardless of their own opinions – if indeed they had any – her quiet independence interested, distracted and occasionally annoyed him. Yet he admired it, and her.

His mother's incessant talking, often about nothing at all, frequently drove him early from the dinner table. Roz was comfortable with silence. No woman had ever intrigued or moved him as she did.

'Mr Casvellan?' As he turned she offered him a letter. 'This was on the table downstairs.' The sunlight on her hair revealed tints of rosewood and mahogany. He had thought her eyes green. But today he saw flecks of gold and bronze. Her cheeks, too often pale, were flushed.

'Thank you.' He smiled, and was briefly surprised when she gave a quick nod and moved away. He read his name penned in his mother's hand. Why would his mother be writing to him? Turning the folded paper over he saw the wafer sealing it and understood the reason for Roz's heightened colour.

His jaw tightened. Every day Ellacott sent over sheaves of documents. Many were private and of considerable importance. His clerk's opinion of Roz Trevaskis's trustworthiness was plain as most of the papers were simply folded and tied in a bundle for ease of carrying. He hoped his mother's letter was of sufficient importance to justify the seal and its implied insult. But perhaps he was being unfair. She had met Roz only once and did not know her.

'Roz,' Davy croaked. 'Come and read to me.' As Casvellan swung round, his brows lifting, Davy added quickly, 'If you're not too busy.'

Putting down the gauze she had just picked up, Roz crossed to the bed. 'No, my sewing can wait. I should much prefer to read to you. Which shall it be? *Don Quixote* or *The Old English Baron*?'

'*The Baron*,' Davy rasped.

'I'm glad,' Roz picked up the leather-bound copy from the bedside table. 'I confess I am keen to know how Edmund goes on in his adventures.'

Watching as she sat on the coverlet Casvellan knew his mother would find such informality improper and shocking. But he understood Roz had done it so Davy did not have to move his head and could more easily hear her.

Turning once more to the window he broke the wafer and unfolded the thick paper.

My dear son, his mother had written. *Deborah tells me Miss Trevaskis has shown more than ordinary dedication to our dearest boy's care during his dreadful illness. I am sure we are all most obliged to her. As you must know, only the delicate state of my own health has kept me from where I most long to be – at his side.*

He inhaled deeply. Containing his irritation

213

took some effort as he gazed across the lawn that bounded the side of the house. Then leaning one shoulder against the wall he resumed reading.

Yet I cannot approve of her continued presence in the house. I will not deny that Deborah speaks well of her. But you must know your sweet-natured sister is possessed by a willingness to see only the best in everyone. For myself, I cannot but wonder at the motives of a young woman so willing to leave her work and home at scarcely a moment's notice. I concede that her speech and manners indicate some care in her upbringing. But if that is indeed the case, why then was she employed in a tavern?

Such concerns are natural to a loving mother. But when I raised them with Dr Avers he quite dismissed them which I consider most unfeeling. In truth he appears to harbour an admiration for this girl I cannot think at all proper.

Although I am relieved that under your watchful gaze my dearest boy is receiving the best care, I would be failing in my duty if I did not point out to you the dangers of your situation. Isolation from your normal life and business, anxiety about your brother's condition, and proximity to this young woman are circumstances in which it would be only too easy to imagine an attachment. Indeed, who could blame Miss Trevaskis for wishing this change in her fortunes might be permanent, and employing every effort and charm to achieve it. But I beg you to consider the damage – particularly to your sister's prospects – of a liaison so totally unsuitable. Do not allow yourself to be beguiled, even briefly,

214

for you may be sure she would talk of it. Such girls always do.

Now that the period of greatest danger is past I urge you most strongly to send Miss Trevaskis home – where no doubt she has been much missed – and allow Davy's valet and groom to take care of him.

Casvellan's fingers crushed the letter as he stared blindly out of the window, incandescent at his mother's interference. He remembered all too clearly her refusal to acknowledge his father's appalling behaviour until the scandal made it impossible to ignore. Even then she had blamed the unfortunate girls, insisting *they* had done the seducing.

She had the gall to lecture him? Such effrontery was insupportable. Nor was there any comparison between him and his father.

Roz was not responsible for their kiss. Though the fact that it had occurred added greater strain to an already complicated situation. *Because he wanted more.*

The moment his lips touched hers he had realized he was the first man she had granted such an intimacy. His fierce pleasure in the knowledge had surprised him. Then all thought had been swept aside by a deep and powerful hunger that found its echo in her soft generous mouth, her grip on his shoulders and the pliancy of her body against his. Releasing her, putting distance between them, had been one of the hardest things he had ever done. For she was no lightskirt to be used, discarded and forgotten.

Fuelling his rage was the bitter knowledge

215

that, where Deb's future hopes were concerned, his mother had a point. He could not ignore the wider impact of his actions, both on his family and his position as a Justice. Roz Trevaskis might have the manners of a lady, but illegitimacy barred her from society. Meanwhile her mother, a gentleman's daughter, had sunk to the gutter and appeared determined to remain there.

Rubbing the throbbing ache in his forehead he turned, and their eyes met. He was practised at hiding his emotions. But something of the turmoil inside him must have shown for her tentative smile wavered. He guessed at once that she believed he was regretting what had happened. He didn't, but could not tell her so. He needed time to think.

She continued reading but the underlying strain in her voice made Casvellan want to smash something. Crossing to the fire he tossed the letter into the flames. 'Forgive my interruption, Davy. Miss Trevaskis, would you be so kind as to send word to my groom to saddle Raad? I will be down directly.' Disappearing into the bedroom he closed the door.

Panting slightly from the headlong gallop, Casvellan leaned his weight back and used the pressure of his legs to slow the stallion to a canter then a prancing walk. He was proud that the horses he had bred and reared at Trescowe all retained a soft mouth and responded to the lightest touch on the rein.

That was one more reason not to sell Raad to Pengarrick, whose heavy hands would ruin the horse within a week. He patted Raad's arched neck, using his voice to soothe and settle. But the stallion continued to jink sideways, tossing his head.

'I can't fool you, can I?' Casvellan murmured. 'What am I to do? Decisions must be made and I cannot delay them much longer.' With a sigh that felt as if it had been dragged up from his boots, he lowered the rolled brim of his beaver hat to shield his eyes and gazed down on the fields where harvesting had begun.

A ragged line of men wielding sickles worked their way across a field of oats, metal blades flashing in the sun. Behind them more men followed, binding the cut stalks into sheaves. He glimpsed Devlin Varcoe riding along the lane between the turnip and grain fields.

The hot summer weather had brought the crops to ripeness earlier this year. But the thunderstorm had been a warning. Once the weather broke it was likely to remain unsettled. No doubt his home farm tenant, Amos Kestle, had advised Devlin to cut the grain now and stack the sheaves in round arrish mows. There the ears would be protected from any rain until harvest was finished and threshing could begin.

Perhaps it was the need to beat the weather that had persuaded him to put the French prisoners to work with the farm labourers and the miners. For two or three weeks every summer, the miners completed their shifts then came to help with the harvest and earn much-needed extra money.

Even as Casvellan wondered at the wisdom of

the move, a man in the front line swung round. The men either side of him stopped cutting. Others who had been binding straightened up. Suddenly the first man tossed aside his sickle and lunged. Within seconds a fight had erupted.

Even as Casvellan swung the stallion round and urged him down the hill, he saw Devlin kick his horse forward. Turning from the mow where he had been stacking sheaves, Lt Phillippe sprinted towards the melee.

Casvellan caught his breath as his agent and the French officer waded in. A fist caught the lieutenant. The split skin above his eyebrow gushed blood. But though half-blinded he didn't falter. Bellowing for order, Devlin and the lieutenant dragged the fighting men apart and hurled them away. Standing back to back, they roared at the two groups of men who glared at each other, then bent their heads, some bitter and sullen, others sheepish.

Casvellan halted Raad a short distance away. 'Mr Varcoe, Lt Phillippe, a word if you please?'

'My fault, sir.' Devlin muttered, wiped his sweating forehead with his forearm. 'I shouldn't have tried to work them together. Amos warned me.'

Recalling the resentment with which his tenant farmer had greeted the new agent's appointment, Casvellan raised an eyebrow.

Devlin grinned. 'We reached an understanding.'

Casvellan nodded. 'I'm glad to hear it. Where is he?'

'One of the prisoners cut his leg with a sickle.

He was bleeding like a stuck pig. Amos took him back to the farm so Dolly could sew him up.'

Casvellan frowned. 'Why didn't he send his boy?'

'Reuben's ploughing.' Devlin pointed up the hillside. Stepping closer he lowered his voice. 'Sir, this shouldn't have happened and I take responsibility for it. But the miners resent the prisoners taking their work. They're afraid they'll get less money.'

With a nod, Casvellan turned to the lieutenant. 'Your men will take no further part in the harvest. They will sow turnips and dig potatoes. When the harvest is complete and the miners have gone, they can assist with the threshing. However, if there is any repetition of today's behaviour they will be locked inside.'

He switched his gaze to Devlin. 'Inform the miners that every one of them will forfeit a day's pay. I am aware some weren't involved in the fight. But losing money will serve as a warning.' The sun burned through his coat and his shirt clung damply to his skin. 'Let every man have a drink then put them back to work.'

With a nod he wheeled the stallion round and headed back towards the house.

Leaving Raad in the stable yard he walked briskly to the house and let himself in through the side door. Hot and thirsty, a dull ache gnawing at the base of his skull, he removed his hat as he climbed the back stairs. Opening the sickroom door he saw Roz pouring lemonade into a glass. She glanced up and as swiftly looked away, colour climbing her throat to warm her cheeks.

'There's a can of water and fresh towels in—next door, sir.'

On the narrow table between the windows he saw a tray containing bread, fruit, cheese and a tankard. 'For me?'

Her gaze darting to the tray, she nodded. 'Yes, sir. It occurred to me that as the day is so warm you would prefer ale to wine. But if—'

'No, that's fine. Thank you.' He heard his mother's voice. *She will employ every effort and charm. But do not allow yourself to be beguiled.*

'Excuse me.' He strode into the bedroom and shut the door. Dropping his hat and gloves on the bedcover, he peeled off his coat and tossed that after them. His waistcoat, collar and neckcloth followed. Rolling back his shirtsleeves he tipped the can into the basin. After he had soaped and rinsed his hands he scooped water over his face several times, then wiped his wet hands around the back of his neck where the muscles felt like knotted rope.

Drying himself, he dropped the towel and raked both hands through his hair. Then, still in shirtsleeves, he returned to the sickroom. He ate and drank while reading the papers sent across by his clerk. Papers Roz had stacked neatly beside the tray. He made notes, jotted replies to queries, wrote instructions, and when he could sit still no longer he got up and moved to the window.

He could sense her behind him, sitting at an angle in the armchair, sewing yet more lavender bags. She must be bored to sobs, yet she had not uttered one word of complaint.

Tense and restless, he returned to the bedroom and stared for several moments at his coat and waistcoat, both still lying where they had fallen. He shouldn't be here. *Where else should he be? What was more important than his brother?* Davy was going to live. He could believe it now. While Davy convalesced he would resume his normal life and duties. The crisis was past and all was well. Nothing had changed. Yet every-thing was different.

The following afternoon while Davy dozed, Roz stood up after tending the fire and wiped her hands down her coarse apron. Casvellan sat at the table writing, his back to her. Despite the open window the room was warm. He wore a clean white shirt of fine lawn open at the throat, the full sleeves rolled up his forearms. His black hair curled on the nape of his neck. He pushed his fingers through it then braced his head on one hand, the movement emphasizing the width of his shoulders while he continued to write.

Captivated, Roz watched him. She knew he sought escape in work, as she did. For when neither was occupied, the air seemed to shimmer and vibrate with tension. There was no way of undoing what had happened. Nor, even if it were possible, would she want to. When she looked at him she quivered inside. His kiss had been everything she imagined, and more. He knew who and what she was – *though not all of it* – yet he had kissed her. With his mouth on hers and his arms around her she had thought *I am home,*

I am safe.

It made no sense. Their lives could not be more different. They had met only because he was a Justice and her mother a felon. She loved him. She knew that now. Knew, too, it hopeless. For though so far she had evaded capture, she had broken the law. Her only escape from the ache of longing and grinding fear was sleep. But it was an uneasy rest, plagued by dreams.

During these weeks of isolation she had learned to read him, knew he too was fighting battles, though whether they involved her she had no idea. He had become distant, withdrawn. Afraid he regretted their kiss, dreading the moment he would tell her to leave, she took her cue from him and concentrated on her tasks for Davy.

Moistening dry lips, she cleared her throat. 'Forgive me for interrupting,' she spoke softly, her heart leaping as he swung round, revealing dark smears of weariness under his eyes.

'Yes?'

'May I go outside for a little while? I need more woundwort.'

'Of course.' He turned back to his papers. 'You also need fresh air.'

Standing in the ditch, she bent to pick velvety leaves and dropped them in her apron. Through her bodice the sun warmed her back. Her faded calico skirt was hot and uncomfortable. But both muslin gowns had required laundering and neither had yet been returned.

'Miss Trevaskis, how glad I am to see you!'

Straightening up, Roz saw Deborah hurrying

towards her, a shallow basket full of lavender over her arm. 'Good afternoon, Miss Casvellan.'

'Will this be of use to you?' She indicated the basket.

'Indeed, it will,' Roz said with a smile. 'Your younger brother has finally admitted it is very soothing in his bath.'

'Cook tells me he is taking gruel. *Gruel*. We are both astonished.' Deborah laughed. 'What threats did you employ?'

'None were necessary,' Roz said. 'He was bored with barley water. When I explained that the oatmeal would help him regain his strength, and when properly flavoured is very palatable, he was minded to try it. Indeed he finished an entire bowl just an hour ago. When I came out he was sleeping peacefully.'

Deborah smiled. 'This is wonderful news and will surely relieve my mother's anxiety. I can only believe that her determination to expect the worst was an attempt to prepare herself in case—' She stopped, took a deep breath. 'But that is past now. If Davy is taking solid food again surely all will be well.'

'No doubt Mr Casvellan's reply to your mother's letter will add weight to your reassurance.'

A line appeared between Deborah's brows. 'My mother wrote him a letter? How very odd. She did not mention it. I shall go to her at once with the good news. I think you have worked a miracle, Miss Trevaskis.'

'You are very kind. But I only did what Dr Avers—'

'Dr Avers has not set foot on Trescowe since confirming Davy's illness. In all that time, except for these rare interludes to gather herbs, you have not left his bedside. You must allow me to decide who deserves my gratitude.'

'Mr Casvellan—' Roz said before she could stop herself.

Deborah blew a sigh. 'My mother is constantly telling me that men have no place in a sickroom. I daresay that in most cases she would be right. But had she seen him yesterday – I'm glad she didn't. I confess, Miss Trevaskis, I feared for him. He's a superb rider,' she added quickly. 'But his stallion is headstrong and powerful. Watching the pair of them my heart was in my mouth.' She shook her head as if mocking her own foolishness. 'Do you ride?' Even as the words left Deborah's lips, Roz saw a faint blush colour her cheeks and knew she wished them unsaid.

'I – forgive me. That was thoughtless.'

'Please don't apologize,' Roz said quickly as her head filled with images of a dark narrow path, a string of mules, uniformed figures leaping out and the stinging lash of a whip slicing into her skin.

'I am told you work at the Three Mackerel,' Deborah said quietly. Her fingers played with the twisted handle of the basket. 'However, it is clear to me you were born to a very different life and this is why I find myself at ease with you.'

'No,' Roz blurted. 'You do not know me. Your mother would not wish you to know me.'

Deborah's chin rose. 'I hope I am a good and

224

dutiful daughter, but I am no longer a child and reserve the right to choose my own friends. Our acquaintance leads me to believe I should enjoy your friendship very much. But I will not press you.' She set down the basket of lavender a short distance from the ditch. 'I must go or my mother will begin to fret. What a relief it is to have good news for her.'

Don't mention me. Roz pressed her lips together to hold back words that were both a warning and a plea. If asked to explain, what could she say? Deborah's declaration had touched her deeply. To have such a friend ... But no, it wasn't possible. What did they have in common – other than their love for her elder brother?

No matter what Deborah knew, or had heard from gossiping servants, or thought she understood, she didn't have the full facts. Only she, her mother and Will Prowse knew the entire wretched truth.

Mrs Casvellan didn't want her here and would press for her removal the instant Davy was well enough to be looked after by household staff. Every day that passed brought that moment nearer. It was best for everyone that she left. But how would she bear it?

'Roz! Roz!'

Looking round she saw Tom running towards her leading Deborah's mare.

'Tom? What?'

'I just come back from the village. I had to take Miss Deborah's mare to blacksmith.' His thin chest heaved as he gasped for breath. 'I passed Ma on the track. She's coming here. Roz, you got to stop her.'

'You're sure she's coming here?' Roz demanded.

'Yes!' Though Tom was vibrating with anxiety, he held the mare's rein loose and stroked her muzzle gently with a small grubby hand. 'She told me. Said she needed to see you.'

'Has she been drinking?'

Tom nodded. 'If she make trouble, Mr Casvellan will send me away. Roz, I love it here.'

'Hush now, Tom. You won't lose your job.'

'I will if you don't stop her.'

Roz looked at his sweating face, reddening from the effort of holding back tears. Pulling her apron undone she lay the bundle down on the verge. She had to head off her mother and persuade her to go back home. But she couldn't possibly run all the way, not in this heat.

'Tom, I need to borrow the mare.'

He passed her the rein then linked his fingers. 'I'll give you a leg up.'

Her heart swelled. She put her foot into his cupped hands and with strength that surprised her he heaved her up and she swung her leg over the mare's bare back.

'You will stop her, promise?' He ran alongside as she gathered the reins and clicked her tongue.

'I promise.' She urged the mare into a canter, hoping desperately she might reach the trees that lined the drive without being seen.

In the sickroom, unable to settle, Casvellan had risen from his chair at the desk and wandered to the window. Was it yesterday he had caught sight of her as she bent to pick the herb?

He had grown used to seeing her busy at some task, or sitting sewing or reading to Davy. He missed her when she went out. *How foolish was that?*

He gazed down at the lawn and the grassy ditch where the herb grew and watched her as she talked with his sister. Then Deb left and he saw young Tom running towards Roz, dragging Deb's mare. Moments later, Roz was astride the mare's back and hurtling towards the drive.

His frown deepened. Where was she going? Fast and fearless, she rode like a boy. Leaning forward to urge the mare on she reached the trees. Then all he caught were glimpses of light, shadow and movement. Something tugged at his memory. He couldn't grasp – then suddenly – *a dark path ... a string of pack animals.* Shock punched hard, stopping his breath.

If he needed a reason to have nothing more to do with her, he had it now.

Fifteen

Roz had left the drive and was on the moor when she spotted her mother stumbling along the stony rutted road. Dreading the inevitable row but determined to stop her, Roz cantered the mare forward.

As she drew closer she was appalled at her mother's appearance. A grubby fichu filled the neckline of a stained bodice. Her petticoat was filthy, the hem and her scuffed shoes all coated with dust. She had bundled her hair beneath a cap edged with ragged frills, but escaped strands trailed untidily down her neck.

Drawing the mare to a stop, Roz slid to the ground on trembling legs. She moistened her lips. 'Mama! What are you doing here?' The powerful reek of stale sweat and brandy fumes caught in her throat. Guilt at the disgust she was struggling to hide fought with anger that her mother would shame them both by appearing in public in such a state.

'Coming to see you. Which wouldn't have been necessary if you had any consideration,' Mary-Blanche snapped. 'I'm hot and tired and—'

'Why, Mama?' Anxiety and frustration tightened Roz's nerves. Where had her mother obtained the brandy? How had it been paid for? Instantly she shied away from possibilities she couldn't bear to imagine. Hopelessness swamped her. How naïve, how *stupid* she had been, imagining their reunion would be enough to stop her mother drinking.

'What do you mean, *why?* You know perfectly well *why*. You're living in luxury with the Casvellans, and I'm left in that cottage without a penny. I could be starving for all you care.'

Picturing the spartan room in which Davy lay Roz rested her forehead against the mare's warm neck. Had she heeded her grandfather she would have spared herself two years of anxiety and stress. But she would not have met Branoc Casvellan, or worked alongside him, or slept in a bed still warm from his body. Or been kissed, or fallen deeply and hopelessly in love. Soon she would leave Trescowe to return to a life that had been difficult enough before. Now it would be intolerable.

'You needn't look at me like that either,' Mary-Blanche was defiant. 'It's all your fault. You should be home with me. I don't like it on my own.' Despite the hot sunshine she rubbed her arms as if chilled, and muttered, 'I see things.'

Swallowing her wretchedness, Roz softened her voice. 'I'll speak to Mr Casvellan directly about some money.' Her stomach clenched at the prospect. 'But you must go home now.'

'What if I don't want to? You're *my* daughter but I haven't seen anything of you for weeks.'

Roz fought to remain calm. 'Mama, I told you in my letter why I needed to remain here. Davy

Casvellan has the smallpox and none of the staff could nurse him. Because I've had cowpox I was safe from infection. Dr Avers insisted we remain isolated to make sure the disease didn't spread.'

Mary-Blanche eyed her, sullen and suspicious. 'How is he? The boy? Will he live?'

'I hope so. But it's still too soon to be sure.'

'So how much longer are you going to be here?'

Not long enough. 'I can't tell you exactly.'

'Well, that's no good to me. I've got no money, no food—'

'How did you buy the brandy, Mama?'

Mary-Blanche's self-pity switched instantly to aggression and she fisted her hands on her hips. 'Who said I bought it?' she said, glaring. 'I never said I bought it. Anyway, your letter said Mr Casvellan was going to pay you.'

'He will.'

'When? I need money now. There's not a crust of bread in the place, nor even a tallow dip. As for—'

'I'll get you money,' Roz broke in desperately. 'Go home now and I'll send it to you.'

'I've come this far, I might as well come back with you to the house.'

'No.' Roz's tone, flat and abrupt, made Mary-Blanche jump. 'Please, Mama. You shouldn't stay here. It's not safe for you. If the constable should see you—' she stopped. 'Go home. You will have money by tonight.'

'Promise?'

With no idea how she would achieve it but determined her mother should not take one step

230

nearer Trescowe, Roz nodded. 'Yes, I promise. Please, Mama, go on home.'

'I don't know if I can walk all that way,' Mary-Blanche whined. 'My feet are killing me.'

Roz knew she had already been away too long. But if the only way she could get her mother home was to mount her on the mare and lead her back to the village then that was what she would have to do. The clop of hooves and rumble of wheels on the stony track made dread rise like sickness in Roz's throat. She forced herself to look round. Seeing Tamara Varcoe, her closest friend, she could have wept with relief and shame.

Perched on the seat of a small dogcart Tamara reined in the pony, a smile lighting her face. 'Roz, what a lovely surprise! It is so long since I have seen you. But I know how busy you have been. How is young Mr Casvellan?'

'A little better.'

'Devlin says everyone is convinced he would have died but for you.' At Roz's silent, anguished plea Tamara switched her gaze to Mary-Blanche. 'Good afternoon, Mrs Trevaskis. You must be very proud of Roz. Are you going back to the village? You are very welcome to ride with me.'

Flashing her friend a look of deep gratitude, Roz turned to her mother. 'Do go, Mama. It will save you the walk.'

'I wouldn't be out here now if—'

'Mama,' Roz broke in, burning with embarrassment. 'We must not keep Mrs Varcoe waiting in this heat.'

'All right, if I must. But you make sure I hear from you by tonight, or—'

'I gave you my word.' Releasing the mare's rein, Roz helped her mother up into the dogcart, then looked past her to Tamara. 'Thank you.'

Tamara nodded. 'When you are no longer needed at Trescowe do come and see me, Roz. I miss you.' Shortening the reins, she clicked her tongue and the dogcart rattled away along the track.

Roz watched it go, needing to be sure. As it rounded a curve and disappeared from view she led the mare over to a rock, re-mounted, and hurried back toward the house. Tom waited anxiously at the entrance to the drive, hopping from foot to foot.

'Has she gone?'

'Yes.'

'Honest?'

'Truly. Mrs Varcoe came along and took her up in the trap.' Jumping down, Roz handed him the rein. 'Hurry now. Mr Eathorne will be wondering what has become of you.'

As Tom scampered away with the mare trotting beside him, Roz hurried to where she had dropped her apron. Gathering up the bundle of herb, she used one corner of the white cotton to wipe her hot face.

As she turned toward the house some instinct made her look up. Branoc Casvellan was standing at a second-floor window. His frown made her heart lurch. He would want to know why she had been away so long. Taking a deep breath, she crossed cool grass and crunching gravel to the side entrance. When she reached the sick-room, she wiped a damp palm down her petti-coat then opened the door.

Casvellan crossed the bare floor, grasped her upper arm and forced her into the bedroom. Pushing the door almost shut he swung her round to face him.

'Where have you been?' Low-pitched and soft, his voice sent chills down her spine. But she met his gaze.

'Tom was returning from the blacksmith in the village with your sister's mare. He came upon our mother. She was on her way here. He–he wanted me to persuade her to return home.'

'And did you?'

Her mouth was bone dry, her swallow audible, and she had to push her tongue between her teeth and upper lip to free it. 'Yes. Fortunately Tamara – Mrs Varcoe – arrived in her dogcart on her way to the village. She kindly offered my mother a ride home.'

'Why was your mother coming here?'

Mortification burned. 'She has no food or candles. I promised her I would send some money to her by tonight.'

His gaze bored into hers. 'And once she has the money, do you really believe she will buy food?'

Roz's chin rose. 'What am I supposed to do? Leave her to starve? If I were there I would shop. But I'm not. She's alone, and she doesn't cope well by herself.'

'How convenient for her. So you must dance to any tune of her choosing.' Before she could reply, he swung away, rubbing the back of his neck. 'I promised you payment for nursing my brother. I will have part of the agreed sum delivered to her this afternoon. If that is what you wish.'

'Thank you.'

He continued as if she had not spoken. 'Or you could prepare a list of provisions you think she will need. I will send a servant with the list and money, and instructions to the shopkeeper to deliver the goods.'

'Yes, yes, that would be best. Thank you. You are very kind.' She started for the door. 'I will go and—'

'Stay where you are.'

Startled, Roz glanced round. Cold fingers gripped her heart and squeezed. She had seen him angry. But never like this.

'What? Oh no. No, not Davy. Truly, I did not intend to be out so long.'

Casvellan shook his head. 'His condition has not changed.'

Relief weakened her. 'Then what?'

'Remind me,' he invited with lethal calm. 'How did you obtain that scar on your face?'

Roz felt the blood drain from her head. The room swayed and black spots filled her vision. She staggered, groped for the bed, and sank onto it, clutching the brass foot post as icy perspiration dewed her face and body. Pins and needles stabbed her hands and feet. Then scalding heat rushed like a breaking wave from her toes to the roots of her hair.

He must have seen her jump onto his sister's

mare. Something about her riding had jogged his memory, betrayed her. He could not prove anything. But if she lied to him now she would forfeit his trust forever.

'Well?' His tone was harsh.

She raised her head. In his eyes, behind bitter fury, she glimpsed grief. 'From the lash of your whip.'

His expression pierced her soul. 'I thought I had missed. You made no sound.'

'It would have betrayed me. I thought only of escape with what cargo had not been taken by the dragoons.'

He raked his hair, strode toward the window, then whirled round once more. 'You lied to me.'

'I had no choice,' she cried. 'Every single day I have regretted—' tears clogged her throat and she threw up one hand in a gesture of hopelessness. How could she expect him to understand?

'Why in the name of all that's holy did you get involved in smuggling?'

Tears spilled over her lashes and tracked down her cheeks. She dashed them away impatiently, clinging to the rags of her pride. 'How else was I to pay my mother's fines, and rent for the cottage, and still put food on the table?' *Even then it hadn't been enough. She'd had to borrow from Will Prowse.*

'Bran? Roz?' At his brother's raspy shout Casvellan's breath hissed in frustration.

Roz stood up. She felt as fragile as fine glass. But she would say it before he could. 'You will wish me to leave.'

He looked down his nose at her. 'Do not

235

presume to make my decisions.' As her face flamed he continued with cutting disdain, 'I will not have my brother upset. Until he is out of danger you will remain here and continue nursing him.'

'Bran! Where are you? Roz?'

'I will attend to him,' Casvellan said. 'Meanwhile, you write the list of your mother's requirements.' Reaching the door he called to his brother. 'One moment, Davy. I'm on my way.' Then he looked back over his shoulder. 'Despite what I have learned this afternoon,' his throat worked and she saw a muscle jump in his jaw. Then he inclined his head with a formality that left her utterly desolate. 'You will always have my gratitude.'

'That's not what I—' she managed to stop just in time, before she betrayed herself and embarrassed him.

One dark brow lifted. 'Then what *do* you want? Ah, of course. Money.'

Roz flinched as if he had slapped her. But he was at the doorway and walked through without looking back.

Davy's illness had made considerable physical demands on her. But she and Casvellan had worked as a team. That was then. It was different now. Before, sharing tasks had deepened understanding and nurtured friendship. Now there was coolness and distance.

Each night when she fell into bed she wondered if she could go on. When she woke and forced herself up to begin another day, she dreaded facing him. But Davy still required nursing and his bed changed every morning. The floors and surfaces, bowls and buckets, even the bath, required disinfecting after every use.

She *could* leave. Casvellan would not physically restrain her. And being a man of honour he would pay her as promised. Which was why she could not go. She was too much in his debt to walk out on him while he still needed her.

Davy continued to make progress. She left the compresses off, exposing his hands and feet to the air so that scabs might form more quickly, and read to him until she was hoarse to take his mind off the itching. As his appetite improved she ordered steamed fish and lightly boiled eggs to supplement the creamed oatmeal.

'This is invalid food,' he grumbled.

'You have been very ill,' she replied. 'But your feet are healing well and I think it won't be long before you are able to take a turn about the room. Now, for your dessert this evening I suggest a milk pudding flavoured with nutmeg, cinnamon and cloves. It's a favourite recipe of my grandmother's. She claims it's the best thing she knows for calming the mind and strengthening the blood.'

When she set the tray before him he ate every scrap.

But even while she tried to remain focused on her daily tasks and on whichever book she was reading to Davy, every nerve and fibre of her body quivered as taut as piano wire with awareness of Casvellan.

He carried buckets and trays, tended the fires, lifted his brother, and helped fill and empty the bath. The rest of the time he worked at the table, dealing with the piles of work his clerk sent over every morning.

By unspoken agreement they tried for Davy's sake to carry on as before. But very soon Roz noticed Davy frowning as his gaze darted between her and his brother. Desperate to avoid questions she did not know how to answer she made a valiant effort to appear cheerful and divert his attention. It had worked – so far. But last night, the third in a row, she had crawled into bed with a blinding headache.

Casvellan folded the razor and set it aside. He rinsed off the remaining lather then picked up the towel and buried his face in it. If he needed further reason – as if her mother were not enough – to have nothing more to do with her, he had it. Roz Trevaskis was a smuggler. *No, she had simply led the string of pack animals.* Had anyone else offered that excuse in mitigation would he have accepted it? No, he would not.

But nor could he have proven her involvement. He had no witness. The men caught and questioned had remained stubbornly silent. His only evidence was a fine scar and her resemblance to a boyish rider he had glimpsed fleeing the dragoons.

She could have lied. Many would have. Yet she had not. A dark flush had replaced the pallor of shock. But despite her shame – and there was no doubting it – she had held his gaze and told him the truth.

Her scar was his doing. His whip had sliced

Casvellan's mouth. 'I believe it is. It is from a Captain of Dragoons called Visick. He says he is newly posted to the area after service abroad. And he is interested in my young stallion.' Crossing to Davy's bed, Casvellan sat on the side of it. 'He learned of Raad's lineage from Charles Kerrow of Trenarwyn.'

'Didn't Mr Kerrow buy Raad's great grandsire from our grandfather?' Davy asked.

'Indeed he did. Captain Visick has come into an inheritance. He wants to buy Raad to race him. Should Raad win—'

'Which he will,' Davy interrupted, his eyes bright with excitement. 'He was called lightning for a reason.'

'We'll see.'

'If he did win, he'd be hugely valuable as a stud horse.' Davy paused, fingering the sheet. 'But he wouldn't be yours any more.'

The emotions chasing across his brother's face echoed Casvellan's own. 'True, but I'd have money to invest in the estate and farms.'

'That's not ... I mean, I know it's important, but...' Davy slumped back on the pillows. 'Would he not take Bourkan instead?'

'Bourkan's a stud horse. He's been out of training for too long. He wouldn't be suitable for racing.'

'But Raad, he's your favourite, Bran.'

Concerned at the febrile glitter in his brother's eyes, Casvellan smiled. 'Perhaps the Captain and I might be able to work out an agreement that would allow me to retain an interest.' He stood up. 'First things first. I shan't be making any decisions until I've met him. Now drink your lemonade.'

Davy snorted, muttering, 'Lemonade.' And the moment passed. But as Casvellan moved to the table to read the rest of his mail, he saw Roz wring out a muslin cloth in fresh water and lay it on Davy's forehead.

'What's that for?' Davy demanded.

'I'm sorry, is it too cold?' Roz enquired.

'No,' he allowed. 'Actually it's quite nice. Refreshing.'

'That's what it's for,' she said with a smile. As she turned away Casvellan caught her eye and gave an imperceptible nod of thanks. It wasn't until he was breaking the wafer on the next letter that he realized. *Davy had noticed what he had not. Her eyes: she had been crying.*

Anger churned inside him. Whose fault was that? He would ignore it, and her. That was what she wanted, wasn't it? Why wouldn't she look at him? What else could he do?

Bombarded by an unsettling sense of guilt – an experience he disliked intensely and didn't know how to combat – he opened the letter and recognized his clerk's handwriting. Why had Ellacott sealed this but none of the others? His gaze skimmed over the neat lines, but because his mind was still on Roz he wasn't fully concentrating.

Then he saw Mary-Blanche Trevaskis's name, followed by that of Sir Edward Pengarrick.

242

Sixteen

Roz swirled a lavender bag in the water and squeezed it several times to release the fragrance and soothing properties. Soaking another cloth she wrung it out and lay it on Davy's forehead in place of the first.

'You're putting scent on me again,' he grumbled but didn't open his eyes.

'Many fashionable gentlemen wear cologne,' Roz countered as she straightened the covers. Casvellan did. She recalled the faint hint of it in his justice room: subtle, astringent, and perfect for him. During their isolation here he had foregone it. Instead they shared a cake of soap, its fragrance recognizable yet different on his skin. Misery wrenched her heart and she forced her attention back to Davy, her tone light. 'It is considered quite the thing.'

'Not lavender, they don't.' His voice slurred.

'Don't worry,' Roz said softly. 'You will soon be well, then you may choose something more suitable.' She hoped he would sleep for at least an hour. Bored and frustrated with his confinement, he was pushing himself beyond his strength.

'Miss Trevaskis?' The abruptness of Casvellan's tone made Roz swallow involuntarily. 'I need a few moments, if you please.'

Straightening, she saw that he had moved towards the bedroom door. What could he want? Surely everything had been said?

He gestured towards the open door. She noticed he was holding a letter. Wiping her hands down her white apron she glanced back at Davy who had drifted into sleep. Her pulse quickening, she passed Casvellan who followed her into the bedroom.

Crossing to the window, Roz folded her arms in an instinctive gesture of self-protection and turned to face him.

Casvellan looked once more at the letter then lowered it. 'I ... There is no easy way to...' He drew a breath. 'Ellacott informs me that your mother was arrested for drunkenness and disorderly behaviour, and was taken before Sir Edward Pengarrick. He has sentenced her to be whipped at the cart's tail.'

As shock jerked her, Roz's hand flew up to cover her mouth.

'I'm sorry to bring you such—' He broke off with a muttered curse. 'Are you all right? Would you like some water?'

Fighting shame that made her want to run and hide, she forced her head up and met his gaze. It was nearly her undoing, for his face was tight with anger.

'When?' It emerged as a hoarse whisper forcing her to clear her throat.

'At noon on Saturday. Tomorrow.'

'Does he say where? Will it be in Porthinnis?' *Please, please, let it be the village.* But Cas-

244

vellan was already shaking his head.

'Helston.'

Roz closed her eyes: a whipping in the town centre at the busiest time of the busiest day of the week. Her mother – daughter of a respected clergyman and justice – was to be a public spectacle. Stripped to the waist, tied to the tailboard of a cart and dragged through the main street while the constable administered a whipping. A punishment supposed to act as a warning to others, yet also a deliberate invitation to scorn and mockery.

Perhaps it was as well that Casvellan's discovery of her smuggling activities had snuffed out any possibility of even friendship between them before news of this latest embarrassment.

'I'm sorry,' he said stiffly. 'And I bear some responsibility. Pengarrick will be aware of your mother's past record, and that the sentences I passed failed to curb her behaviour.' He looked away. 'Had I been more stringent—'

'It would have made no difference,' Roz spoke through trembling lips, appalled at the deliberately degrading nature of the sentence. Where had her mother obtained the brandy? What had driven her out into the street? *What kind of disorderly behaviour?* Surely her mother must have known the constable would be called? Or, frightened of being alone, was she beyond caring?

'You were kinder than she deserved. If she had only responded...' Roz shook her head. 'But she didn't, or couldn't. The responsibility is hers, no one else's.'

'And she will pay. However, I cannot absolve myself entirely. Pengarrick's sentence is also a calculated insult directed at me. He ... We do not get on.'

Roz clasped her arms more tightly. 'I know.' As he looked up she explained. 'The whole village knows. Sir Edward is neither liked nor respected in Porthinnis.' *Unlike you*, she wanted to say, but held back, fearful he might think she was trying to curry favour. 'Even so, I would not have you assume responsibility for something not your fault.' She moistened her lips. 'Mr Casvellan, I must be with her. I cannot let her face this alone.'

'Why?' He frowned. 'She deserted you. And since coming back into your life she has caused you nothing but trouble and sorrow. Why are you willing to stand by such a woman? Why would you wish to?'

'Because...' Roz shrugged helplessly. 'Because despite all that she is still my mother. And because she has no one else.'

'Whose fault is that?' he hissed, his voice vibrating with anger and the effort of keeping his voice low. 'She ran away and left you.'

'She had no alternative.'

'So *she* says.' He was scathing.

'No one leaves a *happy* home,' Roz cried. 'No mother *willingly* abandons her child.'

'Do you say that because you believe it?' His voice was harsh. 'Or because the alternative is too painful to accept?'

She rubbed her arms, cold despite the summer heat and the fire burning in the grate. 'Do you imagine I have not asked myself a thousand times? Why did she go? Had she no feelings at all for me?' She raised her chin. 'I know what most people think. I see it in their faces. But I am not so poor that I would beg for sympathy, especially yours.' She turned her head away, blinking to dispel burning tears before they could fall.

'I beg your pardon. I should not have...' Muttering a violent oath he raked his hair.

She barely heard him as she fought for control, her throat painfully stiff. 'Have I your permission to go to Helston on Saturday?'

'Of course. But how will you get there? I will speak to my sister. I'm sure she would be willing to—'

'No,' she said quickly. 'It is very good of you, but I will find my own way.'

'As I know you to be very resourceful I have no doubt you'll succeed,' he retorted bitterly. 'But in your determination not to accept any assistance from me, you appear to have forgotten something. It's unlikely your mother will be capable of walking back to Porthinnis.'

His words stung and she flushed. 'I had not forgotten.' She raised her eyes to his. 'Nor will I ever forget the great kindness your sister has shown me. That is why I cannot accept.'

He gestured impatiently. 'What?'

'Please, hear me out. Sir Edward has shown considerable interest in your horses. It is possible he may be in Helston. Not to watch: I doubt my mother is sufficiently important, or that he would even recall her face. But if he should see

Miss Casvellan, or recognize her mare ... Roz took a breath and forced the words out. 'Any connection with my mother and me can only cause your family embarrassment.'

There, she had said it. Since her first visit to his justice rooms and during the precious days she had spent here with him caring for Davy, even when common sense mocked her foolish fantasies she had allowed herself to hope that *perhaps, maybe*. But the dream was over, burned away by the searing heat of reality. She forced herself to continue.

'Jack – Mr Hicks – goes into Helston on Saturday mornings to pick up provisions. I am confident he will allow me to ride in with him and we can bring my mother back on the cart.'

'Then it appears everything is settled.' He was suddenly distant.

'Thank you.'

'I would be obliged if you will remain here until the morning.'

'Of course,' Roz said, surprised. 'Once I have taken my mother back to the cottage and tended—'

He silenced her with a gesture and turned away, gazing fixedly at the hearth. 'It is likely she will require considerable attention. Under the circumstances...' He turned his head away and she heard him clear his throat. When he looked at her his face was expressionless. He had withdrawn behind an impenetrable barrier. 'This would be an appropriate time to conclude your engagement here. Davy is recovering well and Avers can tell me what is required for his convalescence. I will have Ellacott prepare a purse of the money you are owed.'

Each word rocked her like a hammer blow. She gripped her hands so tightly the bones hurt. But focusing on that small pain enabled her to hold herself straight. Obviously he wanted to be rid of her. Her usefulness could no longer counter the embarrassment of her continued presence.

Grief threatened to choke her. She cleared her throat. 'As you wish, sir.'

With a terse nod he walked out.

Her legs buckled and she sank down on the bed. She could not – did not – blame him. She had known her stay here was limited to the duration of Davy's illness. Yet leaving would be the hardest thing she had ever done, far harder than leaving the security of her grandparents' home. But she had survived that and she would survive this.

She heard a chair scrape against the floorboards. The sickroom door opened, closed. In the passage his footsteps headed toward the back stairs.

She woke at dawn still tired after a restless night.

When she got up to take her turn sitting with Davy, he had immediately sent her back to bed, his tone and manner allowing no argument. Determined to complete her usual tasks before she left, she pushed back the covers and saw, just inside the door, a copper can of hot water. Tears welled, spilling down her cheeks before she could stop them.

Scrubbing them away, she washed, then pulled

on a clean shift and stockings. The freshly laundered blue muslin hung over the back of the chair where she had laid it the previous evening. The apricot one was rolled up ready to be washed. Both gowns reminded her of Deborah's offer of friendship: a gift offered in all sincerity but impossible to accept. Turning away, Roz put on the print bodice and calico petticoat she had been wearing the day she brought Davy home, then tied on the dowlas apron. After tidying the bedroom, she picked up the copper can and entered the sickroom.

Davy was still asleep. As she started forward Casvellan rose from the armchair and she caught her breath. The shutters were folded back and the early light was paling from grey to primrose.

She lifted the water can. 'Thank you.'

'I was awake. There's chocolate,' he gestured toward the narrow table. There were two cups beside the jug, and a drawstring purse of fine soft leather.

Setting down the can she crossed to the table, lifted the jug and glanced at him. 'Shall I pour you—?'

'Later.' He was brusque. 'Drink it while it's hot.'

She poured steaming chocolate into a cup. Standing at the window with her back to him she cradled it between trembling hands and lifted it to her mouth. The thick sweet liquid slid down her parched throat and curled warmly in her stomach, soothing the ache that had kept her awake for much of the night. Each time she stirred she had heard him moving about, and the

250

low murmur as he read to his brother.

Draining the cup, she set it down carefully. Already she felt stronger. Making an effort to smile she turned to thank him. But her throat dried as he looked at her.

'No doubt,' he said carefully, shifting his gaze towards his sleeping brother, 'you will have things to do at home before you leave for Helston.' She saw his throat work as he swallowed. 'That being the case, you should leave now.'

Roz looked at him, about to protest, to remind him of all the jobs she did each morning while he slept. Then she pressed her lips together. She didn't need to remind him. He knew, and would already have made alternative arrangements.

'Tom should be waiting on the drive with Deborah's mare.' His gaze remained fixed on his brother. 'He can ride behind you as far as the village, then bring the mare back here. I must have my way in this,' he insisted before she could speak. 'God knows it is little enough—' He broke off, inhaled deeply. 'Today will be difficult for you. Do not make it more so.'

With the choking lump in her throat making speech impossible, Roz could only nod. Swallowing repeatedly, she picked up the purse and walked blindly past him to the bedroom pulling off the dowlas apron. Removing the pretty kid slippers, she pushed her feet into her boots and quickly tied the laces while her chest heaved with sobs. She had arrived with nothing. She was leaving with less, for her heart would remain here. *She didn't want to go. He didn't want her to stay.*

251

She wiped her wet face on the towel, and straightened her spine. Right now it was too painful to look back, to find comfort in memories. She must focus on the next few minutes, on leaving with dignity.

Once outside she would think only of seeing Tom and riding across the moor to the village. Each small parcel of minutes was manageable. She would cope. *She had no choice.* Filling her lungs slowly, she held the breath, then released it and returned to the sickroom.

Casvellan was standing by the window, feet apart, arms folded. As she entered he turned.

'Sir—' Roz began and fell silent at his abrupt gesture.

'No, Roz, no *sir.*' At his weary smile she felt her heart break.

She gave a brief nod, knowing exactly what he meant. In here where they had shared so much, formality had no place.

She saw him hesitate. Would he come forward? Offer his hand? She wanted him to, longed for one last touch. But feared it as well. For it would only remind her of sensations and longings best forgotten. The tension in his jaw revealed his own inner battle. There was one last thing she could do for him.

'Goodbye,' she whispered. Then turned and left.

As she crossed the grass she glanced back. He was standing at the window. But through her tears his face was just a blur.

'Be all right will you, girl?' Jack Hicks demanded as Roz climbed down from the cart.

She nodded and reached up for the basket. It contained a pot of woundwort salve and strips of linen, the least dirty of her mother's bodices, flour, tea, a loaf and vegetables she had paid for with money from the purse Casvellan had left for her.

'Want to leave the basket with me?' he offered.

Roz shook her head. 'I still have things to buy. It's not yet eleven, so I've at least an hour before...' she couldn't continue.

'All right, my bird. Listen, soon as I'm done I'll go on down by the market. I'll watch out for 'ee.' Clicking his tongue he urged the cob away.

Eggs, butter, meat, soap and candles. Roz silently recited her list as she made her way towards the main street. Despite the smallpox, Helston town centre was as crowded as she had feared. While women shopped and children clustered hopefully at the sweet stalls lining the wide sloping street, tradesmen led pack animals or drove loaded wagons through the throng.

Farmer's wives wearing crisp white bodices and calamanco petticoats bustled past well-to-do ladies dressed in high-waisted muslins and feathered turbans lingering to look at the window displays of milliners, drapers and haberdashery shops. Gentlemen in well-cut frock-coats, pale pantaloons and highly polished hessians shared pavements with farmers and miners in shirtsleeves and waistcoats, coarse breeches and working men's lace-up boots.

Roz went quickly from shop to shop, pushing her way through the milling people, mentally ticking off each item as she filled her basket. Then it was time.

The gaol was situated between the Coinage Hall and the Duchy Officer's house. Shock sent an uncomfortable tingling along her limbs as she approached and saw a horse and cart waiting outside. Her mouth suddenly dried while perspiration prickled her forehead and the back of her neck. She forced herself forward while her heart thumped harder and faster against her ribs.

She didn't recognize the constable standing by the open door. In his forties, ruddy-faced and stocky, he was slapping a cudgel rhythmically against his palm as he looked up and down the street. As she crossed the road the clock struck noon and a younger constable led her mother out.

Her hands were cuffed in front of her with iron shackles. Dirty and unkempt, shaking uncontrollably, she was wearing only a dirty shift, a stained black woollen petticoat, grey stockings and down-at-heel leather shoes. Her stays had been removed.

Burning with shame and wrenched by pity, Roz eased past people who had stopped to watch, and reached the constable who had shoved his cudgel into his belt and put out a hand.

'Stay back now,' he was sharp. 'No one allowed near the prisoner.'

Flushing, Roz stood her ground. 'This lady is my mother.'

'Some lady,' the constable sneered. 'Now get back out of it, or I'll—'

'Please,' Roz spoke quietly. 'May I speak to you? I promise I won't make trouble. Please?' Tempted to invoke Casvellan's name, she resisted. He had been more than fair to her mother. It would be wrong to embroil him in this.

Snorting impatiently, the constable clicked his tongue. 'Go on then, say what you got to say and be quick about it.'

'You look like a fair man, and you hold a position of trust. In the name of charity, please let me walk with her. Surely a public whipping is disgrace enough?'

The constable frowned, then jerked his chin forward. 'I dunno.'

'Please?'

He sniffed. 'All right. But you don't touch her,' he warned. Then after a quick glance round he muttered. 'Better for you if you made yourself scarce. You stay and you'll be part of the show.'

Roz shrivelled inside. She knew only too well. 'I can't abandon her.' She looked at the woman who had given birth to her, walked out of her life, and now stood trembling as she gasped for air. 'I can't. Whatever she's done she's still my mother.'

The constable shrugged. 'More fool you.' He eyed her basket. 'You'd better put that in the back of the cart.'

While Roz did as he suggested, the constable passed a rope through the shackles. As he tied it to an iron ring screwed into the top of the tailboard, it pulled Mary-Blanche's arms up in front of her at shoulder height. People were stopping

255

to stare and murmur.

Roz turned to face her mother, her back to the tailboard. 'Mama?'

Shuddering, Mary-Blanche didn't respond.

'Mama!' Roz pitched her voice low but loud enough to carry. 'It's Roz, Mama. Look at me!'

Mary-Blanche raised her head. For an instant she seemed bewildered.

'It's me, Mama.'

'Roz?' Her voice sounded rough and hoarse, as if she had been shouting. 'What are you doing here? This is no place for you. You shouldn't have come.' Mary-Blanche's face crumpled and tears left tracks down her grimy cheeks.

'I couldn't let you face this alone.' Even as she spoke a part of Roz wished she were somewhere – anywhere – else.

The cart rocked as the driver climbed up onto the seat. The constable caught Roz's eye and gave a brief nod. Then stepping forward he took hold of the back of Mary-Blanche's shift and ripped it apart from neck to waist. Roz dug her nails into her palms as gasps and murmurs rippled through the crowd.

'I'm going to stay with you.' Somehow she kept her voice level while dread quickened her heartbeat.

As the cart moved forward pulling her with it, Mary-Blanche stiffened, her eyes widening. The constable pulled a short leather-covered handle out of his belt and shook the coiled lash loose.

Feeling sick, Roz swallowed hard. She wanted to run, get as far away as she could, until it was all over. But if she did, how would she live with herself? She couldn't. She positioned herself so she was just ahead and to one side of her mother.

'Mama.' Her voice was soft, urgent. 'Look at me.'

The constable's arm rose and fell, the lash whistled through the air. As it lay across her bare skin, Mary-Blanche cried out in shock and pain, arching her back. There was a collective intake of breath from the crowd.

'Ma, what's that man hitting her for?' a child cried.

'She been bad,' his mother replied. 'That's what 'appen when you do bad things. So you mind what I tell you.'

Roz held her mother's terror-stricken gaze. 'Look at me, Mama. Keep your eyes on mine.'

'I can't—' Mary-Blanche's wail was cut short by a gasp.

'You can. Come on. Look at me. I'm here and I'll stay with you.'

The lash struck again and again. Surrounded by the watching crowd, sensing their disgust and their avidity, Roz saw every stroke. She heard her mother's cries turn from gasps of shock to shouts of agony and eventually cracked screams. Roz wanted to scream herself. Sobs trembled in her chest but she kept swallowing them down.

By the time the cart reached the bottom of the street, her mother was semi-conscious and whimpering. As the driver pulled the cart to a halt Mary-Blanche's eyes rolled up in her head and she collapsed in a dead faint, her head lolling between her outstretched arms. Blood oozing from flesh scraped raw by the shackles trickled in crimson rivulets down her arms.

Roz dived forward, holding her mother's body off the dung-strewn street. 'For the love of God, surely that's enough?' she cried.

The constable nodded, avoiding her eyes as he coiled the lash and jammed it in his belt. Then he untied the rope. The crowd who had watched with mingled horror and fascination turn away in search of other amusement. Mary-Blanche moaned with pain as he removed the shackles.

'You didn't ought to 'ave stayed,' he muttered. 'But you're some brave maid, I'll say that for 'ee. How you going get 'er 'ome?'

'A friend – down at the cattle market.' Despite the heat Roz was cold to her bones and her teeth were chattering.

'Well, you can't carry 'er.' He sighed and let the tailboard down. 'Get on the cart and pull 'er up. Janner'll take 'ee. Janner!' He shouted and the driver glanced over his shoulder. 'Take 'em down the market.'

'Thank you,' Roz managed. Sitting on the bare boards, holding her groaning mother face down across her lap, Roz's head throbbed. Tasting blood where she had bitten through her lip, she reached for the pot of salve in her basket and smeared it gently across the welts criss-crossing her mother's back. After laying strips of linen on top she shook out a kerchief and arranged it around Mary-Blanche's shoulders.

Roz saw Jack, as Janner stopped the cart. 'Thank you,' she called. 'We're very grateful.' As she jumped down her legs were so shaky she would have fallen had she not clutched the tailboard just in time. She placed her basket by her feet, then carefully helped her mother to the ground. Mary-Blanche moved slowly, her face grey as she sucked air through her teeth. Huge drops of sweat trickled down her temples and her hair was plastered to her forehead.

Jack reached inside his coat and pulled out a pewter flask. Unscrewing the top he thrust it at Roz.

'Drink. Don't argue. Look like death you do.'

Roz swallowed, coughing as the brandy burned her throat. But as the spirit's heat warmed her stomach and crept along her shaking limbs she felt better. When her mother seized the flask and gulped several mouthfuls, Jack caught Roz's eye and shook his head. But neither had the heart to stop her.

Seventeen

Making her mother as comfortable as possible among the sacks and crates in the back of the cart, Roz wedged in her basket then climbed up beside Jack for the drive back to the village.

'How's young Casvellan? Be all right will he?' Jack asked, urging the cob into a brisk trot.

Bracing herself as the wheels rumbled over hard-baked ruts and gullies, Roz's grip on the wooden seat tightened. 'I believe so.'

'Justice would've been in some bad way but for you. I hope he paid you proper.'

Roz nodded. 'He was very fair.'

Jack lowered his voice. 'Well, 'tidn for me to say,' he glanced over his shoulder, jerking his head towards her mother. 'But if you leave she get her hands on it,' he hissed air through his teeth, 'be gone quicker'n snow on a fire, it will.'

'I know.' Roz reached into the waistband of her petticoat and pulled out a cotton square knotted to form a small pouch that made a muffled clinking sound as she passed it to him. 'Our quarter's rent is wrapped in the gauze,' she spoke softly. 'The rest will pay off what I owe Will Prowse. Will you see he gets it?'

With a brief nod, Jack put the bundle in his coat pocket. 'Nell 'ave missed you awful,' he said after a while. 'Annie been good as gold doing extra shifts and all. But that Keren,' he rolled his eyes. 'Daft as a carrot 'alf scraped, she is. 'Ow's young Tom going on?'

Picturing her young half-brother, Roz felt the tension in her neck and shoulders ease a little. 'Very well. He's blissfully happy.'

Jack nodded. 'Best place for'n if you ask me, specially if Dan Eathorne 'ave taken a shine to 'n. Good ol' boy, Dan is. He'll work the lad 'ard. But what Dan don't know 'bout 'orses idn worth knowing. So,' he added. 'I can tell Nell you'll be back to work Monday?'

Roz forced a smile. 'Yes.'

Jack drove round to the rear of the inn. Toby hurried out, nodded a greeting, and held the cob's head while Roz jumped down. Once the tailboard was lowered she lifted out her basket and set it aside. Then she and Jack helped her mother off the cart. Mary-Blanche moved stiffly like a very old woman, clutching the kerchief around her and wincing with every step as she clung to Roz's supporting arm.

'Manage, can you?' Jack frowned.

'Yes.' Roz nodded. 'We're fine now. Thank you so much for the ride back.'

'You get on inside quick,' he urged. 'Afore some nosy beggar come out to see what's on.'

Reaching the cottage, Roz dropped her basket, opened the door and guided her mother to a wooden stool. 'Just give me a moment to light the fire, Mama.'

'It hurts,' Mary-Blanche moaned.

'I know.' Roz closed the door. The cottage had

only one small window at the front and normally the door was left open to let in more light. But dressing her mother's wounds demanded privacy. 'As soon as the kettle boils I'll make you some tea.'

'That won't help.'

'No, but hot compresses will.'

Once the wood was burning she pulled the filled kettle over the flames and emptied her basket onto the table. Lighting two spermaceti candles from the bundle she had bought, she put them in holders on the shelf above the fire.

She carried a cup of tea to her mother whose hands trembled as she reached for it.

'You haven't got a drop of brandy, have you?'

Covering her mother's hands with her own, Roz helped her lift the cup to her mouth. 'No, I haven't. Can you hold it by yourself?'

'Where are you going?'

'Just to get things ready. As soon as you've drunk your tea I'll attend to your back.'

Pouring hot water into a basin, Roz set out large squares and strips of old muslin and the pot of salve.

'Here.' Tremors shook Mary-Blanche's hand as she held out the empty cup.

'I'll make some more as soon as we're finished.'

'It hurts so much, Roz.'

'I promise I'll be careful. Nothing could be worse than what you've already endured. You were so brave,' Roz said as she removed her mother's petticoat, stockings and shoes. The smell of stale perspiration and a body too long unwashed was unpleasant. *The stench of small-pox had been far worse. And yet ...* Roz shied away from memories still too raw to revisit.

With great care she soaked the bloodstained strips of linen and the torn remnants of shift from her mother's back, clenching her teeth as she revealed criss-crossed scarlet welts sur-rounded by crimson and purple bruising. Trying to ignore her mother's gasps and cries she bathed the lacerated skin and very gently dabbed away oozing blood.

Soaking two large squares of muslin in hot water, she wrung them out and spread salve on one, placed the other on top of it and laid the poultice gently on her mother's back. As she bound it in place, Mary-Blanche rested her fore-head against Roz's shoulder.

'It's too much,' she sobbed. 'Roz, for the love of God get me some brandy. I can't cope with this. I can't.'

Roz felt as if she were being ripped in half. She remembered the fiery stinging pain of Casvellan's lash across her face. Her mother's wounds were far worse. If she was asking – beg-ging – Roz to get brandy, then clearly there was none in the cottage. But brandy was the reason for her whipping, and the cause of her degrada-tion. To give her more – even in such desperate circumstances ... 'Mama, I can't.'

Turning away she gathered up the blood-stained cloths and dropped them onto the flames.

'I'm in agony!' Mary-Blanche shouted, her voice clogged with tears. 'But you don't care! You're spiteful and mean and cruel!'

Roz sank into the wooden armchair by the fire and buried her face in her hands. This was what she had come back to?

When she reached the cottage that morning and opened the door she had gagged at the foetid smell. Seeing the mess and squalor she had wanted to turn around and walk away. But she couldn't, for she had nowhere to go. Though she had left her heart at Trescowe, this, for better or worse, was her home. And today her mother had needed her more than ever before.

So she had gone inside and started work. After cleaning out the overflowing grate she had re-lit the fire, emptied the chamber pot and ashes down the stinking cesspit and tidied the room. It had taken three kettles of boiling water to scrub all the filthy pans and dishes, and another to clean the accumulated grease, spills and grime from the table and shelves. She had brushed the hearth, washed the floor, shaken the rug, and brought in more kindling and logs.

Then she'd just had time to wash, change into a clean bodice and petticoat, and put on her straw bonnet ready to ride into Helston with Jack.

'What's wrong?' Mary-Blanche demanded. 'Roz?' Her voice was edged with fear. 'I didn't mean it about you being cruel. But the pain – my back feels like it's on fire.'

Sucking in a breath, Roz made herself sit up, wiping away tears with her fingertips. 'It will ease, Mama. And I promise you the poultice will help. I'm just tired, that's all.' Pushing to her feet she refilled the kettle. As she set the pitcher

264

down and turned to the table, she heard footsteps outside. Then with a crash that made her jump the door flew open and Will Prowse stood framed in the opening.

'So, you're 'ome, are you? 'Bout bleddy time.'

He had come for the money. Roz ran her tongue over paper-dry lips. 'Mr Prowse, my mother is unwell—'

'Your mother 'ave just been flogged at the cart's tail,' he snarled.

Roz drew herself up. 'Then you will understand that this is not a convenient time.'

'Tis never a *convenient* time with you,' Will mimicked savagely. 'Well, too bleddy bad.'

'Please, go and see Jack. He has—'

'I'll see Jack when I'm ready.' He pointed at Mary-Blanche. 'Her and me got some business to settle.'

'I can't talk to you now. I'm in pain,' Mary-Blanche whimpered. 'Roz, make him go away!'

'We made a bargain,' Will persisted. 'I kept my side of it. But I'm still waiting.'

'What bargain?' Roz pressed fingers to her throbbing head.

'Don't listen to him,' Mary-Blanche shrieked. 'He's lying.'

'*I'm* lying? You wouldn't know truth if it bit you in the arse,' Will spat.

'Stop it!' Roz cried. Then she turned to the smuggler. 'What are you talking about, Mr Prowse? What bargain?'

'Brandy, of course. Good stuff it was too. Finest cognac.'

Roz didn't understand. 'You sold her brandy?

But—'

'Sold? 'Ow could I do that when she never got a farthing to scratch 'erself with? She 'ad it for free. Two bleddy tubs. She promised if I gived 'er brandy, she would see to it that you married me.'

'What?' Roz shook her head. 'I don't believe you.'

'Ask 'er,' Will gestured. 'Go on. I aren't the one lying.'

Roz swung round. Her mother's shrug mingled defiance and desperation. 'What was I s'posed to do? I needed it. But you wouldn't give me the money.'

Roz stared at her mother, realizing with horror and wrenching shame that Will Prowse was telling the truth. 'We didn't *have* the money, Mama. Every penny I earned went on food and rent and your fines.'

'That's right,' Mary-Blanche cried. 'Blame me.'

Feeling sick, Roz turned back to Will. 'I'm sorry, Mr Prowse. You wasted your brandy. You already had my answer.'

'But she said—'

'She had no right to make promises on my behalf. And I'm certainly not bound by them.'

'Roz,' Mary-Blanche wailed.

'You owe me,' Will shouted at her. 'I been good to you. I gived you work and loaned you money. Any'ow, tidn like anyone else is after you. Promised I'd see you right, didn't I? C'mon, maid,' he wheedled. 'I'll even take she as well,' he jerked his head towards Mary-

Blanche.

'Roz,' Mary-Blanche wailed again.

'Please, Mr Prowse. Don't say any more,' Roz begged.

'What's wrong? 'Tis a fair offer.' His face darkened. 'You should be bleddy grateful.'

'I cannot accept.' Roz clasped her arms protectively across her body. 'Surely,' she tried in desperation, 'you would be happier offering for someone who would welcome your proposal?'

'I don't want someone else. I want *you*!' he shouted, his face flushed, eyes glittering.

Stretched beyond bearing, Roz's control finally snapped. 'But I don't want you. And it doesn't matter how many times you ask, my answer will be the same.'

'Think you're too good for me, do you? Bleddy nerve! With a mother like you got? Anybody's for the price of a drink? I want you, maid. And I'm 'aving you. Need showing what's what, you do.' He lunged at her.

'No! Stay away from me!' With a gasp of fear Roz stumbled back. But her heel caught on the frayed edge of the rug and she staggered. Unable to stop herself she fell to the floor. Will dived on top of her, trying to grab her flailing arms, his face looming close. 'You owe me,' he muttered.

'No!' she shouted. 'I gave Jack the money.'

'I 'aven't seen it,' Will panted. 'And debts got to be paid. Now be still, maid, 'less you want me to hurt you. Which I don't mind doing. Too proud you are. Need a man to tame you.'

Terrified, desperate, Roz fought with all her strength, thrashing her head from side to side to avoid his mouth. His breath was foul and her stomach heaved. Forcing his knee between hers he scrabbled at her petticoat, pulling it up over her thigh. But as he shifted his weight to reach for the flap of his trousers, Roz managed to bend her knee and kicked out as hard as she could.

Her booted foot caught him in the stomach, driving the air from his lungs with a grunt. Frantic to escape she kicked out again, this time with both feet, and he tumbled backwards. His head hit the stone hearth with a sickening crack.

Sobbing and gasping for air, her racing heart threatening to burst through her ribs, she scrambled away. Too shaken to try to stand, afraid she would vomit, she remained on the floor, staring in blank horror at the still figure.

'Oh Lord, Oh God,' Mary-Blanche keened. 'You've killed him.'

Roz pressed shaking fingers to her mouth. *He couldn't be dead. What if he was? Why hadn't he listened? She'd given Jack the money. Why didn't he move? He'd been going to ... In front of her mother...*

'Shake his foot,' Mary-Blanche whispered. 'See if he...'

'No.' Roz rasped. Her throat was painfully dry. She couldn't touch him.

'You must do something. We can't just—'
Will groaned.

Sick and shaking, weak with relief and the aftermath of her terror, Roz climbed to her feet. Her legs were so unsteady she had to lean on the table to hold herself upright.

He groaned again. As his eyes fluttered open

he raised one hand to the back of his head. When he withdrew it there was blood on his fingers.

'Roz,' Mary-Blanche urged. 'Don't just stand there. Help him up.'

Roz didn't move as Will struggled to his feet.

'Roz!' Mary-Blanche urged desperately. 'Help him.'

She shook her head. 'I can't.'

'Don't you come near me. You stay away,' he warned. 'Tried to kill me you did.'

Roz gaped at him. 'No!'

'Did too. Look!' He touched his head again then brandished his bloodied hand at her.

Roz kept shaking her head. 'No. It was an accident.'

'Bleddy wasn't.' Will's face was pale, his eyes glassy. 'You and your thieving mother both owe me money. You'd do anything sooner than pay. But it didn't work, did it? You think you're so special, Roz Trevaskis.' His face was twisted with rage and bitterness. 'But you done it now. I'll see you hang. Then I'll dance on your grave.'

As he staggered out, slamming the door behind him, Roz's legs gave way and she sank to the floor, her eyes wide and blind.

'Roz, listen. Roz! For pity's sake, girl. Pull yourself together!'

He couldn't mean it. Raising her head, dazed and disbelieving, Roz looked at her mother.

'Go back to Trescowe. It's your only hope. Go on, quickly! Before Will has time to find the constable.'

Swallowing, Roz licked her lips. Her mouth tasted of metal. 'I can't.' Her breath caught on a sob and she almost choked. 'Mr Casvellan doesn't need me any more.'

'You can't stay here. It won't be safe. The whole village knows Will Prowse wanted you. You refused his offer, but you still borrowed money from him.'

'I know, but—'

'You aren't *listening*,' Mary-Blanche shouted. 'He's mad as fire, he's bleeding, and he'll swear blind you tried to kill him.'

'But I *didn't*,' Roz cried. 'I just wanted to get away, to get him off me.' She shuddered violently.

'If he goes round the village telling *his* tale of what happened, who do you think they'll believe?' Mary-Blanche demanded. 'He's lived in Porthinnis all his life. And now Devlin Varcoe is out of the trade, it's Will who brings in the tea, tobacco and brandy. I'm telling you they'll take his side. You've got to go. It'll be all round the village by now where I've been today, and what was done to me. Sir Edward passed that sentence. If you appear before him you'll fare far worse.'

'Perhaps—' Roz began with desperate hope.

'Will Prowse might have second thoughts? If he does they'll be even nastier. Get up those stairs and pack a bag. You have to reach Trescowe before he finds the constable. Please God, Colenso isn't home.'

It was late afternoon when Roz reached the house. Her shoulders ached from the weight of the bag into which she had thrust what was clean and within reach. The handle felt slippery in her damp palm as she crossed the turning circle to the building housing the Justice's rooms.

To her relief the front door stood open. Though it was Saturday someone was inside. Mr Ellacott? Or maybe a maid doing some cleaning? Could she persuade whoever it was to carry a message to Mr Casvellan?

As she trudged up the stairs, the bag thumping against her weary legs, she remembered all the other times she had climbed them. Then she had come to plead for her mother. Now she was here to plead for herself. Her shift and bodice clung damply to her skin. Her feet were hot and sore from the long walk. Fear as much as thirst had parched her mouth and throat.

She dreaded seeing him, dreaded his scorn, feared he would assume she expected favours. She didn't. She wanted only that he should believe her. But would he? As she reached the landing Casvellan emerged from his clerk's office carrying an open ledger.

At her gasp he looked up, his thoughtful frown was fractured by shock and concern.

'I didn't expect – I thought – I'm so sorry. I wouldn't have – but there was nowhere else...'

'What is it? Your mother?'

'No, she's at home.'

'You'd better come in.' Indicating his room he took her bag, dropped it beside his paper-strewn desk, and gestured for her to sit. 'What's happened?'

Roz sank into the chair and pulled off her bonnet. 'I shouldn't have ... You've already had so much to ... But there's nowhere else, and—'

'Miss Trevaskis,' he interrupted.

At his formality her head jerked up.

'Slowly and clearly, if you please?'

'Yes,' she whispered, trying to moisten her lips but even her tongue was dry. 'Of course. I'm sorry.' She took a breath and tried to order thoughts that leapt and flew like sparks. 'We got back from Helston at about two. While I was tending my mother Will Prowse came into the cottage and refused to leave. He–he told me he had an arrangement with my mother.'

Casvellan's brows climbed. 'And this was?'

Roz swallowed and her face grew hot. 'He supplied her with brandy. In exchange for it she–she was to persuade me to accept his offer.'

'Prowse made you an offer? Of marriage?'

Glancing up, Roz nodded. 'Months ago, and I declined it.' She couldn't prevent a shudder and fought sickening memories. 'When he burst in today he kept saying that we owed him. But I *didn't*. I had already given Jack Hicks the money to clear my debt on the way back from Helston. Jack – Mr Hicks – promised he would pass it on.'

'You owed Prowse money?'

Burning with shame, she pressed her fingers to her pounding temples and nodded.

'Why?'

'There was no one else I could ask. I had planned to pay him back with what I earned from the last smuggling run. But the dragoons were waiting – you know all that. Yet even though I managed to hold onto some of the kegs he refused to pay me anything. He even accused me

272

of betraying—'

Swivelling his chair he stood up, the sudden movement making her jump. Arms folded, he turned to the window, then swung round and glared at her across his desk. 'When I asked *why*, I meant what reason did you have for borrowing money from this man?'

She met his angry gaze with bewilderment. 'I told you. I didn't have enough for my mother's fines. She was terrified that if I couldn't pay, you would send her to Bodmin gaol. I couldn't let—'

He silenced her with a gesture. 'Yes,' he said quietly. 'You did tell me.' Resuming his seat, he leaned back, resting his elbows on the chair arms and steepling his fingers. 'Please continue.'

Roz couldn't think. It was as if her head was full of mist. 'I'm sorry, I don't remember where I was.'

'Prowse claimed to have an arrangement with your mother.'

She moistened her lips again. 'I told him my mother had no right to make such a bargain, nor was I bound by it. Then he–he attacked me.'

Shaking with fury and remembered fear, Roz bolted up out of her chair, hugging herself tightly as she paced. She glanced at Casvellan and saw that he had turned his chair and was watching her.

'We struggled. He was on top of me and tried – he intended – I ... I kicked him. It was the only way I could ... He–he fell backward and hit his head. I thought ... Her voice faded to a whisper. 'I thought...' She relived the agonizing moments

273

– the instant of fierce relief – when she had believed him dead.

'Then his eyes opened. There was blood on the back of his head. He said – he said I tried to kill him. But I didn't, truly I didn't. I only wanted to get away, to get him off me.' Her voice broke. 'I'm sorry.'

He rose from his chair. *'You're* sorry?' His implacable expression and the hard glitter in his eyes tightened her skin. She shivered.

'I know you don't want me here. But he was going for the constable and my mother says everyone will believe him, not us, because he has lived in the village all his life and – and they all depend on him for – for—'

'Smuggled goods?' Casvellan said, standing perfectly still. 'I'm well aware of his activities. But knowing and proof...' he waved the subject aside. 'Did anyone else witness his assault on you?'

'Only my mother,' Roz said with a sigh. She rubbed her sweat-dewed forehead. The floor seemed to be rocking gently. She didn't feel at all well. Though hot and clammy, her teeth were chattering. 'She said if I was arrested and taken before Sir Edward, he wouldn't believe me.' She raised her head. 'Please – Oh – I'm so sorry,' her voice trailed off as the world went dark and she felt herself falling.

Opening her eyes, Roz found herself lying on the floor. She pushed herself up, her apology unspoken as she realized the room was empty. She was alone. Climbing unsteadily to her feet she reached for the nearest chair and sat down.

She pressed her knees together, rested her elbows on them and held her head in her hands feeling utterly wretched.

She knew she wasn't strong enough to face another walk back across the moor. Her thoughts tumbled wildly. She heard footsteps on the stairs and sat up just as Casvellan strode in.

His frown softened as he saw her. 'Hush,' he said as she opened her mouth to apologize. 'I have sent a maid to find my sister. She will help you across to the house.'

Panic welled. 'No, please, I didn't—'

'You cannot remain here,' his gesture encompassed the room. 'You are clearly unwell.'

As she started to speak he silenced her with a look. But the words would not be held back.

'I am so very sorry.'

'Enough!' he was brusque. 'No more apologies. But for you my brother might have died. My family owes you a debt—'

'No!' she interrupted.

'Forgive me.' He was cool. 'I should have remembered. You do not appreciate gratitude.'

'I do, indeed I do,' Roz blurted. 'But it's not necessary, not from you. I would do anything—' she broke off, dipping her head as the betraying blush climbed up her throat to burn her face. 'I beg your pardon,' she whispered.

'Roz,' He took a step towards her, stopping at the sound of feet on the stairs.

'Bran? Where are you?'

'In here.'

A moment later Deborah hurried in. 'Daisy said you wanted me urgently.'

275

'Deb, Miss Trevaskis will be our guest for a while longer. Would you escort her over to the house and up the back stairs to—'

'The same room as before? Of course.'

It was so smoothly done, so tactful, that had Roz not known them both she would never have noticed the brief but speaking look they exchanged.

'Have a jug of lemonade sent up at once.' He turned to Roz. 'Have you eaten since this morning?'

She shook her head.

'Oh good heavens, you poor soul!' Deborah said, instantly sympathetic. 'And you walked here from the village? You must be exhausted. Indeed, you look very pale. Mrs Hambly shall prepare you a light repast. Bread and butter, cheese, cold meat, perhaps a slice of cake and some fruit?'

'You are very kind,' Roz managed, a lump forming in her throat. She wasn't sure she would be able to eat half of it.

'Not at all. I know Davy will be happy.'

'Deb,' Casvellan interrupted. 'Miss Trevaskis has suffered a severe shock—'

'Your sister deserves to know the truth,' Roz told him quietly, then turned. 'Miss Casvellan,' – her swallow was audible, 'My mother was whipped for drunkenness in Helston this morning. I had brought her home and was attending to her wounds when–when a man known to us burst into our cottage. He–he—' she coughed.

'Attacked her,' Casvellan spoke through gritted teeth.

'But he is claiming I tried to kill him.'

'Oh my dear,' Deborah said. 'How utterly dreadful for you. It is no wonder you are so pale. Did you hurt him? I do so hope you did.'

'Deb!'

'I didn't intend – I just wanted to...' Reliving her desperate struggle to escape Will's crushing weight, foul breath, and the terrible fear of what he planned, she gasped, 'To get away. I kicked him and he fell backward. He hit his head. There was a lot of blood.' She shuddered again. 'When he regained his senses he–he...' Her voice wobbled and her gaze sought Casvellan's, desperate that he believe her. 'He said I would hang and–and he'd dance on my grave.'

'What a thoroughly unpleasant person,' Deborah was brisk. 'It seems to me a shame he regained whatever senses—'

'Deb!' Casvellan warned again.

'Well, his claim is ridiculous.' She turned to Roz, her smile warm. 'You must not give it another moment's thought. Come, pick up your bonnet. I'll bring your bag. Here, take my arm.'

Roz felt as if a crippling burden had been lifted from her shoulders.

As they left the room she glanced over her shoulder. Casvellan was seated behind his desk and reaching for his pen. She mouthed a silent *thank you* and received a nod in return.

As they entered the sickroom, Davy looked up, his blotched face breaking into a smile. 'You're back. I thought ... but no matter.' He flapped one hand. 'I'm relieved to see you. Deborah is hopeless at reading aloud.'

277

'Later, Davy,' Deborah called over her shoulder as she propelled Roz into the bedroom. 'Don't worry,' she reassured softly. 'I shall tell him you walked here from the village, were overcome by the heat, and need a few hours in which to rest and recover.'

Daisy arrived with a tray on which stood a jug and two glasses. Unsettled by the sympathy in her glance, it was a moment before Roz realized that while Daisy could not possibly know of Will Prowse's attack, news of her mother's whipping would certainly have reached Trescowe.

Setting the tray on the small table in the bedroom, Daisy listened to Deborah's instructions then bobbed a curtsey and left.

'Are you sure you're not hurt?' Deborah's voice mirrored the concern on her face. 'Shall I send for Dr Avers?'

'No! You are kind, and I appreciate the thought.' Seated in the chair beside the window, Roz alternately sipped the drink then rolled the cool glass against her forehead. 'But I–I don't want to talk—' She broke off, shaking her head.

'It's all right,' Deborah touched her shoulder. 'I do understand.'

As Daisy returned with fresh towels under her arm and another tray containing several covered dishes, Deborah chatted lightly.

'Though the last two growing seasons were terrible, this year's yields look very promising. That should help keep prices down which will be of great help to everyone.'

When the maid bustled out she rose as well. 'I shall leave you now. Daisy will bring hot water shortly. Just rest, and try not to worry.'

'You have been very kind, Miss Casvellan.'

'Please call me Deb.'

As Roz started to shake her head, Deborah laid a gentle hand on her arm. 'My brother trusts me. I would deem it an honour if you felt you could too. I can only guess what a dreadfully difficult day you have endured.'

Roz's face crumpled in anguish and she turned away as tears too long held back poured down her face. 'Your mother would not wish—'

'I am four-and-twenty years old, Roz,' Deborah interrupted quietly. 'I like to think I am a dutiful daughter. But I have learned not to trouble my mother with matters of which she has little understanding and less sympathy.' She patted Roz's shoulder. 'As for that horrible man's ridiculous accusation, no one who knows you could possibly give credence to it.' She paused. 'These recent weeks will have been very draining. And I hope you will not think me impertinent if I say that I imagine life was difficult for you long before that. But you are safe here. If there is anything you need, just ask Daisy. May I come and see you in the morning?'

Deeply touched by Deborah's tact in treating her as a guest, Roz nodded shyly. 'I should like that very much.'

'Until tomorrow, then.' With a reassuring smile she closed the door softly. Roz heard her talking to Davy.

Alone, Roz ate a little of everything. Daisy

279

brought the water, knocking before she entered.

'If you got anything needs laundering, Miss, just leave it out in the passage with the tray, save me bothering you.'

'Thank you.'

After closing the bedroom door, Roz stripped down to her shift. She filled the basin and washed her hair thoroughly, desperate to rid herself of every trace of Will Prowse's foul smell and touch. Squeezing the water out she wrapped her head in one of the towels. Then she bathed. To stop herself reliving what had happened, she concentrated on the warm water, the sweet scent of the soap. Then, dry and blessedly cool, she put on a clean shift, a cream linen bodice and an apple green dimity petticoat. Unwrapping her hair she combed out the tangles and left it loose over her shoulders to dry.

The nausea had eased so she ate a little more. She had just finished what was on her plate when she heard Davy calling.

'Roz? You must be feeling better now. I'm bored. Come and read to me.'

After several trips to put trays, slop pail, water can and her bundle of clothes outside the door, she closed it and crossed to Davy's bed.

'I'm glad you're back,' he grinned. 'Deb's hopeless at reading aloud.' He studied her. 'Your hair's all curly. It looks nice loose like that.'

'Thank you. Which book would you like?'

'Robinson Crusoe.' He settled back against the pillows. 'Start at the beginning. Deb read a couple of pages this morning, but—'

'That was kind of her,' Roz interrupted gently.

'No doubt she has many other demands on her time.'

'None as important as me,' he replied with total confidence.

Seating herself on the side of the bed near the foot, Roz opened the book to the marked page. 'Chapter One.'

Releasing a contented sigh, Davy closed his eyes.

Eighteen

The following morning, woken by Daisy bringing hot chocolate and sweet buttered rolls, Roz bolted upright, first dazed then guilt-stricken at sleeping so long. What state would her mother be in this morning? She ought to be with her, tending to her back. But even as guilt gnawed she knew she could not have stayed. As soon as Will had made his complaint, Sir Edward would have sent a constable to arrest her. Considering the punishment he had dealt her mother, the least she could have expected was remand to gaol. Only here was she safe.

'Miss?'

'What?' Roz looked at the maid. 'I'm sorry, I...'

'I was just asking if you need anything else?'

'No, thank you.' Roz rubbed her face with both hands, trying to wake herself up.

'Beg pardon, Miss, but you're still looking some fagged. When you've had your breakfast, how don't you try and sleep a bit longer? Family's going church directly and Master Davy's still sleeping like a baby.'

But not for long; Roz knew he would wake soon. 'Thank you, Daisy. I'd rather get up.'

'If you say so, Miss. I'll bring your hot water.'

Roz drank her chocolate and ate the rolls. Exhausted by the heights and depths of emotion she had experienced in recent days, now she was simply numb. Daisy came back with the copper can.

'Mr Casvellan said to tell you Preece will see to Master Davy. Right behind me he is.'

Twenty minutes later Roz was ready for the day. Checking her appearance in the hand mirror she saw pale cheeks and haunted eyes with dark circles under them. A stark image softened only by escaped curls that feathered softly on her forehead and in front of her ears.

Through the closed door Roz could hear Davy talking to the valet. She emptied the basin and remade the bed. Then, overcome by sudden weariness, she sat in the chair by the open window and listened to the faint sound of church bells. The air was beginning to warm as the sun burned off the dew. The wind had backed round to the southeast and she thought she could smell the sea.

At the sound of the sickroom door opening and closing she looked round. She heard a female voice, Davy's muffled reply, then with a brief knock, the bedroom door opened. Deborah whirled in, pretty in white figured muslin, a short jacket of pale blue velvet with a frilled collar, white gloves and white kid slippers.

'Good morning,' she beamed. 'No, stay where you are.'

But Roz rose to her feet. Remaining seated didn't feel right.

'I thought to find you still in bed. That is

where you should be,' Deborah scolded.

'I am not ill,' Roz said gently. Nor would she take advantage.

'No, but you look tired still. Though that is no surprise, nor is it polite of me to remark upon it. I beg your pardon. Have you had some breakfast?'

'Yes, thank you. Daisy is looking after me very well.'

'Good. Casvellan is driving us to church in a few minutes. But before we go I thought I'd see if you need anything. Some books perhaps?'

'I'd be very grateful for some paper and a pen. I should write and let my mother know I am safe.'

'Of course. Daisy will bring it to you in just a few minutes. I must go or my mother will wonder where I am.' With a brief wave she disappeared.

Casvellan followed his mother and sister out of the cool church into breezy sunshine. Though he had not heard a word of the service, he paused to speak to the vicar.

'I'd appreciate a few moments of your time, Dr Trennack. Tomorrow afternoon, if that's convenient?'

Reassured that it was, Casvellan bowed and moved on. Scanning the groups of people chatting and smiling, aware of sidelong glances and ignoring them, he saw Constable Colenso who was clearly anxious to speak to him.

Casvellan spoke softly, touching his sister's arm. 'When she's finished talking, take mother to the carriage. I'll be with you shortly.'

Sending his wife and children on ahead, Colenso moved a short distance off the main path into the shadow of a towering yew.

'Thought you should know, sir,' he spoke quietly as Casvellan joined him, 'Will Prowse come hammering on my door yest'day afternoon. Said I should go and arrest Roz Trevaskis. Talking wild he was. Some nonsense about her trying to kill'n. I told'n I wasn't going to arrest nobody without a complaint being made. So he said he'd go uplong to Chyrose and make the bleddy complaint, begging your pardon, sir. I told'n he should come to you, but he wadn' having it. Well, I thought it best to go with'n. Which I did, but 'twas a waste of time.'

'In what way?'

'Made me stay outside, didn't they? Sir Edward's man said there wad' no need for me to go in with Will while he said his piece.'

Controlling his anger, Casvellan nodded. 'Go on.'

'When Will come out, I asked the secretary for a copy of the statement. But he refused.'

'You surprise me.' The irony in Casvellan's tone could not mask his frustration. 'Were you able to persuade him?'

'I done me best, sir. I told'n that as the alleged offence took place in Porthinnis, which is under your jurisdication, it should have been you that heard the complaint. I said Will had no business coming to Chyrose, and it was very strange Sir Edward hadn't told'n so and sent'n packing. That being the case, 'twas only common

285

courtesy for a copy of 'is statement to be given to yourself, which I would undertake to do.'

'What was his response?'

The constable shook his head. 'Still wasn't willing, sir. So I said – and I hope you don't mind me taking the liberty, sir – I said you'd prob'ly have to report his refusal to a higher authority. Which, seeing as several of Sir Edward's recent judgements been overturned on appeal to Quarter Sessions, might give'n troubles he'd sooner be without.' He made a sound of disgust. 'Didn't make a scrap of diff'rence. He wouldn't even let me see the complaint, never mind give me a copy. Truth to tell, sir, looked to me like he wad'n all that happy but didn't dare go against Sir Edward's orders.'

Casvellan nodded. He had expected no less. 'I am obliged to you, constable.'

'But that id'n the end of it, sir. Sir Edward want to speak to Mary-Blanche Trevaskis. I got to take her up Chyrose tomorrow afternoon so he can question her. But I seen Jack Hicks last night. He brung Mary-Blanche and Roz back from Helston yesterday and he said Mary-Blanche was in some poor way. She'd be hard put to cross the street. Only if she don't go, Sir Edward'll have her for contempt.'

Casvellan nodded. 'Hire a mount for her from the blacksmith.' Reaching into his waistcoat pocket he withdrew a silver coin and passed it over. 'As Sir Edward seems disinclined to observe the courtesies, you would oblige me by calling on Mrs Trevaskis tomorrow morning and taking a detailed statement from her concerning the events of Saturday afternoon.'

'Yes, sir.' Knuckling his forehead the constable hurried to join his family.

Casvellan turned to where his mother and sister waited. The baronet was reputed to be a major investor in contraband cargoes and would want Prowse available. By hurrying to Pengarrick and laying a formal complaint of attempted murder against Roz, Prowse had established himself as the victim and forestalled any complaint she might make against him.

Loathing the baronet's overt croneyism and the harshness of his sentences, Casvellan had battled increasing frustration at his powerlessness to intervene. Reporting the most blatant cases to Quarter Sessions had achieved some redress but earned him disapproval from those who should have backed his stand. He'd had enough.

When they reached Trescowe he immediately excused himself.

'Where are you going?' his mother demanded.

'I have business that cannot wait,' he said over his shoulder, sending his sister an apologetic glance.

In the sickroom Davy was wrapped in a blanket and seated in a chair by the window. Roz was reading to him. As the door opened they both looked round.

'What a welcome sight,' Casvellan said, smiling at his brother. 'I think it will not be long before you are taking the air outside. I'm sorry to intrude on your story but I need a few words with Miss Trevaskis. Will you excuse us?'

'If you must, but don't be long.'

Casvellan glimpsed anxiety on Roz's face as she closed the book and rose to her feet.

In the bedroom he explained what he wanted her to do. 'Exactly as it happened. Make your description accurate and detailed.'

Remembered horror haunted her gaze as she nodded and it cost him enormous effort not to draw her into his arms, hold her close and promise that never again would anyone hurt or upset her. 'You have sufficient paper and ink?'

She nodded again. 'Yes, thank you. When...?'

'As soon as possible.'

Mary-Blanche lay face down. Apart from crawling out to get a drink and a bite to eat or answer a call of nature, she hadn't left her bed for two days. But she had slept little, kept awake by the fiery pain from her back. It had faded to a deep nagging ache, with the occasional sharp sting as scabs caught on the linen bandages or split open again if she moved too suddenly.

Sober now, there was no escaping her guilt over Will Prowse's attack. He had been about to rape Roz, knowing Mary-Blanche could not – or would not – try to stop him. Was this the level to which she had sunk? Selling her own daughter for two kegs of brandy? She squirmed and sweated with shame.

Held captive by her pain, unable to sleep, she had been tormented by memories: begging Roz to pay her fines so she could avoid the filth and fever of Bodmin gaol. Now, because of her, Roz might be sent there: Roz, who had kept a roof

288

over their heads and food on the table. Since coming to the village Mary-Blanche had felt safe for the first time in years. Roz had been company and she'd taken responsibility for Tom.

Mary-Blanche thought of her son. She had no idea who his father was. Terrified when she realized she was pregnant, with no idea how she would cope, she had tried to abort him. But even then he'd been stubborn.

After he was born some remnant of conscience had forbidden her to abandon him as she had Roz. Instead, she carried him with her when she went begging, and always got more money than the other rag-clad wretches.

A quiet baby, he rarely woke when she brought a man back to the squalid room in a back-street hovel in Penzance. Ten years ago there had been plenty of men. And for a price, hating them all as she hated both her father and the only man she had ever loved, she had done what they wanted. Afterwards she had deadened the shame, disgust and guilt with brandy. Never gin. Gin was common.

Tom had grown into a quiet watchful child, wary as a wild animal. Mary-Blanche could not remember seeing him smile until Roz came.

Though she needed Roz, she had still resented her. Resented the kindness she knew she didn't deserve. Resented Roz's willingness to work hard, her attempts to make things better. *Couldn't the girl see she wasn't worth it?*

When guilt and hopelessness became unbearable she had drowned them in cognac. But when she sobered up and realized – when she could remember – what she had done, the sadness on her daughter's face made her even more ashamed, and she would do anything, anything at all, to escape into oblivion.

Now she was alone and there was no escape, no way out. Colenso would be coming shortly to escort her to Chyrose. When he'd come this morning she hadn't wanted to open the door. But when he told her Justice Casvellan needed her statement in order to help Roz, she had crept from her bed to the door and let him in.

Moving carefully to avoid re-opening the healing wounds, she sorted through her clothes to try and find the least grubby bodice and petticoat. Roz usually did the washing. But while she had been at Trescowe, Mary-Blanche hadn't bothered. So it had just piled up. And now, when she needed to make a good impression, she hadn't a clean garment to her name.

Removing her shift made her cry out, and it took her almost an hour to wash and dress. She dragged a comb through her greasy hair, plaited it into a braid and pinned it at the back of her head. Then she put on a cap and tied a straw hat over the top.

Her mouth was dry, her head pounded, and she would have sold her soul for a large glass of blood and thunder to stop the shakes and give her courage. But she had no money, and knew nobody in the village would lend her as much as a farthing.

A brisk tap on the door made her start violently. Then Constable Colenso's voice called, 'Miz Trevaskis? You ready?'

Unable to keep still, Casvellan tapped restless fingers on the arm of his leather chair. He had not yet told his clerk about the call he had paid on Dr Trennack. Lasting an hour, the visit had proved to be more productive than he could have hoped. As they had shaken hands on the vicarage doorstep, he felt an unaccustomed lightness that made him realize how heavy the burden had become. There was still much to do but he had set the wheels in motion.

Ellacott coughed delicately. 'Sir, I abhor gossip. But it appears to be common knowledge that Sir Edward is a major investor in Prowse's free trade enterprises.'

Casvellan nodded. 'Yet that doesn't explain his refusal to allow Colenso a copy of Prowse's complaint.' Rising from his chair he crossed to the tall window. 'I cannot hear the case. Pengarrick would delight in citing Miss Trevaskis's presence under my roof as evidence of my corruption.' Folding his arms he gazed out. 'I cannot – will not – allow him to use her as a weapon in his battle against me.'

'You could request an adjournment to Quarter Sessions,' the clerk suggested.

'No.' Casvellan shook his head. 'A six-week wait would be intolerable.'

Ellacott cleared his throat. 'Then might I suggest a letter to the Bench chairman?'

Casvellan sat down again. The same thought had occurred to him. 'Go on.'

'Were you to lay *all* the circumstances before him – Miss Trevaskis's care of your brother, Sir Edward's enmity, which I cannot believe has escaped the chairman's notice – I believe Mr Morley-Noles would consider it his duty to sit. Because of the seriousness of the charge it is unlikely he will sit alone. But even if Sir Edward is on the bench, Mr Morley-Noles will have seniority.'

'Thank you, Ellacott.' The deep groove between Casvellan's brows softened as he nodded. 'I shall write to him directly.'

Roz turned the page and glanced up. Why had Casvellan wanted a written statement? As soon as Davy had fallen asleep she had seized the opportunity. It had taken her almost an hour, and by the time she had finished she was shaking. Folding the closely written sheets, she had taken them down the back stairs, rung the bell and asked Daisy to take them immediately to Mr Casvellan.

As she returned to the sickroom Davy had stirred, demanding a drink and more of the story.

'I'm awake,' he said without moving. 'Listening with my eyes shut helps me see it all happening. I like the way you read, you make it—'

The door opened and his mother swept in, elegant in a long-sleeved gown of lilac figured muslin. A frilled and gathered kerchief of fine white lawn was draped about her shoulders. Her hair was drawn up in a series of complicated coils topped by a small lace cap.

Rising quickly from the bed, Roz dropped a

polite curtsey as Davy's eyes opened.

'My dearest son,' Mrs Casvellan gasped dramatically, stretching out both hands to him. Glancing at Roz she nodded coolly. 'You may leave us.'

'Mama.' Davy appeared more irritated than delighted to see his mother.

'I have been so anxious about you,' she cooed, perching on the foot of the bed and wafting a cologne-soaked handkerchief beneath her nose. She made no attempt to touch or kiss her son.

'If you knew how many sleepless nights I have endured, worrying if you were being properly cared for.'

'I didn't know much about it,' Davy said. 'But I must say it is a confounded nuisance that I still feel as weak as a kitten.'

Wondering if she should wait in the bedroom, Roz decided against it and went out into the passage, quietly closing the door behind her. Still smarting from the abrupt dismissal, she wasn't sure what to do. As this was the first time Mrs Casvellan had seen her son since he was taken ill, her visit would probably last for half an hour at least.

Casvellan had forbidden her to walk far from the house. The sun was hot as she shut the side gate and crossed the gravel to the grass. The cool shade of the beeches beckoned. She longed to go and see Tamara. But how could she lay this load of anxiety on a friend, especially one in Tamara's condition? She would go and see the horses instead.

Approaching the stables she paused to watch

293

two chestnut fillies in a large paddock, cantering after each other with much head tossing and tails held high, then abruptly changing direction as if playing. In another paddock two pewter-gray mares, one heavily pregnant, one much younger, cropped grass, their tails twitching to keep flies away.

At the entrance to the stable yard four men stood in conversation. Roz recognized Casvellan instantly. Not wishing to intrude, or even to be seen, she turned away.

'Roz! Roz!'

As Tom raced towards her, a grin splitting his grimy face, the anxiety that lay like a weight in her chest lightened.

'You'll never guess what I've been doing!'

'I'm sure it's something important.'

''Tis too. Mr Eathorne only let me polish Raad's tack. What do you think of that?' His smile was so wide and so proud that Roz felt her eyes prickle.

'That's wonderful! He must think a great deal of you to trust you with such an important job.'

Tom nodded. 'He said it had to be spotless because Captain Visick was coming. That's him over there, with Mr Casvellan and Mr Eathorne.' Tom pointed to a slim man in a beautifully cut brown frock-coat, buff breeches and polished top-boots. Wearing his holly green coat, Casvellan looked taller, broader, and to Roz's eyes infinitely more attractive.

'And the other gentleman?' Roz indicated a man standing apart watching the fillies. She wanted to keep her young brother's gaze directed elsewhere while the heat in her face, caused by a quickened heartbeat and hopeless yearning, subsided.

'That's the captain's farrier. Captain Visick brung—'

'Brought,' Roz corrected gently.

'Brought him along because he wants to buy Raad. He says what his man don't – *doesn't* – know about horses isn't worth knowing. I don't think Mr Eathorne liked that. I wish Raad wasn't being sold,' Tom said wistfully. 'But when Mr Casvellan put him through his paces the captain was really taken. He tried not to show it, but I could tell.'

Recalling the bond between man and horse on the beach, Roz knew what a wrench it would be for Casvellan to part with the stallion.

'Anyhow,' Tom gave a gusty sigh. 'The farrier examined him and couldn't find anything wrong. Which he wouldn't, 'cos Raad is perfect.'

Glancing up, Roz noticed the farrier watching her and Tom. Beginning to feel uncomfortable, she was about to send her brother back to work and return to the house when one of the grooms came out of the stable yard. The farrier caught his arm, asked a question that had the groom looking over.

'I think you'd better go back to work now,' Roz said, lightly tugging the brim of his cap.

'All right.' He beamed at her. ''Bye.' He scampered away, waving at the groom who was beckoning impatiently.

As Roz started to turn away she heard her

name called.

'Miss? Miss Trevaskis?'

She hesitated, turned back and saw the farrier hurrying towards her. He stopped, snatching his hat off, holding it in front of him. Oddly it was his nervousness that eased her own.

'Beg pardon, Miss.' He dashed a hand across his face. 'I–I used to know someone called Trevaskis who lived at Lanisley. I don't suppose ... would you happen to know that family?'

Roz nodded. 'Yes, I know them.'

As he passed the back of his hand across his mouth she saw he was trembling. 'The Reverend Dr John Trevaskis?'

'He's my grandfather.'

'Then you must be acquainted with his daughter, Mary-Blanche?'

'My mother. I'm afraid you have the advantage of me, sir. Who—?'

He coughed. 'Spargo, Miss. My name is Derry Spargo.'

Roz's breath caught on a gasp and her hand flew to her face. She knew the name as well as she knew her own; knew it from her mother's drunken, tearful rants. This man, this stranger, was her father.

Nineteen

Roz reached the top of the back stairs carrying her straw bonnet by its wide brim. The ribbon ties hung loose and fluttered as she walked. Her emotions were in turmoil. She had suffered one shock after another. This latest, though not unpleasant, had left her deeply shaken.

Daisy emerged from the sickroom, her anxiety softening to relief. 'Oh, there you are, miss. I was looking for you.'

'Here I am.'

The maid wiped her hands down her apron. Roz recognized the gesture. How often lately had she betrayed her own nervousness in exactly the same manner? *What now?*

'Mrs Casvellan wants to see you in her sitting room.'

'Thank you. I'll just—'

'No, miss. She said the minute you come back.'

'Very well. Where is her sitting room?'

'Best if I show you. Take that for you, shall I?' She indicated the bonnet.

Handing it over, Roz raised both hands to her hair hoping it was tidy. What did Mrs Casvellan want? She certainly hadn't seemed inclined to conversation earlier. In fact, her abrupt dismissal had verged on rudeness. But perhaps she had been worried about Davy and the possibility of disfiguring scars.

As they reached the landing Daisy pointed. 'Just along there, miss. Second door. Wait for you, shall I?'

Roz shook her head. 'No, thank you. I'm sure I can find my own way back.'

As Daisy bobbed a curtsey then bustled away down the main staircase Roz straightened her spine. *She had just met her father.* Diffident, polite, he was not at all the callous heartbreaker of her mother's bitter ravings. And despite initial wariness, her instinct had been to trust him. Had she done the right thing? But he had pleaded, promising he meant no harm. So after warning him her mother wasn't well, and despite anxiety about what he would find, she had given him the cottage's direction.

Reaching the door Daisy had indicated she knocked and hearing a faint 'Come' opened it. She stopped on the threshold, overwhelmed by the contrast between this opulence and the plain rooms in which she and Casvellan were nursing his brother.

The spacious room was full of late afternoon sunlight streaming in to illuminate an astonishing amount of furniture. There were small slim-legged tables, chairs with floral tapestry seats, a bureau, a small inlaid chest and a tilting fire screen. One side of a mahogany workbox stood open to reveal a swirl of rainbow-coloured silks. On the wall opposite a marble fireplace a large mirror hung amid portraits and landscapes in heavy gold frames.

Mrs Casvellan was seated on a sofa upholstered in green and gold damask. She held a round embroidery frame in one hand and continued placing tiny stitches with the other. A tea set of flowered bone china had been placed on a small table to one side.

She glanced up, impatience flitting across her features. 'Come in and close the door.'

Roz did as she was told then waited, her hands linked in front of her. 'You wished to see me, ma'am?'

'Yes.' Mrs Casvellan returned her gaze to her sewing and placed another stitch. 'My younger son tells me he is now able to leave his bed for short periods.'

Roz knew at once that to be left standing was no oversight. It was intended to make clear her position as servant rather than guest. *Was she to be forever an outcast?* Yet what right had she to complain? Though the circumstances of her birth were not her fault, her involvement with smuggling was. A choice driven by desperation had led to unimaginable consequences.

'Yes, ma'am. He takes a turn about the room and sits in a chair while his bed is changed. He is still very weak and it may be some time before he fully regains his strength but he is making excellent progress.'

Resting the frame in her lap, Mrs Casvellan looked at Roz with an expression of puzzlement. 'That being the case, I fail to understand why you are still here.' Her tone was mild, her smile bemused. But her eyes betrayed her. 'Surely you are needed at home?'

Hot colour flooded Roz's face as she looked away. On the mantelpiece between two silver candlesticks stood six small plates decorated in delphinium blue and gold. It reminded her of a similar display in her grandfather's study. Quickly she pushed the memory away.

Had Casvellan mentioned the hearing? No, he would not have done. Nor would Deborah.

'I beg your pardon, ma'am. I have stayed because Mr Casvellan thought it best that I should.'

Lisette studied her embroidery, angling the frame to catch the light. 'In recent weeks you have spent considerable time in the company of my elder son. Indeed, I would not think it strange to learn that you had formed an attachment to him.' She glanced up, her coy smile inviting confidence. But her gaze held very different emotions.

Roz said nothing.

As the silence stretched Mrs Casvellan's features hardened. 'You would be very foolish to nurture any hope of such dreams becoming reality. Your circumstances...' Her mouth pursed in distaste. 'I need not elaborate.'

Roz dug a thumbnail into the palm of her other hand. But her voice held steady. 'Forgive me, ma'am. I do not take your meaning. My grandfather is a clergyman and a justice. My upbringing in his household was everything proper.'

Twin spots of angry colour appeared on the older woman's cheeks. 'Indeed? Then why, with such apparent advantages, do you choose to work as a barmaid at the Three Mackerel inn? Hardly a suitable occupation for a young lady, would you say?'

I had no choice. The words rushed to Roz's tongue, but she could not say them. Doing so would provoke more questions, and she would find herself forced to relate the events that had brought her to the village.

'Perhaps not, though it is honest work.' She stopped, unable to continue as her memory threw up vivid images of her wild flight leading half the string of pack ponies, her face streaming blood from the lash of Casvellan's whip. *Honest work?*

'My dear, I don't doubt it. I'm sure you are *most* obliging.'

The condescension stung. Then Roz recognized the deeper meaning in the remark. Anger flared, hot and bright as flame. From her first day at the inn she had walked a fine line, taking care to be pleasant to Jack's customers while quietly but firmly rebuffing the liberties some men considered their right.

Wanting to protest, she bit her tongue. A response would only play into the older woman's hands. Silence was more dignified, but it cost her dearly.

'Casvellan is a fine looking man,' his mother continued, picking up a skein of sapphire silk, laying it across the frame and studying the effect. 'I could not blame any young woman for believing herself in love with him. Nor is it surprising that someone such as you might mistake gratitude for a warmer emotion.' She

301

looked up. 'But my son holds an important position in society. When he marries, which I believe will be soon, duty and preference will ensure he chooses a bride from his own circle.'

Each word stabbed like a finely honed blade. But Roz didn't flinch. Hadn't she always known it? 'That being so, I don't understand the reason for this conversation.'

Setting her embroidery down on the sofa Mrs Casvellan rose, folding her hands at her waist. 'Miss Trevaskis, your job here is done. Go home.'

'Believe me, ma'am, it gives me no pleasure to remain where I am not welcome. But I am not free to leave. If you wish to know more,' she added, as her inquisitor's eyes narrowed, 'you must ask Mr Casvellan.' With a brief curtsy Roz walked to the door.

'Wait!'

Roz looked over her shoulder. 'You can have nothing more to say to me. And I must return to the sickroom. Good afternoon.' She wrenched open the door and almost collided with Casvellan.

'Roz?' he murmured, frowning.

'Excuse me.' Lips pressed tight to stop them from quivering, she slipped past him. He watched her run along the landing and vanish round the corner.

He wanted to follow. But first he would find out what had upset her, though he feared he could guess. Reining in his temper he pushed open the door.

'Branoc! How unexpected! And such a plea-

302

sure.' His mother's smile was too wide, her colour unnaturally high. 'Let me ring for tea. This has sat too long and is quite cold.'

'You did not offer Miss Trevaskis a cup?' His enquiry was deceptively mild.

'Good God, no! My dear, I know she has been useful. But I do feel it's time she left Trescowe.'

'And you took it upon yourself to tell her that?'

'Yes. I thought to spare you such a trifling detail. I have been to see Davy, and now he is so much better Preece can take over—'

'Enough!' he snapped. 'Miss Trevaskis is here at my invitation and will remain until I decide otherwise. You would oblige me by not meddling in matters that do not concern you.'

His mother's eyes widened and her mouth fell open. One hand flew to the gauze folds over her bosom. He knew exactly what would happen next. Right on cue tears welled, spilling down her cheeks. 'Meddling? How can you say that? Of course it concerns me. You are head of the family. Your actions reflect on us all.'

'As did your husband's, madam,' he snapped, and immediately regretted it. She was not responsible for his father's behaviour. *Any more than Roz was responsible for her mother's.*

'How can you speak so to me?' she sobbed, drawing a small lace-edged square of lawn from her sleeve. She dabbed her eyes. 'My only concern is your wellbeing.'

'Then kindly confine yourself to your own affairs and leave mine to me.'

'Do you imagine I *enjoy* being worried to

death? Have I not suffered enough? Losing your father, Deborah's tragedy, and now Davy's illness. My nerves are in shreds. Ever since that girl entered the house you have not been yourself.'

'How would you know that? I've scarce seen you for weeks.'

'A mother senses these things,' she declared. 'And it is perfectly clear to me that she believes herself in love with you. I do not blame her for that. You are, after all, a brilliant catch. But such a match...' She threw up her hands. 'The very idea is insupportable! I do not approve of gossip as you know. But what I have heard about her mother does not bear repeating.' She shuddered.

'Then spare yourself the discomfort.'

'Someone must warn you of the danger.'

'You cannot tell me anything I don't already know.'

'Then why do you not send her home? If not for me, then do it for Deborah. At four-and-twenty her chances of making a match are fast diminishing. You have a duty—'

'Excuse me.' Bowing abruptly he turned to the door.

'You cannot go. Casvellan, I insist that you—'

He closed the door, shutting his eyes for an instant. He'd handled that badly. But she would try the patience of a saint. As he strode briskly along the landing his mother's words echoed. *She believes herself in love with you.*

Mary-Blanche dipped and squeezed the shift in water now scummy with soap and grime. Turning her head sideways she sniffed back a sob, using her upper arm to wipe her face of tears that would not stop. She felt wretchedly ill and wasn't sure if the bread and butter she had swallowed an hour ago would stay down.

Wringing water from the shift she added it to the pile on the table beside the wooden tub. The door stood open letting in fresh air and the afternoon sunshine. Flames leapt beneath the big kettle. She had been working since dawn. She had to keep busy or she would go mad.

She had emptied every drawer and cupboard, wiped them out and put everything back neatly. Then, boiling kettle after kettle, she had started on the washing. Already her hands were wrinkled like dried plums, her chafed wrists sore and her arms red to the elbows.

She wiped her eyes once more. Scooping water out of the tub with a bucket, she carried it outside and emptied it onto the long grass by the hedge. After another bucketful the tub was light enough to carry. Her back ached dreadfully. The stinging was so fierce she feared she had opened up some of the wounds again. But she deserved the pain. And didn't dare stop.

Filling two buckets at the pump, she rinsed shifts, nightgowns, stockings and bodices with the clear water. She'd give anything for a bumper of brandy. *She had sold her daughter for it.*

'I'm sorry. So sorry,' she whispered, tears spilling from swollen eyes. Sniffing hard, she gathered up the rinsed garments and dumped them into an empty bucket. She would hang them out then make a pot of tea. Roz had bought some in Helston: decent tea, not cheap Bohea, and groceries. At least with food in the larder she didn't have to go into the village. Didn't have to face the stares, sidelong glances and whispers.

She swung the kettle back over the flames. As she took down the lidded tin from the shelf above the fireplace, she heard boots on the path and looked up to see a man framed in the door-way, blocking the light.

Instantly fearful, she folded her arms. The scabs on her back pulled and split making her wince. 'What do you want?'

'Mary-Blanche Trevaskis?'

'Who wants to know?'

He removed his hat. 'Don't you know me, Mary-Blanche?'

'No. Why should I?' But even as she spoke, she realized there was something vaguely familiar in his voice, the way he stood. A memory from the past rose like a bubble. As it burst, her heart gave a painful thud as shock took her breath.

'No – it can't – I don't believe...' She was terrified it might be and equally terrified it wasn't. *'Derry?'*

'Can I come in?'

She moved towards him, still unsure. The clamour of questions made her head hurt. She stared at the man, trying to recall the youth. *Twenty-one years without a word.* A harsh sob rasped her throat and she slapped his face with all her strength, wanting to hurt as she had been hurt. But tearing pain from the sudden movement made her cry out and, trembling violently, she reached for her chair. She didn't dare take her eyes off him, afraid that if she did he would vanish.

The blow had rocked him. She could see the imprint of her fingers dark red on his weathered skin. He would go, and she would never know *why*. What did it matter anyway? It was too late. It was all too late. But he hadn't moved.

'Please, Mary-Blanche, let me come in. I've so much to tell you.'

'Now? After twenty-one years? Why bother?' She had meant it to sound scathing. But what emerged was hopeless desolation.

'Don't you want to know what happened?'

'I should listen to you tell me a pack of lies?'

'Why would I? I never lied to you, Mary-Blanche.'

'You abandoned me!' She hugged herself as scars far deeper than those on her back broke open afresh.

'I swear to you on our daughter's life, it wasn't my choice.'

Our daughter. She flinched at the words. 'Roz? You've seen Roz?'

He nodded. 'At Trescowe. She told me where you were.'

Lifting the corners of her apron, she wiped her eyes. Her head pounded and her back throbbed. 'You'd better come in.' He wouldn't stay. When he learned what she'd done, what she had become, he would go and she would never see him again. But he was here now and she needed to know what only he could tell her.

'Can I close the door while we talk?' He waited with his hand on the latch. 'I'll leave it open if you'd rather.'

She gave a bitter laugh. She had no reputation to protect. 'No, close it.' Her emotions lurched wildly from joy that he had come back, to despair. It was too long. Too much had happened. She had fallen too far. But at least he had not found her drunk, and the cottage was clean and tidy.

Then she glanced around, seeing the room through his eyes: the trivet on one side of the ash-strewn hearth and the hook holding the big black kettle, the wooden tub and the bucket of wet washing on the old scarred table. Her gaze flew over the grubby rag rug, battered wooden chairs, walls desperately in need of lime-wash, the old curtain hiding her bed in the alcove and the steep narrow staircase with its worn treads.

Her gesture encompassed the room and the poverty it embodied. 'This won't be what you're used to.'

'I've lived in far worse,' he said quietly. 'We've not long been back—'

'Back? Where have you been?'

'America, India, then France. Can I sit down?'

Gesturing at the other chair she moistened dry lips and forced herself to ask. Might as well know the worst. Get it over with.

'Who's *we*? Your wife?'

He dropped his hat on the table then paused, his hand on the chair back. 'I'm not married.'

'Did she die?'

He shook his head. 'I never did marry. When I

said *we* I meant Captain Visick and me.' He pulled out the other chair and sat facing her. 'He's a cavalry officer. I served with him as his farrier. When he came home I came with him.'

'How long for?'

'We're back for good. The captain came into an inheritance and resigned his commission. He's going to train horses for racing and wanted me with him.'

'Nice for you.' *He'd never married?* His face was brown. Grooves scored his forehead and bracketed his mouth. More lines fanned from the outer corners of eyes the colour of bluebells. His cropped hair, once fair, was now threaded with grey. A dark coat fit snugly over broad shoulders and a barrel chest. A clean neck cloth was tied in a simple knot.

He looked well. Whereas she – she dared not imagine what he was seeing as he looked at her.

'Mary-Blanche, why didn't you answer my letters?'

Her head flew up. 'What letters? The last I heard from you was when you left me at the Red Lion. You said you were going to the post office to see if the special licence had arrived. Why didn't you come back? How could you just go and leave me like that?'

'It wasn't my choice, Mary-Blanche. I swear it. My father had tracked us down. I don't know how because he refused to tell me. But the clerk had started looking at me strangely each time I went in.'

'You never said.'

'I didn't want to worry you. Anyway, I'd just

come out of the post office and there was my father in the street. I begged him to let me return to you but he refused. He said your father would be taking you home.'

Mary-Blanche remembered the shock of her father's arrival, his icy anger, his accusations of monstrous selfishness and moral degeneracy. Terrified, not knowing where Derry was or why he had left her, she realized then that in her father's eyes she had fallen so far she would never redeem herself.

'Two weeks later I was in the army and sailing for America to fight the colonists. That first year I wrote you fifteen letters.'

'You did?' Propping her elbows on the table, Mary-Blanche covered her mouth as tears slid down her cheeks and through her fingers. 'Truly?'

He nodded. 'I know it doesn't sound like many. But we were never in one place long. I had to send them to your parents' house. I didn't know where else...' He lifted the palm he had laid flat on the table. 'I put in a note to them saying how sorry I was for the trouble we had caused. I knew they were angry. So were mine. But my pa was very bitter that your father blamed him for us eloping.'

'He said your family wasn't good enough.' Mary-Blanche's breath caught on a sob. 'I did much better for myself, didn't I?' She bent her head and her tears dropped onto the table.

'I hoped the fact that I kept writing would prove to your parents that I was serious, and that I meant well by you. And I wanted you to know what had happened: that I hadn't just walked away. Every time mail reached us I hoped. But after a year and no reply I gave up.'

Mary-Blanche couldn't contain her sobs. 'I never saw them. Not one.' For over twenty years she had believed herself worthless, unloved and unlovable. 'I thought you had abandoned me.'

'How could you believe I'd do that?'

'What else was I to think? You went out that morning and you never came back. I didn't know where you'd gone, or why.' As she relived the anguish it was as if her heart were breaking all over again. 'Then when I found out I was having Roz...' She shook her head.

'Bad, was it?' His voice was gruff.

She searched his face, expecting him to look away, unable to hide his disgust. But his gaze remained steadily on hers. In it she saw sympathy and deep sadness.

'You can't imagine. And it just got worse. My father rarely spoke to me. My sisters kept telling me I had wrecked their lives.'

'Yet they ... I'd have expected them to put the baby up for adoption.'

Mary-Blanche shook her head. 'Father's principles wouldn't let him. I was the sinner, not the child. My mother was shocked and angry at first. Then she told me she'd had two more babies after Beryan, my youngest sister. But they'd both died. She loved having a baby in the house. Roz cried whenever I...' She swallowed. 'Even my own baby was happier with my mother than with me. In the end it was just too ... I couldn't ... So I left Roz with them and ran away.' Her face felt hot and tight and her mouth was dust-dry. 'Do you want some tea?'

'Please. You got anything to eat? I was that nervous about seeing you...' he said with an embarrassed shrug.

'Heavy cake?'

He nodded, 'Handsome.'

As she pushed herself to her feet and turned to the fireplace she heard his sharp intake of breath.

'There's blood on your back.'

She stood for a moment, then turned and faced him. 'Last Saturday in Helston I was tied to the tail of a cart and whipped down the length of the main street.'

His hand on the table curled into a fist and she heard him swallow. 'Why?'

Mary-Blanche took a breath. 'I drink. And when I drink I behave badly. I expect you'll want to go now. Leave the door—'

'I'll go if you want. But you offered me tea and cake.'

She buried her face in her hands. A moment later his chair scraped on the floor. Then she felt his hand under her forearm as he led her back to her chair.

'Hush now, my bird. Sounds to me like you've had a terrible time. How about I get the tea? I can cook too. We had to do for ourselves while we were on the move.'

Wiping her face, Mary-Blanche looked at him. 'Oh Derry, you haven't heard the worst of it.'

Crouching to stir the embers and add more coal, he looked over his shoulder. 'I don't need to.'

'Yes, you do. Nothing happens in this village without somebody knowing about it. You'll have been seen coming here. If I don't tell you, someone else will.'

He made the tea, took the cake tin from the shelf and cut two slices. Then sitting at the table he listened without interrupting while she told him everything, not sparing either of them. When she had finished she was exhausted. But as she reached with shaking fingers for her cup, she felt cleansed.

He glanced across the table. 'Do you blame me?'

'I did,' she acknowledged. 'But if I hadn't been so unhappy at home I would never have eloped with you in the first place. Then none of this would have happened. But maybe I wouldn't have had Roz.' Her voice wavered. 'I don't deserve her.'

Derry smiled. 'She's a brave pretty maid. I had some job persuading her to tell me where you lived. Had to promise I wouldn't upset you.' He paused. 'You don't mind that I came?'

Mary-Blanche gazed at him. 'No.' She swallowed. 'But you probably wish you hadn't.'

He nodded at the door. 'That's still closed. I'm still here.' His gaze met hers. 'And glad to be.'

Despite her exhaustion Mary-Blanche felt a gentle flutter under her ribs. 'Why were you at Trescowe anyway?'

'I went with the captain to look at Mr Casvellan's stallion. While we were there I heard Dan Eathorne, Mr Casvellan's head groom, telling the captain about a stable boy called Tom

Trevaskis having a rare gift with horses. Then this young woman came to watch and someone said she was the lad's sister. Anyway, I thought it couldn't hurt to ask if she knew your family. When she said you were her mother...' He shook his head. 'You could've knocked me down with a straw. I told her my name and I could see she knew who I was. So I knew you must've spoken of me.'

'I hated you,' Mary-Blanche whispered. 'But I never forgot. I tried. God knows I tried.'

Derry swallowed a mouthful of cake. 'What's she doing at Trescowe?'

Mary-Blanche related the events of the past six weeks.

'When's the hearing?' he asked when she had finished.

'I don't know.'

'I'll find out.' Derry rose to his feet. 'Thanks for the tea.'

'You're welcome.' Mary-Blanche stood as well, not daring to hope.

Picking up his hat from the table he turned it between his fingers. 'Mary-Blanche, we can't go back, nor undo the past. But I'll be living at Trenance, that's Captain Visick's place. It's only two miles from Porthinnis. Can I come and see you again?'

Touched by his formality and unable to tear her gaze from his craggy weather-beaten face, Mary-Blanche smiled. It felt strange. 'If you want.'

314

Twenty

Casvellan decided it was time his mother paid a visit to her sister in Truro. Even if all went well over the next two weeks – which it *must*, for he could not contemplate failure – her demands that he heed her unwanted advice were past bearing. He would send one of the maids with her and keep Deborah here. His sister deserved a rest.

As he ran down the sweeping staircase he caught sight of his butler in the hall.

'Bassett, my brother is now sufficiently recovered to return to his own room.'

'That is excellent news, sir. When would you like Preece to collect him?'

'This afternoon. Before dinner.'

If the butler was surprised he did not show it. He simply bowed. 'I shall have a fire lit and his bed made up immediately.'

'I'm much obliged to you.'

Turning to the side table the butler lifted a small silver tray beside a vase of yellow roses. On it lay a folded document sealed with scarlet wax. 'This has just arrived, sir. The messenger left but ten minutes ago.'

Casvellan picked up the letter and turned it over. He recognized the elegant penmanship of Mr Morley-Noles and anxiety tightened his stomach. Breaking the seal, he crossed the hall to his bookroom then closed the door behind him and unfolded the thick paper.

When Preece arrived carrying a quilted green silk banyan Davy was delighted.

'I'm to go now?'

'Yes, sir. Before dinner, Mr Casvellan said.'

Closing the book she had been reading to him Roz laid it on the side table. 'I'll leave you to get ready.'

'I shall still want you to read to me,' Davy announced, pushing back the covers and slowly moving his legs over the side of the bed.

The likelihood of his mother permitting that was remote. But Roz simply smiled and retreated to the bedroom. Leaving the door ajar she gazed out of the window. The breeze had dropped and leaves drooped, dusty and unmoving in the heavy heat of late afternoon. Without Davy to nurse, how would she fill the days until the hearing? Though much better he was still very weak. Why had Casvellan decided to move him now?

The silence told her they had gone. Returning to the sickroom, needing to be busy, she stripped the bed. She rolled sheets, pillowcases and towels into a bundle and placed it by the door. She had just started folding the blankets when she heard footsteps in the passage.

Her heart gave an extra beat. She hoped it might be Casvellan, but feared what news he might bring. She fought disappointment as Daisy walked in carrying a loaded tray.

'Here, I'll do that, miss. You sit down and have

your dinner. There's lamb and peas, a slice of game pie, a lovely ripe peach, some raspberries and a dish of cream.'

Dropping the blankets onto the bare mattress, Roz turned quickly to the side table, moving books, paper, pens and inkpot to one side.

Setting the tray down the maid frowned, hands fisted on her ample hips. 'Don't mind me saying, miss, but you're still looking awful tired. Still, be easier for you now Master Davy have gone.'

No it won't, Roz wanted to shout. *I'll have far too much time to think and worry.*

'Fancy anything else, do you? 'Tidn no trouble.'

Roz glanced at the food, felt her stomach revolt, and turned quickly, forcing a smile. 'No, this is lovely. Thank you.'

Sympathy puckered Daisy's round face. 'We heard 'bout your mother. But 't won't do you no good fretting yourself to a shadow. No disrespect, miss, but cook said she seen more meat on a butcher's apron. Right, I'll leave you be. Anything you want, just ring the bell.' Picking up the bundle of linen, the maid dropped a curtsey and bustled out.

The evening light was golden and the setting sun cast long shadows. Sitting by the open window in the faded velvet armchair Roz watched swallows swoop and soar. They would leave soon, and so would she. But where would she be going? Back to the cottage and her mother? Or – she shivered in dread as gooseflesh prickled her skin – to Bodmin gaol?

Hearing the door open she assumed it was

317

Daisy with a fresh jug of lemonade and did not turn. The maid had sharp eyes and would see at once that she had been weeping.

'I hope I'm not intruding,' Casvellan said quietly, adding as she jerked round, 'Please, stay where you are. May I join you?'

Her face hot, throat suddenly dry, she could only nod.

Lifting the other chair as if it were weightless he set it down opposite hers. 'Forgive me for not coming sooner. There were certain matters to be dealt with that could not wait.' Flicking his coat tails up he sat, leaning forward, apparently studying his linked fingers.

Her gaze roamed from the unruly waves of his dark hair over the broad shoulders filling his well-cut coat to his hard-muscled thighs in close-fitting breeches. Swamped by a passionate yearning for him she moistened her lips. 'I hope your brother is comfortably settled?'

Glancing up he nodded. A smile lifted the corners of his mouth. 'He would never admit it, but the move has exhausted him. Still, I'm told he ate a good dinner. I've just spent twenty minutes watching him struggle to keep his eyes open while we talked. In the end pity demanded I leave. He was asleep before I reached the door.'

He straightened, crossing one booted leg over the other. 'I had another reason for coming to see you.'

Her heartbeat quickened as anxiety roared through her. 'The hearing?'

He watched her from beneath black brows. 'It has been arranged for Friday.'

'This Friday?' Her voice cracked.

He nodded. 'In the upper room of the Market House in Helston. The seriousness of the charge means it must be heard by a panel of three justices.'

'Will you—?' She broke off, black dread welling as he shook his head.

'I can't. You have been living under my roof. Sir Edward would use this to throw doubt on my integrity.'

'So who...?' Her throat was too dry to continue.

'Mr Morley-Noles of Boscarn, Sir Edward Pengarrick, and the Reverend Dr John Trevaskis.'

'M–my grandfather?' she gasped, shock swiftly followed by panic. 'Then I am lost.'

'No.'

'Oh yes. He will think the worst of me. How could he not? My mother left me in his care. But I left his house without permission or blessing to go to her. I ignored his advice and disobeyed his instruction. He will believe I have inherited all her undesirable traits of character.'

'Stop that!' His harshness made her flinch. He was instantly contrite. 'Forgive me. But I cannot allow ... No one who knows you could ever think such a thing.'

Roz stared at him, desperately wanting to believe him. But Sir Edward and Mr Morley-Noles did not know her as Casvellan did. Sir Edward had ordered her mother whipped. With her grandfather and Sir Edward already disposed against her, what chance did she have? Fear and hopelessness rolled over her like a wave, sucking her into deep despair. She turned her head away, desperate not to break down in front of him.

He stood up. 'I want to apologize for any discomfort my mother may have caused you this afternoon.'

Her throat stiff, Roz swallowed hard and rose to her feet. She cleared her throat. 'You are her elder son and she wants the best for you. No one could blame her for that.'

'As always your generosity does you credit. But I will decide what is best for me.' About to say more, he appeared to think better of it, and averted his gaze. 'I must go.'

Utterly desolate she bobbed a curtsy. He half-turned then reached for her hand. As he raised it to his mouth her breath caught. The warmth of his lips on her knuckles made her heart quake.

'I–I want you to know,' strain and longing made her voice husky, 'how much I apprec—'

Silencing her with his forefinger against her mouth he shook his head, smiling. Her own mouth widened in tremulous response and they murmured simultaneously, 'No gratitude.'

Still holding her hand he drew her closer, lowering his head so it was next to hers. Closing her eyes, she rested her temple against his cheek and felt his warm breath on her neck. Here she was totally safe. If she could only stay ... His head turned, lips brushing her cheek. She yearned for his mouth on hers; longed to forget everything outside this room; ached to lie with him, love him, offer him her heart and soul.

Had he professed to love her ... But he had not.

320

He was an honourable man and would not say what he did not feel. Besides, his mother loathed her. If on Friday the worst happened, she might be leaving Helston for Bodmin gaol.

Though she loved him with every fibre of her being she could not live as her mother had. Now her job here was done further contact with her would only damage him. Flattening her hand against his chest she stepped back. It felt as if she was ripping away a part of herself.

'Roz, I–I must go.' His voice was rough and he still held her hand.

She looked into his eyes, the respect, admiration and passionate love she felt for him demanding release. But knowing the damage Sir Edward could inflict should gossip link them, she stayed silent.

'When this is over—'

Swiftly pressing her fingertips against his mouth she shook her head. 'No, please don't. I would not have you say what you might regret.'

His features hardened. In his gaze she glimpsed a reflection of her own turmoil. Then suddenly distant, unreadable, he released her hand.

'I beg your pardon.' With a brief formal bow he strode out.

Roz turned to the window, hugging herself, rocking as scalding tears slid down her face. She knew she had done the right thing. So why did it hurt so much?

Later that night, woken from restless sleep by a sudden spattering against the window, Roz stared into the darkness and listened to the wind sigh and groan through the trees while rain hissed onto thirsty earth.

In the morning, Roz stood once more at the open window wondering what to do. The air was cool and fragrant with the scent of flowers and warm moist earth. Raindrops glittered like scattered diamonds on the emerald grass. Washed clean of dust, trees of every shade from pale lime to warm russet whispered and shimmered, stirred by a faint breeze. In the ditches, cow parsley frothed around pink spikes of valerian and patches of bright yellow celandines. Overhead the sky was a clear periwinkle blue.

After a quick knock, Deborah popped her head round the door. 'May I come in?'

'Yes, of course.'

She wore a *bergère* hat with blue flowers around the crown and blue ribbon ties that matched her long-sleeved gown of spotted muslin.

'I am walking down to the stables. Mr Eathorne says Farasha is soon to have her foal. Will you come with me?'

'I'm not sure—'

'Roz, you cannot stay shut up in here all day, and I should so enjoy your company.'

With an effort Roz smiled. 'I'll just put on my boots.'

Wary of further antagonizing Deborah's mother, Roz refused to use the main staircase. 'I will meet you on the carriage drive.'

'I wouldn't hear of it,' Deborah said, and led the way down the back stairs, calling a greeting to the cook and Daisy as they passed.

Once outside, Deborah chatted as they walked

towards the stables. 'Farasha is my brother's favourite brood mare. Flight, the chestnut filly, is one of hers. So is Raad. Bran says Raad is the best horse he's ever bred.' She did not seem to expect a response, which relieved Roz who had felt guilty at contributing nothing to the conversation.

They stopped at the first of the paddocks and watched the two fillies chase one another, then moved on past another paddock where a black mare and a bay colt grazed. 'That's Leila,' Deborah said. 'Her name means night. Her colt is called Lamaan. It means flash or brightness,' she explained.

Hearing their voices the colt raised his head. His coat was the colour of molasses, his legs long and slender. He held his head high, curved ears forward.

'Isn't he beautiful?' Roz breathed.

'Arabian horses have such lovely faces,' Deborah said, leading the way into the yard.

It was shaped like an open square. Gaps at each corner allowed access to paddocks, fields, and the main and back drives. In front of them was a long building with a wide door at either end. These stood open. A lad emerged from the furthest doorway wheeling a barrow laden with soiled straw with a fork on top. Turning left he pushed it out of the yard.

Another boy followed with a second barrow. Roz recognized Tom. Seeing her he grinned but kept going, visibly struggling with the weight of the barrow but determined. Her heart swelled with love for him. He was pluck to the backbone. Another lad stood at the well filling water buckets.

Outside the left-hand block, Captain Visick stood talking to Dan Eathorne and Derry Spargo. When Derry caught sight of her and bowed politely, Captain Visick glanced round. A smile lit his face. Seeing Deborah blush deep-rose, Roz suddenly understood her desire to walk down here, and the reason behind her nervous chatter. As the captain excused himself to the head groom and came towards them, Roz turned aside to give Deborah and the captain a moment's privacy.

Casvellan strode into the yard from the top end, hesitating for an instant upon seeing Roz. As she dropped a curtsey, he inclined his head. Then with a brief smile for his sister, he nodded to Derry and shook hands with the captain before questioning Dan Eathorne. The head groom unbolted the door and stood back to allow Casvellan to go in first. With a quick word and a smile to Deborah the captain followed. Deborah remained on the threshold, moving to one side so as not to block the light.

As Derry Spargo walked quickly towards her, Roz was touched to see him tip his hat in greeting.

But how was she to address him? She couldn't call him *father*. He was still a stranger. Yet *Mr Spargo* sounded so formal. Hoping he would understand she simply smiled. 'Good morning.'

'Lovely one, isn't it?' He beamed, his eyes crinkling at the corners. Though the hard conditions of his years abroad had left their mark he was still a good-looking man. But there was more to him than a pleasant appearance. She sensed solidity and kindness.

'I've been to see your mother.'

'How is she?'

'Still suffering with her back. But she's all right. When I arrived she was doing a pile of washing.'

'Really? You're not saying that to spare me—'

'Look,' he said gently. 'I know what's worrying you. She hasn't touched a drop since the day you came back here.'

Roz's face flamed. 'She told you?'

'Everything. She said if she didn't, someone else was bound to. Anyhow, I asked if I could call on her again and she said yes. So I want you to know I mean well by her. She's missing you awful. And...' He hesitated.

'What? Please tell me.'

'She's beside herself for all the trouble she gave you.' He glanced back towards the stable. 'I'd better go.' He tugged the brim of his hat once more.

Roz touched his arm. 'Thank you.' For two years she had struggled under a crushing burden of responsibility. Now Tom had a job he loved, it appeared that her mother had finally stopped drinking, and after twenty-one years her parents were reunited. Watching Derry Spargo walk away, Roz's emotions see-sawed between amazed relief at the change in her mother, and a sense of something like bereavement. Of *course* she was happy for them. But where did all this leave her?

Twenty-One

Friday dawned sunny but cool. By the time Daisy arrived with her hot chocolate Roz had begun to tremble. Still tired after a restless night she tried to force down some bread and butter. But when she couldn't swallow, she set it aside.

Washed and wearing a clean shift she was putting on her stockings when there was another knock and Deborah looked in.

'I won't ask how you are feeling. Will you allow me to lend you one of my gowns?'

'You are very kind. But I have this.' Roz indicated her primrose chemise of figured muslin lying across the rumpled blankets.

'It's very pretty,' Deborah said. 'Oh Roz, I wouldn't offend you for the world, but—'

'It's old-fashioned,' Roz finished, to spare her. 'I know. But for two years I have been working at the Three Mackerel. If I appear in something smart and fashionable – which your gowns are – people like Sir Edward Pengarrick will want to know where I obtained the money to pay for it.'

'You haven't bought it,' Deborah argued.

'Were he told that, he would demand to know why you, a young lady of good family, would lend a gown to a tavern wench.'

'You're not...' Realization, discomfort and

326

sympathy crossed Deborah's face like clouds before the sun.

'I am, but no matter. The point is,' Roz said gently, 'accepting your generous offer might cause embarrassment for you and your family. I won't have that happen. Please understand. I can't accept.'

Deborah sighed. 'I suppose you're right. It's just – I so wanted to do something to help you feel better.'

Dropping the chemise over her head, Roz retied the ribbon that gathered the neckline. She reached for her comb. 'You already have. Your kindness during my stay here has meant more to me than...' Realizing she was about to lose control of her voice she tilted her head so Deborah could not see her face and swept the comb through her thick curls.

Deborah watched from her perch on the bed. 'I'm so angry on your behalf. I have not known you long, but I am absolutely certain you would never deliberately hurt anyone. Indeed, Davy might not be here now but for your dedication and kindness. If there were any justice...'

Roz glanced at her. Did Deborah not realize? 'This hearing is not about justice.' Dropping the comb on the bed, Roz gathered her hair at the nape, twisted it into a neat coil and pinned it. 'It's about revenge. Will Prowse's revenge on me for refusing to marry him, and Sir Edward's revenge on Mr Casvellan for being a more honourable justice and a far better man.' As shock widened Deborah's eyes, Roz turned away to reach for her ribbon sash, her face hot. 'I am just a pawn.'

'But that–that's appalling!'

Hoping Deborah's outrage had deflected her from perceiving what could only embarrass them both, Roz picked up her kerchief. Quickly folding it, she swung it over her shoulders then crossed the ends in front and tied them at the back.

'It is also the truth.' Saying the words brought home to Roz the enormity of what awaited her in the Market House. Sinking onto the side of the bed she closed her hand around the comb. The teeth dug into her palm.

Deborah sat beside her. 'Let me come with you.'

'You are very kind, but no.' Roz tried to smile but the muscles in her face wouldn't work properly. 'In any case, your mother would never allow it.' As Deborah opened her mouth, Roz pressed on. 'And she would be right. The gossips will be out in force. Will Prowse will have made sure of that. You should not be seen in my company. Not only would it harm you, it might rebound on me.'

'How so?'

'It is certain that Sir Edward will question why I was permitted to remain here at Trescowe instead of being remanded to prison.'

'You were nursing my young brother through smallpox!'

'He will care nothing for that. Truly, it would be better for you to remain here.'

'If that is what you want, then that is what I shall do. But as soon as the charade is over, you

328

must come back for I shall want to know everything.'

A knock on the door made Roz start. As Deborah went to open it, Roz stood up on legs that trembled, shook out her full skirts, and reached for her simple straw hat. As she heard Casvellan's voice her heart gave a great thud. When he came in he was alone, breathtaking in a dark blue coat, fawn breeches and top-boots polished to a mirror shine. Still damp, his unruly hair curled against a snowy neckcloth.

'Good morning.' His expression was unreadable. 'Are you ready?'

Not trusting her voice she nodded.

'Mr Morley-Noles has sent a constable to accompany us.'

Her head jerked up. 'You are coming?'

One dark brow rose. 'Of course. A word of warning: the constable is in part an escort for you, but also protection for me, to forestall further accusations by Pengarrick regarding my integrity.'

Her gaze flew to his and behind his cool detachment she glimpsed a fury that made the back of her neck prickle.

'As Mr Morley-Noles is a man of great thoroughness, the constable will also have been instructed to watch, listen and report anything that indicates collusion between us.'

'I understand.' Her voice cracked. If she said nothing she could not betray herself or embarrass him.

'I have saddled Deborah's mare for you. She insisted. You can ride sidesaddle?'

As swift colour flooded her cheeks, Roz nodded and turned away to put on her hat. He had seen her on horseback twice. The first time disguised as a boy, the second on Deborah's mare. On both occasions she had ridden bareback and astride, as far removed from ladylike behaviour as it was possible to get.

Tying the ribbons with fingers that shook, she was glad the brim hid her face as he escorted her along the passage, down the main staircase and out of the front door. She held herself rigid, expecting at any moment to hear Mrs Casvellan's shrill voice. They were halfway down the drive before she felt free to properly release the breath she had been holding. The mare responded immediately and Roz patted her neck in silent apology.

As the constable plodded along behind them, Casvellan glanced across at Roz. The quick flare of colour had ebbed, leaving her pale. He recognized the fragility of her composure. Yet her back was straight and her hands light on the reins. Tipping his beaver hat further forward to shade his eyes, he knew without doubt that he had made the right decision.

Riding into the busy centre of Helston, Casvellan turned off the main street into the stable yard behind the Angel Hotel. He dismounted then handed the stallion over to an admiring ostler. Casvellan turned to help Roz but she was already jumping down. His heart lurched as she staggered. But she recovered instantly, her hat hiding her face as she shook out her skirts. The ostler led Raad and the mare away.

Casvellan looked up at the constable who was red-faced and perspiring. 'What were your instructions?'

'To take Miss Trevaskis directly to the Market House, sir.'

Dipping long fingers into his waistcoat pocket, Casvellan withdrew a silver coin. 'Kindly see that she is offered some refreshment, and have a pint of ale yourself with my compliments.'

The constable palmed the coin, knuckling his forehead. 'That's 'andsome of 'e sir. Much obliged, I'm sure. This way, miss.'

Unable to watch her go for fear of betraying himself, Casvellan entered the stables and spoke quietly to the ostler. Another coin changed hands. Then he entered the hotel, his boots loud on the stone flags. As he approached the private room where the Justices usually met he heard Pengarrick shouting and paused to listen.

'...a mockery!'

'I am well aware of Dr Trevaskis's relationship to both the accused and the main witness,' Oliver Morley-Noles replied in frigid tones. 'He would not have sat had there been another justice available. However, as I told him, and I repeat now, I have absolute faith in his integrity. The matter is closed.'

Opening the door, Casvellan saw the Reverend Dr John Trevaskis standing near the empty fireplace, clasping a tankard. The wretchedness etched on his face caused Casvellan a very unworthy pang of satisfaction. The man deserved to suffer.

Pengarrick was slumped in a chair, his booted

legs splayed out in front of him. Casvellan wondered if the baronet's hectic complexion was the result of heat, anger or cognac.

Seeing him, Pengarrick drained his tankard and lurched to his feet.

'What's this I hear about you selling that stallion of yours to young Visick?'

'You are mistaken.' Casvellan did not raise his voice but his tone carried. He nodded to the other two. 'Good morning, gentlemen.'

'What d'you mean?' Pengarrick demanded.

'I mean that I have not sold him. Captain Visick will train and race the stallion and once he is proved I shall breed from him.' Ignoring Pengarrick who snorted, muttering under his breath, Casvellan addressed the bench chairman.

'The constable has just taken Miss Trevaskis across to the Market Hall.'

'How is she?' Beneath the white wig proclaiming him a man of the cloth, Dr Trevaskis's long face was haggard. Concern for his granddaughter or merely discomfort after a long ride?

'As you might expect.' Despite his level tone, Casvellan felt anything but cool. He looked round as the landlord appeared, wiping his hands on his apron.

'Pint of ale for you, sir?'

'Yes. I'll come down.'

'No need for that,' said Mr Morley-Noles. 'It's still twenty minutes short of the hour. Join us.'

'Another time perhaps.' Sharing a drink or meal before hearings was supposed to increase friendly harmony between Justices who often found themselves in professional disagreement.

Today just the thought was enough to choke him.

With a bow to the chairman and Dr Trevaskis and a nod to Pengarrick, whose gaze held an unholy blend of hatred and glee, Casvellan left.

The constable put his head round the door of the small bare room where Roz sat alone listening to passing footsteps and voices. 'Time to go in, miss. All right, are you?'

'Yes.' Her heart leapt and fluttered like a frightened bird as she stood up. Dry-mouthed, she walked ahead of the constable up the wooden stairs. He crossed a wide landing then opened one of a pair of double doors.

The room beyond was long. Though there were windows down both sides they were small and set low. Sunlight streamed in through those on the right and fell in bars across part of a double row of benches that faced each other. Those on the right were empty. On the left, she was vaguely aware of three men sitting in the back row, but the constable's sturdy body obscured her view.

With his hand under her elbow – surely he must feel her trembling – he guided her forward to a waist-high wooden bar.

'You stand there, all right?' He backed away.

The three Justices were seated on a raised platform at the far end of the room. Sir Edward slumped in his chair, his paunch straining against his waistcoat. In the centre, Mr Morley-Noles whose profile reminded her of a buzzard, exchanged quiet words with her grandfather who either had not noticed her arrival, or preferred to ignore it. Buffeted by guilt and despair she looked down, desperately blinking away tears while her heartbeat drummed in her ears.

In front of the platform, just below her grandfather, a man wearing a black coat and breeches and a white wig sat behind a table containing several large volumes and writing materials.

Will Prowse was escorted to the witness stand below and to the right of the justices.

The chairman cleared his throat. But it was Sir Edward who spoke.

'I submit that Casvellan be asked to leave this hearing.'

Casvellan? Glancing left Roz saw him. To his right Derry Spargo caught her eye and gave an encouraging nod. She recognized the third man as Dr Trennack, vicar of Porthinnis. What was he doing here?

The chairman frowned. 'On what grounds?'

'The girl has been living in his house—'

'Justice Casvellan has already disqualified himself from sitting,' Mr Morley-Noles interrupted. 'He is present as an observer, as is his right.'

'I still don't—'

'Your objection is dismissed.' The chairman's icy tone implied it should never have been raised. 'We shall proceed.' As the baronet shifted in his chair, clearly furious, the chairman instructed Will Prowse to tell them what had happened on the afternoon in question.

'She tried to kill me.' Will pointed at Roz. 'Her

and her mother was in it together.'

'That will do, Mr Prowse,' the chairman said. 'Mrs Trevaskis is a witness, not a defendant.'

'Begging your pardon, sir, but she id'n no missus. Two children by two different fathers and never been wed.'

'Silence!' Mr Morley-Noles thundered. Roz saw her grandfather flinch as Sir Edward smirked. 'You will confine your answers to the events of Saturday last. Any remarks intended to blacken the witness's character will result in you spending time in the stocks. Do you understand?'

'Sir.' Will nodded but his expression was mutinous.

'Why did you go to the cottage occupied by Miss Trevaskis and her mother?'

'They both owed me money. I went to collect it.'

Roz wanted to interrupt, to tell the magistrates that her debt had been settled. But, about to raise her hand, she caught Casvellan's eye. Seeing his slight frown and the imperceptible shake of his head, she remained silent.

'Explain the circumstances of these loans,' Mr Morley-Noles demanded.

'Roz Trevaskis needed the money because she 'ad to pay a fine and didn't 'ave enough,' Will darted a spite-filled glance at Roz whose face was burning with mortification.

'But this fine had not been incurred by the young lady, had it?' Mr Morley-Noles enquired.

Momentarily startled, clearly wondering how the chairman could have known that, Will glanced at Sir Edward who ignored him. 'No,' he admitted.

'Yet it was Miss Trevaskis who paid the fine.'

'Just said so, hasn't he?' Sir Edward muttered.

'Proceed, Mr Prowse,' the chairman said.

''Er mother and me, we made a bargain. I kept my side of it. Swear to it on a stack of Bibles, I will, sir.'

'That won't be necessary, Mr Prowse.'

'But she never done 'er part. And that id'n right.'

'What was this agreement?'

'That I'd keep 'er supplied with brandy, which I did. Two full kegs she 'ad, and that's God's honest truth.'

'And in return for your generosity you were to receive what?'

'She promised she'd persuade Miss Roz to accept my offer.'

'What were you offering, Mr Prowse?'

Will's expression was affronted. 'Marriage, sir. Willing to wed 'er, I was. And take 'er mother in as well.'

'I see. So why you are accusing Miss Trevaskis of trying to kill you?'

''Cos she did. She said her mother got no right to make any such promise. Then she went for me, sir. Mad as a fetcher she was.'

Roz's gasp at this blatant falsehood was lost beneath the chairman's next question.

'A fetcher, Mr Prowse?'

She gripped the wooden bar, fighting rising panic as she listened.

'Rat, sir, a large rat. Corner 'em with a ferret

or a dog and they go wild.'

'Continue.'

'Punched and kicked me, she did. Knocked me down. I hit my head on the hearthstone. Near cracked 'n open. Out cold I was. When I come round I was bleeding something terrible. I got out fast as I could. In fear for my life I was. I went straight round to Constable Colenso and showed'n what she done.'

'Thank you, Mr Prowse. You may sit down. Usher, bring in Mary-Blanche Trevaskis.'

Watching Will swagger down the room to the long benches, Roz saw him glance towards Casvellan. His smirk melted and he flinched then scuttled into the back row on the right hand side where he tried to make himself as unobtrusive as possible.

Clinging for support to the wooden bar, Roz saw a sneer form on Sir Edward's mouth as a woman passed her. Her grandfather's face was so pale it might have been carved from marble. The constable guided his charge to the stand Will Prowse had just left. She turned and for a moment Roz did not recognize her. She had not seen her mother since dressing the wounds on her back, and had left her in agony face down on her bed.

Wearing a washed-out but freshly ironed bodice, a clean calico petticoat and kerchief, her hair covered by a pristine cotton cap, Mary-Blanche looked clean, tidy and sober. Roz's heart brimmed with gratitude and relief. Trembling almost as much as Roz, Mary-Blanche looked directly at her daughter and her lips flickered in a brave attempt at a reassuring smile.

'You are Mary-Blanche Trevaskis?' Mr Morley-Noles raised an enquiring eyebrow.

Mary-Blanche tried to answer, but no sound emerged. She coughed. 'Yes, sir. I am.'

'You were in the cottage that you share with your daughter on the Saturday afternoon when William Prowse visited?'

'Yes, sir. I was.'

Before Mr Morley-Noles could ask his next question. Sir Edward Pengarrick leaned forward. 'How can you be so sure of your whereabouts on that particular date?'

Beneath his scepticism, Roz recognized chilling spite. Her gaze flew to her mother.

Mary-Blanche swallowed, but her head remained high as she answered. 'Because at noon that day I had been whipped at the cart's tail in Helston. As it was you who sentenced me to that punishment, sir, I have no doubt of where and when it took place.' Roz saw her grandfather's head snap round, naked shock on his face as he looked first at Pengarrick, then at the daughter he had not seen for twenty years.

The chairman gestured. 'Continue, if you please.'

'Roz – my daughter – brought me home. Jack Hicks, landlord of the Three Mackerel inn at Porthinnis kindly let us ride on his cart. My daughter had just finished tending to my back when Mr Prowse burst in—'

'One moment.' Mr Morley-Noles raised a hand. 'I wish to be clear about this. *Burst* in?'

338

'Yes, sir. He didn't knock. He simply flung open the door and walked in. My daughter told him it was not a convenient time, but he refused to leave. He was raving angry and shouting. Some months ago my daughter declined his offer of marriage. That day he asked her again. Once more she refused. But he wouldn't accept it. Then he–he attacked her, knocking her down.'

'Rubbish,' Sir Edward scoffed.

'Continue, if you please,' the chairman said.

'He – William Prowse – kept saying that debts had to be paid, that she was too proud, and needed a man to tame her. It was plain what he intended. Roz was trying to fight him off and I was in no state to help her.' As she looked across, Roz saw her mother's shame and anguish.

'Mr Chairman,' Sir Edward interrupted. 'Why are we wasting time listening to a witness who, by her own admission, had that very day been whipped for drunkenness? She has made numerous appearances before Casvellan. His repeated leniency in the face of this woman's deplorable behaviour merits nothing but scorn. If he has no stomach for the work he would do better to give it up.'

Glancing at Casvellan, Roz saw him murmuring quietly to Dr Trennack who nodded agreement. *Why was he not angry? He should be furious at Pengarrick's public slur on his character.* She didn't understand. *Didn't he care?* A terrible fear began to creep through her. Casvellan looked toward her. His expression was impassive. But what she read in his eyes steadied and reassured her.

'Neither your manners nor your timing do you any credit, sir.' The chairman invested the title with shrivelling contempt. 'The purpose of this hearing is to determine whether the charge against Miss Roz Trevaskis has any merit. You would oblige me by confining your remarks to the matter in hand.'

'Then hear this,' the baronet spat. 'The word of a habitual drunk cannot be trusted. In fact this entire hearing is a charade.'

Oliver Morley-Noles turned toward him. 'You are free to leave if you so wish. I will invite the Reverend Dr Trennack to sit in your place.'

'He can't—'

'Indeed he can,' the chairman broke in smoothly. 'He sat as a Justice in Stratton before coming to the parish of Porthinnis.'

Pengarrick quickly concealed his shock by coughing into a handkerchief. 'No, no. Let us finish and be done with it.'

It dawned on Roz that far more was happening here than her hearing. Then Mr Morley-Noles gestured to her mother.

'Kindly continue.'

Clearing her throat in an effort to steady her voice Mary-Blanche went on. 'Roz managed to kick him away, and he fell backwards. That was when he hit his head.'

'Your daughter was not holding anything that might be considered a weapon?' Mr Morley-Noles demanded.

'No, sir.'

'She had not approached Mr Prowse?'

'No sir.'

'Nor threatened him in any way?'

'No, sir. She suggested to him that he would be happier offering for someone who would welcome his proposal.'

'What was his response?'

'Is this relevant?' Sir Edward demanded impatiently.

'Certainly,' Mr Morley-Noles snapped. 'Mr Prowse has accused Miss Trevaskis of trying to kill him. Yet it appears that not only did he want to marry her, he was prepared to bribe her mother with brandy to bring this about. And despite Miss Trevaskis declining his offer on two separate occasions, he refused to accept her rebuff.' He turned back to Mary-Blanche. 'How did he respond to her suggestion?'

'He shouted that he didn't want someone else, he wanted her. He said she needed to be taught a lesson. That was when he went for her.'

'He physically attacked her?'

'Yes, sir.'

'Thank you, that is all.'

Passing Roz with a shaky smile, Mary-Blanche made her way to the witness bench. She slipped in beside Derry who whispered a few words as he took her hand between his.

Roz watched Mr Morley-Noles speak quietly to the men on either side of him. Sir Edward gave an ill-tempered shrug. Her grandfather nodded, then rubbed his forehead as if it were aching. She remembered him as a confident man of forceful personality, blessed with all the advantages of money and education. A man convinced he knew best, and that his way was the only way. Perhaps in future, having heard something about the reality of life for her and her mother, he might be less judgmental.

'Miss Trevaskis,' Mr Morley-Noles's expression gave nothing away.

Roz gripped the bar tightly.

'Having read statements from all those involved and heard an account of events from both the complainant and a witness, it is our opinion that William Prowse's claim is without merit. I find no evidence that you attacked him, or that you deliberately injured him. His injury occurred as a direct result of his attempt to force himself on you. Therefore responsibility for that injury lies entirely with him. The charge against you is dismissed.'

'What about my money?' shouted Will.

'Be quiet!' Mr Morley-Noles snapped.

Tentatively Roz raised her hand.

'You wish to say something, Miss Trevaskis?'

'If I may, sir.' Roz swallowed, trying to steady her voice, acutely aware of both Casvellan and her grandfather. 'During the ride back from Helston that Saturday afternoon I gave Mr Hicks a small cotton bag containing the money I owed Mr Prowse, and asked him to hand it to Mr Prowse the next time he visited the inn.'

'Did you apprise Mr Prowse of this fact when he entered your cottage?'

'I tried, sir. But he refused to listen.'

Morley-Noles's chilly gaze switched to Will Prowse. 'Has Mr Hicks given you the money?'

Will jerked his head, muttering.

'Speak up!' The chairman snapped.

'Haven't been in there, have I? Any'ow, even if she settled what she owed me, it still don't cover the brandy.'

'Miss Trevaskis, did you have any knowledge of the brandy, or Mr Prowse's arrangement with your mother?'

'No, sir. I did not.'

'Be silent,' he rapped as Will opened his mouth. 'Your evidence this afternoon has been at best unreliable. I am minded to call it a pack of lies. Miss Trevaskis had already turned down your proposal. A man of sense would have accepted that. Just as he would have recognized the futility of bribing someone else in an attempt to have her decision overturned. You are owed nothing but a warning. Should I hear of Miss Trevaskis or her mother being harassed in any way, I would advise her to bring charges against the perpetrator who would be dealt with most severely. I hope I make myself clear?' Waiting, brows raised, until Will nodded, he stood. 'This hearing is concluded.'

Twenty-Two

It was all over. Roz let go of the wooden bar, her knuckles aching from the frantic strength of her grip. Sir Edward, clearly in a foul temper, stomped past without a glance, slamming the door behind him. The chairman had stopped to speak to the man in the black gown who had been writing throughout the proceedings.

She saw her grandfather rise from his seat. He stood for a moment, then started to turn away. Was he angry? Disgusted? She could not let him go without a word. But clearly she would have to make the first move.

'Grandpapa?' As he turned, she bobbed a curtsey. 'I am so sorry for the pain I must have caused by leaving the way I did. I have learned so much during the past two years. They were hard lessons, far harder than I...' She swallowed. 'But I cannot regret them.'

His frown did not lift. His face looked grey. 'I must go. This has been most distressing.'

'No, not yet. Please,' Roz begged. As Dr Trennack approached her grandfather she heard her mother's voice and turned.

'Oh Mama,' she whispered, hugging her gently, mindful of the tender scars on her back. 'Thank you,' she inhaled the scent of soap and fresh linen. Never had it seemed so sweet. 'You were so brave.'

Tears streaked Mary-Blanche's cheeks. 'My heart is too full. I don't deserve...' She choked on a sob and shook her head.

Roz offered her hand to Derry. 'I'm so grateful to you for coming and supporting us.'

'You're my family,' he said simply. 'Where else would I be?'

The warmth drained from his expression as he acknowledged Dr Trevaskis with a nod that hovered between politeness and contempt. Drawing Mary-Blanche's hand through his arm he spoke to Roz. 'Your mother and me have a lot of time to make up. I hope to see more of you as well. I'm that proud of the both of you, I haven't got the words.'

As Roz tried to swallow the huge lump in her throat she heard her grandfather's voice. 'I must go. Good day, Morley-Noles, Trennack. I—'

'Wait.' Mary-Blanche moved in front of her father. 'Why did you keep Derry's letters from me?'

Unused to challenge and clearly uncomfortable, Dr Trevaskis flushed. 'I acted for the best.'

'Whose best? It certainly wasn't mine.' Having expected fury, Roz was startled by her mother's quiet sadness. 'What you did was wrong. Derry loved me.'

The sudden rush of colour had ebbed away leaving Dr Trevaskis paler than ever. But he stiffened. 'You don't understand. He was—'

'The son of a merchant, and therefore not good enough for you. So instead you let me think he

345

had abandoned me, that I was worthless. And I believed it. How could you have done that?'

'You don't understand,' her father repeated.

'No,' Mary-Blanche agreed. 'I don't. And I never will. But who am I to judge others? Excuse me.' Turning, she gripped Roz's hands. 'Come and see me soon.'

Come and see me? Surely her mother expected her to return to the cottage?

'Don't worry.' Derry patted her arm gently. Then he led her mother away.

Dr Trevaskis cleared his throat loudly, re-asserting his authority. 'Now I have found you, Roz, I think you should return with me to Lanisley.'

'Found me? But surely you knew where I was when you were asked to sit for this hearing?'

'Indeed, I was informed.' He stretched his chin as if to escape a collar suddenly too tight. 'But under the circumstances...'

'You felt it best to wait for the outcome,' Roz said quietly.

'I did not wish to worry your grandmother. Surely she has suffered enough over the years?' There was a testy edge to his voice. 'This whole business has been most unfortunate. If you had not been so foolhardy—'

'Do forgive me, Dr Trevaskis.' Roz felt a warm hand cup her elbow, knew instantly who it belonged to, and looked up into Casvellan's face. 'Your granddaughter has been nursing my brother through smallpox. And now this travesty is over she is needed back at Trescowe.'

Bewildered, Roz opened her mouth, felt the

gentle pressure of his fingers on her elbow, and closed it again.

'Indeed, sir?' Dr Trevaskis blustered. 'I am not convinced that this—'

'Be not alarmed, sir. She is in no danger. Good day to you.' Casvellan inclined his head and Roz just had time to bob a curtsey to her grandfather before she was propelled toward the door and down the stairs.

'Why? I thought—' Breathless, her confusion spilled out as he guided her across the street to the hotel.

'Don't be anxious, all is well.'

She wanted to believe him, but he was unsmiling, and his eyes had the same shuttered look she had seen on her visits to his justice room.

'Are you hungry?' She shook her head. 'Come, you must eat something. It has been a long and difficult morning.' He led her upstairs and into a small private room where a table had been laid for two. 'We have a long ride back.'

As he closed the door, Roz whirled to face him, clasping her hands. 'Please, I don't understand. I thought ... You told me I was no longer needed at Trescowe.'

Reaching for her hand he raised it to his lips. 'Never have I been so wrong. You will always be needed there, with me. I can wait no longer. Roz, will you do me the very great honour of becoming my wife?'

As her heart crashed against her ribs ecstatic happiness tumbled into despair. Placing her hand over his, she shook her head. 'I cannot.'

347

He simply nodded. 'Now tell me all the reasons why.'

Her breath caught on a sound that was half-laugh, half-sob. 'Don't tease me. You must know. We have just come from—'

'A hearing at which the charge against you was dismissed.'

'But what if I had been found guilty?'

'Such a mockery of justice could not have occurred. But had I offered marriage before this unpleasant business was settled, you would have used that as a reason to refuse me.'

'Your mother—'

'Is currently enjoying a visit with her widowed sister in Truro. If she decides to return to Trescowe – which is by no means certain – she will live in the dowager house. It is currently being refurbished. And Deborah?' he said before she could, and a smile softened his strong face. 'I think Deb and Captain Visick will have their own plans.'

'Oh, I'm so happy for her. She has shown me such kindness.' Dazed and deeply moved, Roz tried to withdraw her hand, but he would not release it. 'I beg you, think of the damage your reputation will suffer.'

'Why?'

She blinked. *'Why?* Is it not obvious? My mother—'

'Appears to be a changed woman.'

'My involvement in smuggling—'

Laughing, he kissed her knuckles once more. 'My very dear Roz, much of the county is involved in the trade if not as couriers, then as customers. As long as you have no intention of continuing your connection—'

'Of course not!'

'Then the past need not concern us.'

She swallowed to try and ease the painful stiffness in her throat. 'Do you not see? Men like Sir Edward Pengarrick will never allow you to forget it.'

His expression hardened. 'His opinions are of no interest to me. Besides, now I have resigned as a Justice, I need never—'

'What?' Roz gasped.

'I did not do it for you, so do not assume a guilt that is not yours. I did it for me. I have served justice to the best of my ability these past eight years. But it is time for change. I want to breed horses. Captain Visick shares my belief that soon Spain will declare war on England. The British army will need more cavalry horses.'

'All the more reason for you to marry where there is money.'

'I'm afraid that is impossible.'

'Why?'

'Because I will not marry where I cannot love. And as I love you, I cannot marry anyone else.' Laying one hand along her cheek he looked into her eyes. The barriers he had used to keep her at a distance had finally dropped, revealing a need and longing that reflected her own. 'I love you so very much,' he murmured, resting his forehead against hers. Then his mouth found hers in a kiss that told her all she needed to know. For the first time in her life she knew where she belonged.

'Well?' Emotion had roughened his voice. 'For pity's sake, Roz.' He took a breath. 'Miss Trevaskis, will you marry me?'

She flung her arms around his neck. 'Yes, Mr Casvellan, I will, with the greatest pleasure.'

'Soon?'

She nodded, brimming with happiness.

'Would you like a big wedding? Lots of—'

She recoiled. 'Must we? I should much prefer a small gathering.'

Instead of disappointment, his smile widened. Reaching into an inner pocket he pulled out a folded paper. 'Special licence. I did the gentlemanly thing this morning and told your father of my intentions.'

Her father. As shock zinged through her Roz recalled the handshake she had glimpsed in the Market House between Derry Spargo and Casvellan. That was why Derry had told her not to worry as he whisked her mother away.

'That was very...' She stopped, not sure what to say.

'Conventional?' His blue eyes gleamed and as laughter bubbled up she bit her lip.

'Now will you eat something?' He pulled out a chair for her. 'And we must toast our future.'

As they rode towards Trescowe Roz thought of her life at Lanisley, and of all she had experienced during the past two years: anxiety, poverty, exhausting hard work and danger. In trying to help her mother she had seen her own life shattered. Yet that pain-filled twisted path had brought her to this – happiness beyond her wildest dreams. Glancing at the man riding beside her, the man soon to be her husband, she found him watching her.

Smiling, he tilted his head and turned Raad from the main track onto the path leading down to the beach. A few minutes later they reached the shingle. Dismounting, Casvellan looped his arm through the rein so the stallion could not move away, unbuckled the girths and removed the saddle. Joyously Roz followed his lead. As he stripped off his coat and waistcoat and unwound his neckcloth, she loosened the ribbons holding her hat and let it fall to the sand.

'I watched you down here one day,' Roz said.

Casvellan smiled. 'I know. I saw you.'

After giving her a leg up he threw himself onto Raad's back and they headed down towards the hard-packed sand.

He gave her a head start and Roz was determined to keep it as they thundered from one end of the beach to the other, kicking up clouds of spray from the lapping waves. Their laughter floated behind them, carried on the breeze over heather, gorse and warm granite while high above a skylark sang.

D